THE
STOLEN IDOL

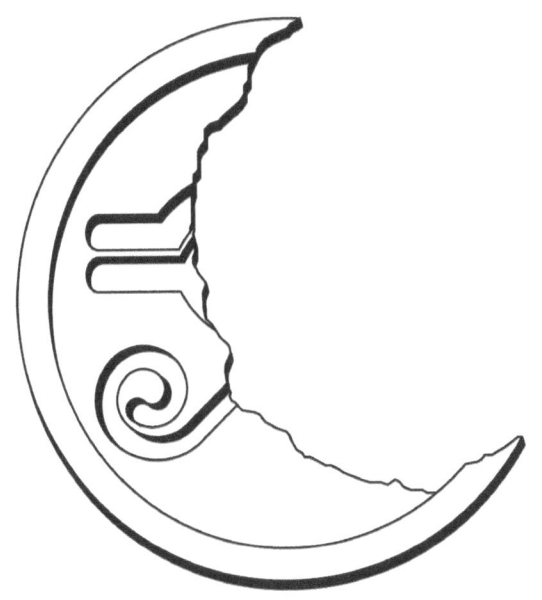

C. WARDE LEE

Jousting
Centaur

First Edition, February 2026

eBook ISBN 979-8-9938548-1-6
Paperback ISBN 979-8-9938548-0-9

To Natalie who supported me while I wrote,
Thom who read the first draft,
Mom who gave her insight,
&
my daughters who asked for a "new" story every night.

1

Fotini

What a stupid sport, Fotini thought as she stared at the fallen knight crumpled in the dirt. The knight could have easily lived the rest of his life in safety and comfort with all his inherited wealth, but instead he lay unmoving somewhere between life and death. The knight's squire placed a finger below his master's nose, paused for a moment, and raised his hand high in the air with a raised thumb.

"Why didn't the knight try to dodge the lance?" Fotini asked her partner, Tragos, who was currently masquerading as her squire. "He rode right into it."

Tragos turned away from his task preparing Fotini for the jousting match and gazed toward the field. The faintest hint of a smile spread across his lips as he watched the knight struggle to his feet with the aid of his squire. "It's seen as cowardly to flinch away from their opponent," he said with a thick Scottish accent.

Without a second glance at the track, Tragos returned to attaching the rusty mess of iron armor to Fotini's mid-section. He brushed his dark brown curls out of his eyes as he checked every piece of her knight costume to make sure it was secure, which didn't look easy for someone barely taller than a child.

"Avoiding injury is not cowardice," Fotini said as she watched Tragos pull and tie hidden ropes tucked beneath a large red and blue checkered cloth covering most of the horse head and neck sitting below Fotini's torso. "Only someone extremely arrogant would trust their armor to that degree. Look what happened to Achilles when he assumed the armor of the Styx would protect him from Trojan arrows."

"Speaking of religion," Tragos said, barely hiding his usual annoyance whenever Fotini mentioned the stories he insisted were myths. "Do you ken what the trophy we were hired to retrieve looks like? Go take a look."

Tragos stepped back and Fotini trotted closer to the entrance of the track where she could see better. She scanned the crowd until she saw a raised wooden structure along the side of the track where an adolescent monarch sat on a gilded cushioned chair. On the wooden railing separating the king from the dirt, sweat, and blood on the field stood a familiar glint of gold.

Even from across a large dusty track Fotini recognized the shape of a golden idol of Artemis, maiden goddess of the hunt, wilderness, and womanhood. The prize showed the goddess holding a bow in one hand while drawing an arrow from a quiver slung over her shoulder with the other. Instead of a long gown, the goddess was always depicted wearing a short tunic so she could easily run through the forest to stalk her prey. A single glimpse of the idol flooded Fotini's mind with memories of visiting the sanctuary with her family as a young child.

"Hey, Fotini!" Tragos yelled Fotini's name to break her gaze from the goddess she worshiped. He heaved a long blue and red striped lance towards her. "You're next."

"How do I look?" Fotini asked.

"Ridiculous," Tragos said while rubbing his head. "I've never seen a knight with a saddle practically on the horse's neck, or one with their legs dangling in front of the poor beast. You look like a crazy person who's never seen a horse, much less ridden one."

Fotini smacked her gauntlet against the oversized hat on Tragos's head and felt the vibration of metal against bone. "This was your idea. I said we should have stolen the prize last night instead of competing for it!"

"Hold your horses!" Tragos said, stepping back before Fotini smacked him again. "You might look insane, but as long as you keep your disguise in place, and keep your mouth shut, we will be fine."

"Yeah, yeah, I'll pretend I'm a stoic, 'manly' knight," Fotini said as she shut the visor of her helmet. "I can't believe I even have to hide my gender from these malakas. I'm still not going to let them hit me."

Tragos shook his head, making his bangs fall back into his eyes. "Just take the hit. Remember, this is a simple vanity tournament for Sir Aberffraw to show off. If you knock him off his horse you win, and we both ken he cannae knock you off yours."

The insufferable whine of a minstrel's horn signaled it was time for Fotini to face the undefeated tournament champion. Tragos walked toward the gate leaving Fotini waiting in the dark of the stadium stables. He muttered under his breath just loud enough for Fotini to hear him say, "Here goes nothing."

Stifled chuckles rolled through the crowd as Tragos stepped onto the track. All the other knights were introduced by squires wearing expensive looking tunics with slim tailored fits and colorful patterns sewn into the trim. Tragos wore an oversized plain green tunic with no artistic flourishes and baggy brown trousers making his body appear misshapen and lumpy. He looked like someone who stole the first outfit they saw off a much larger man's clothesline, which is exactly how Tragos chose his disguise for the tournament.

"Ladies and Gentlemen," Tragos projected his voice across the stadium without a hint of shame for his appearance. "You have seen many knights attempt to dethrone your champion, Sir Aberffraw of the Kingdom of Gwynedd, but none have been successful. I am not surprised. Sir Aberffraw's reputation as the strongest and noblest of knights has spread far enough to reach the ear of my lord, Sir Capall of the Kingdom of Candia across the sea. We traveled a great distance to show how size and strength is no match for skill and strategy. I present to you all, Sir Capall!"

A few claps came from the more inebriated spectators as Tragos bowed and exited the track. Fotini took a deep breath and trotted out of the shadows of the stables knowing all eyes would be on her after Tragos's unorthodox introduction. She expected whispers from the curious crowd, she was always going to be a curiosity as a foreigner, but she was unpleasantly surprised when the stadium erupted in open laughter and shameless pointing. Was her disguise really so out of place?

Fotini momentarily closed her eyes and focused on her breathing. The opinions of the people here were of no consequence. Why should she care what humans, like the ones who stole her from her home in Thessaly, thought? She turned and looked at the golden depiction of her goddess in the distance and her uneasiness turned into resolve. She would defeat Aberffraw, not because she was being paid to retrieve the idol, but because she could not allow it to be in the possession of these pompous asses a moment longer.

Fotini walked the length of the track beside the short wooden fence acting as a barrier between the jousters as Aberffraw sat on a large white stallion trotting the opposite direction. They moved past each other in a slow-motion rehearsal for the game they were about to play. As they passed, Aberffraw leaned over the barrier and whispered, "Forfeit now if you want to live. Just because you are small and riding a foal, don't think I am going to go easy on you."

Fotini kept her mouth shut as instructed.

Fotini reached the far end of the stadium, turned around, and waited for the signal flag. She focused on her breathing and adjusted the grip on her lance. Oh, how she wished she was holding her lightweight spear instead of this heavy blunt stick.

The ripple of a red flag waving at the center of the track signaled the start of the match. Fotini pushed any worries aside and shot down the field in a sudden burst of speed. She was nearly a quarter of the way down the track when Aberffraw kicked his poor horse in the ribs to get him to start running. They both lowered their lances and took aim at their opponent. Aberffraw aimed squarely at Fotini's shoulder while her lance pointed down nearly to the ground. Right before they met, Fotini leaped high into the air above where Aberffraw's lance was pointing and thrust her red and blue striped pole into his shoulder. She felt her lance strike, but at her elevated angle it glanced off Aberffraw's armor leaving him firmly seated in his saddle.

Fotini landed in the dirt and sprinted to the far end of the track in near silence while the spectators processed what they had just witnessed. As she reached the end of the fence dividing the jousting field a mixture of cheers and boos filled the air. She peered down the pitch and saw Aberffraw still riding down the track to where his squire waited for him. He waved his young assistant over with the sharp erratic movements of someone barely containing their rage. After a tense moment of furious whispers, the squire ran over to the King's private box and addressed the king loudly so the whole stadium could hear.

"Your Majesty, King Henry, third of your name, my lord Sir Aberffraw asks for your ruling on the... unconventional tactics displayed by the foreigner Sir Capall of Candia. This dishonorable display is not befitting such a noble sport and should be grounds for disqualification."

Fotini seethed as she listened to the squire. She simply used her agility and speed to her advantage just as Aberffraw used his size! She took a step toward the King to argue why she should be allowed to compete when Tragos appeared by her side and put a hand on her hip.

"Dinnae say a word," Tragos warned. "The King may not agree with Sir Aberffraw, but if you open your mouth, you will surely be disqualified as a woman. Stay calm and let me do all the talking."

Tragos marched over to the King's box looking like a beggar, but with the confidence of someone completely out of touch with reality. "Your Majesty, the rules of this sport are simple are they not? I believe there are no rules about horses jumping over the lance. Besides, is it more entertaining to watch two men hit each other in the exact same fashion all day, or to add an element of surprise to the sport?"

The young King nodded in agreement. "Sir Capall may continue to compete until one of the two knights is knocked from their horse. Let us see what tactics are used overseas in the Kingdom of Candia."

Fotini smiled beneath her visor as she watched Aberffraw throw his lance into the dirt in anger. His temper would make him rash and stupid. She knew then she could beat him with, or without, her hidden advantages.

Tragos approached Fotini with a wide grin. He brushed his bangs out of his eyes and under the bright sunlight Fotini caught a brief glimpse of his rectangular pupils. Hopefully his hair and ridiculous hat cast enough shadow for them to be unnoticed by the King.

"Agility won't be enough," Tragos said, patting Fotini's leg. "You will need to dig in and use his own weight against him. You're going to have to take a hit."

"What if Ailsa's armor doesn't hold up," Fotini whispered so only Tragos could hear.

"Ailsa *promised* the armor would keep you safe," Tragos said. "Do you trust her?"

Of course Fotini trusted Ailsa. The bite sized pain in the ass was capable of almost anything, except lying. It was the one thing Fotini knew Ailsa could not do.

Tragos handed Fotini a fresh lance and she prepared to face Aberffraw again. She pointed her lance skyward and mustered up her remaining courage. It would be okay, she would be fine, the armor will hold up against the lance. Ailsa *promised* it would.

With a wave of the flag, Aberffraw violently kicked his horse forward. Fotini stalled a second and then ran forward at a slightly diminished pace to make it look like she was racing to meet her opponent. She lowered her lance and aimed directly at the center of Aberffraw's chest. He reached full speed just before Fotini skidded to a stop, dropped the reins to grasp her lance with both hands, and braced for impact.

A dull pain spread across Fotini's chest and shoulder as Aberffraw's lance struck. Her armor bent and a fresh dent adorned the cuirass, but it successfully saved her from the brunt of the impact. She felt the vibrations of her own lance cracking against Aberffraw's armor. This time the lance hit the center of the armor instead of glancing off to the side. Unable to move forward, Aberffraw was lifted out of the saddle and pushed backwards as his horse continued galloping down the track. With a thud and cloud of dust the undefeatable champion was defeated.

The stadium exploded in loud boos and a few cheers. Fotini trotted past Aberffraw where he lay on his back like an upside-down tortoise. She couldn't help but let out a small chuckle as he wriggled and cursed while his squire helped him up from the dirt. She nodded to him as she passed, not out of respect but out of pity.

Tragos met Fotini near the end of the stadium gate where they originally entered the match. "You did it! Now just stay quiet and let me do the talking while you accept your prize. Then we can get out of London before anyone thinks too hard about what they just saw."

Fotini nodded and the pair of them walked over toward the King's private box, where the young King sat with uncharacteristic attention as his herald made his way down the stairs with the golden idol of Artemis in hand.

"What an exciting display of strategy!" the herald said as the crowd fell silent. "I have never seen such a unique or entertaining match. I am happy to present to you this statue of the Roman goddess Diana which was recently uncovered in the ruins of the nearby Colosseum. More than just a golden trinket, this prize has value derived from the history of the conquerors who came to England nearly a thousand years ago and laid the foundations of this glorious city. This goddess was revered for her wild spirit, and the King has expressed he cannot think of a more fitting trophy for your performance. Come down from your horse so you may properly receive your prize."

Oh no! Fotini's mind scrambled for excuses as to why she couldn't dismount in front of the King, but before she could open her mouth Tragos stepped forward.

"Good Sir," Tragos said as he bowed. "Unfortunately, a splinter from Sir Aberffraw's lance has gotten lodged in the stirrups and Sir Capall is unable to disentangle himself at present. I ask that we may accept the prize on horseback, and we will sort out our predicament in private."

The herald was unphased but would not be denied in front of the King. "Nonsense. I am sure Sir Capall will be able to come down from his horse if we just undo this strap here."

Before either Tragos or Fotini could react, the herald pulled hard on the newly exposed rope at the base of the horse's neck. Fotini's disguise unraveled, and the horse's head and neck dislodged from her body and fell to the ground with a thud and puff of white flour. Fotini could suddenly feel the breeze on her exposed lower torso where her chestnut fur faded away to her hairless human navel. There was no hiding what she was now.

The herald stepped back in surprise and horror. After a moment of shock he yelled, "a centaur!?!"

Fotini grabbed the idol of Artemis. How dare they use her Roman name instead of the proper Greek! She stuffed it into a pouch hanging around her hip, and galloped toward the gate. Tragos ran after Fotini and leaped high into the air landing on her back as she ran out of the stadium to the outskirts of London.

2

Jaimie

"I hope they catch that monster," John Whitfield said from the back of a perfectly normal horse. John was a large man whose once youthful athletic body was now covered by a thin, but growing, layer of body fat. His formerly vibrant orange hair and beard showed his age with streaks of grey and white. At first glance he appeared friendly and approachable, but up close the corners of his eyes and lips lacked the friendly crinkles made by years of laughter.

John's son, Jaimie, discreetly rolled his eyes as his father ranted about the centaur who competed in the jousting tournament they just left. He looked like a young version of his father. He was still in possession of a youthful frame and a face too young to show a lifetime of emotion, either positive or negative. Jaimie grew tired of his father's obsessive disdain for any creature supposedly created by a pagan god or goddess. He had hoped his father would leave his hatred back in Ireland while doing business in England.

"Not only is it a godless heathen, but it's also a blasted cheat," John continued his rant. "But that's the guard's problem. I have more personal matters to discuss with you, my beloved son and only heir."

Jaimie's heart dropped into his stomach. The only thing worse than his father's tired obsession with unholy creatures was his new focus on ensuring his legacy would continue into future generations. Jaimie found it odd when John asked him to accompany him to England but tried to ignore the persistent thought that it was a ruse to arrange a marriage.

"We are going to meet my dear friend Sir Edward Hastings and his beautiful daughter Elizabeth for lunch at their estate. You no doubt remember Elizabeth from when they visited us while they traveled along the coast of Ireland seven years ago?"

Jaimie's suspicions for why he was asked to join his father in England were confirmed. John had paraded every girl in Ireland past Jaimie ever since he came of age. After three years of polite, but unstimulating, conversations Jaimie had disappointed every young woman on the island. Unfortunately, it appeared England still had eligible bachelorettes.

"I think I remember her." It would have been hard to forget the girl who lived as Jaimie's shadow for a summer when he was only ten years old. She was, in turn, followed by all the other young boys from the village surrounding Whitfield castle. Jaimie was suddenly very popular with all the other children hanging around the courtyard, at least until Elizabeth returned to England. "She had dark brown curls and freckles across her nose."

"That's right," John said with a small hint of a smile, which made him appear happier than Jaimie was accustomed to. "Anyway, her father purchased the last few barrels of our famous ale, so I thought you and Elizabeth should get reacquainted while we wait for Gorm to finish the other deliveries. I hear she has grown into a beautiful young woman, brimming with fertility."

Jaimie wasn't feeling quite ready to be a father, but something else John said caught Jaimie's divided attention.

"Gorm will be there?" Jaimie asked hopefully.

"He should arrive with the last of the ale to deliver sometime after lunch. Then we will all head back to the docks to take the last ship of the day back home."

Lunch still sounded dreadful, but at least Jaimie could look forward to spending the rest of the afternoon with his only real friend. Gorm was John's assistant and a reformed Viking. He came to Whitfield four years ago as part of a raid on the nearby monastery. Jaimie's father happened to be visiting the monks during the attack and immediately got to work vanquishing heathens. Amidst the carnage, he confronted a scared young boy who held a shiny unused sword in a shaky hand. John took pity on the scared Viking who hadn't spilled Irish blood and gave him an ultimatum. He would spare his life if the Viking renounced his pagan Gods and spent the rest of his life atoning for the sins of his upbringing.

Jaimie and John soon arrived at the Hastings estate. It was a large home befitting a noble with an expansive green lawn where Sir Hastings and Elizabeth waited at a sunlit table filled with food and desserts. Sir Hastings was a large man horizontally, but not vertically. He was balding, but the hair he still had was long and hung to his shoulders. Elizabeth, thankfully, still had a full head of dark curly hair and the little weight she carried was deposited in the ideal locations to attract most suitors. Jaimie could see she was very beautiful, and almost any man would be excited to court her. Almost.

"John! It has been too long!" Sir Hastings said as he embraced Jaimie's father. "I am glad you have finally decided to visit. This must be Jaimie! Last time I saw you, you were barely up to your father's elbow."

"And nearly to your chin," Jaimie said in an awkward attempt to make a joke.

"Uh, yes, quite right," Sir Hastings said with a growing twinge of pink in his cheeks. "You might remember my daughter, Elizabeth?"

"Of course," Jaimie said, turning to Elizabeth. "How could I forget the summer we spent together as children? I see you have grown quite... beautiful."

Elizabeth blushed and thanked Jaimie with a small curtsey.

Jamie glanced at his father and noticed a rare smile across his father's normally dower face as he watched Jaimie and Elizabeth's awkward interaction. Hastings broke the tension by addressing John. "Why don't we go inside to discuss the specifics of next year's shipment of ale? We may need enough for a large party within the next year."

"A fine idea," John said before following Hastings inside.

The silence between Jaimie and Elizabeth in the garden was deafening without their fathers present. "Should we sit down?" Jaimie asked.

"Yes," Elizabeth replied. Jaimie politely pulled aside a chair, which Elizabeth gracefully sat in and took his seat across from his surprise date. He hoped Elizabeth would start the conversation, but she simply smiled and stared into his eyes without speaking for an impossibly long moment. Jaimie fought the urge to groan as he searched his mind for appropriate topics of conversation.

"So, the weather is nice today, is this normal for springtime in England?" Jaimie couldn't believe he was attempting to start a conversation about the weather of all things.

"Yes," Elizabeth said without elaboration, although Jaimie couldn't completely blame her since the topic was incredibly dull. Jaimie was of the opinion the only time the weather was an interesting topic was when it was catastrophically bad. The sunshine was nice, but ultimately boring.

Jaimie grabbed a small sandwich from the stack in the center of the table and Elizabeth followed suit without contributing a question or comment of her own.

"I went to my first jousting tournament this morning," Jaimie said, changing topics. "Have you ever been to a tournament?"

"No." Elizabeth batted her eyes and smiled.

Maybe a more open-ended question would get things moving. "Tell me about yourself. What do you like to do? Do you have any hobbies or talents?"

"I like to weave." Three more words than before!

"What sorts of things do you like to weave? Patterns? Tapestries?"

"No, just solid colored cloth."

Jaimie waited for her to say what she did with the un-patterned cloth, but he shouldn't have bothered. He looked up at her mansion and saw both their fathers watching from the window. It appeared watching Jaimie's attempted conversation with Elizabeth was more entertaining than the conversation itself. Jaimie continued to try to get Elizabeth to say more than a single short sentence at a time, but she seemed incapable. What happened to the boisterous young girl who once followed him around the castle spewing a stream of consciousness at anyone with an ear?

He was about to ask her if she had any siblings when the familiar sound of horse hooves and wagon wheels filled the air. Jaimie looked down the lane and saw a very welcome sight.

A young man just shy of twenty steered two horses from atop a cart with only a few remaining barrels of ale strapped inside. The man had wavy golden hair hanging in curtains around a strong jaw accented with a few days' worth of stubble. When the wind caught his hair, scandalous pagan tattoos were revealed on his neck giving him an air of danger and a mysterious past. His bright blue eyes reflected the sun like flashes of lightning as they gazed in Jaimie's direction and soft lips pulled back into a welcoming smile. Gorm had finally arrived.

"I hope I'm not too late," Gorm said as he steered the cart next to the table where Elizabeth and Jaimie sat, the one-sided conversation finally concluded. Gorm's wide smile disappeared when his eyes flitted toward Elizabeth. "You must be Lady Hastings?"

"I am."

"Nice to meet you," Gorm said with an expressionless nod of his head. "Lord Hastings has ordered several barrels of Whitfield Ale, where should I take them?"

"I will ask my father," Elizabeth stood and walked inside.

"Sorry for interrupting your date," Gorm said with an unapologetic tone as Elizabeth disappeared into the house.

"Thank you for the interruption, she is the most boring person I have ever talked to," Jaimie said. "Either she is completely uninterested in me, or she has never been allowed to speak before. I hope it's the former."

Gorm's shining smile reappeared. "I doubt that," he said with exaggerated emphasis, "she's probably just nervous. Some people have trouble speaking when in the presence of such a wealthy and handsome man."

Jaimie felt a slight warmth in his cheeks.

John, Sir Hastings, and Elizabeth appeared inside the doorway, putting an end to Jaimie's private conversation with Gorm.

"You can place the barrels here and I will have someone take them inside," Sir Hastings said to Gorm with a slightly sour look as he stared at the neck tattoos. Jaimie suspected he would normally ask for the delivery to be taken inside but did not trust Gorm to leave empty-handed.

Gorm unloaded the cart as John and Sir Hastings talked about business while Jaimie stood awkwardly next to Elizabeth as she smiled blankly. When the cart was unloaded, Jaimie climbed up on the driver's bench next to Gorm's usual seat. "We probably should be heading out if we want to make the last ship."

John reluctantly agreed and gave Sir Hastings a firm embrace before climbing in the back of the empty cart where the ale was previously stored and turned back to Sir Hastings. "You and Elizabeth should come to Ireland before the end of the summer. We can continue our conversation then."

"I will make the arrangements," Sir Hastings said. After a few awkward goodbyes Jaimie, Gorm, and John headed down the path toward the docks.

3

Tragos

"Get off my back!" Fotini yelled as Tragos held on to her shoulders for dear life. An arrow whizzed past them as she galloped down the road outside of London. "I'm not a damn horse!"

"You ken that's only half true!" Tragos yelled over the wind and clopping of hooves against the hard dirt road. "I'm not nearly as fast as you are with only two legs! It's your pride or my life! Which is it!?!"

Fotini pushed forward without responding, but she stopped complaining. Tragos gripped Fotini's shoulders as more and more arrows whizzed past. He looked back and saw five guards on horseback getting closer. One of the riders looked Tragos in the eyes as he took aim and pulled an arrow back against his bowstring.

Tragos's vision suddenly blurred as an arrow slammed through his hat into one of his hidden horns. A sharp sting pulsed where the arrow hit, but thankfully he was mostly unhurt. He yanked the arrow free and tossed it by the roadside along with the unbearably hot hat he wore as part of his human disguise. He ran the fingers of one hand through his sweat-dampened hair, and along the curve of the black horns sprouting from his skull until he felt a rough hole where the arrow pierced the bone.

"Mhac Na Galla shot me in the head!" He swore. "Can you go any faster!?!"

"I'm running... as fast... as I can..." Fotini said between tired breaths as she ripped her helmet off her head releasing a loose braid of warm brown hair. "Get this... armor off me..."

Tragos gripped Fotini's back with his thighs and frantically started undoing the straps keeping the iron plate armor in place around Fotini's humanlike torso, but the bumping and jostling of Fotini's galloping didn't make it easy. He pulled out a small knife and started slicing away every leather strap he could find wrapped around Fotini. Bit by bit, the armor fell away with an unpleasant clang, like an old church bell hitting the ground, until Fotini was only wearing a knight's simple wool undershirt. In his haste, he accidentally cut the strap to Fotini's leather pouch she kept around her hip and watched it bounce down the road, releasing a handful of raspberries into the air as it went. Tragos swore under his breath knowing Fotini would be unbearable once she noticed her treats were gone.

Without the weight of the armor weighing her down, Fotini gathered speed and the guards from the city stopped gaining on her and Tragos, but they weren't falling behind either.

"Turn there!" Tragos yelled as he noticed a familiar tree next to the path. "Follow the plan!"

Fotini pivoted and the pair shot off the road into the tall grass of a field at the edge of the forest. The guards couldn't change direction as quickly as Fotini, but they were far from giving up their pursuit. They steered their hulking horses off the road and continued the chase, though at a slightly slower pace with the uneven terrain.

Tragos turned away from the guards and focused on the shadowy tree line they were quickly approaching. He recognized a large boulder at the edge of the forest as the spot where they stored the weapons and supplies they couldn't easily hide in their disguises for the tournament. Tragos's precious sword was less than a hundred yards away waiting behind the large stone.

Tragos scanned the shaded tree line behind the boulder until he finally saw what looked like a pair of shining eyes among the branches. He smiled; the reflective bits of scrap metal he had hammered into the tree earlier in the day looked just like a monstrous pair of eyes peering out from the shade of the trees. Hopefully these men would be just as superstitious as Fotini.

They skidded to a stop in the shadows beneath the trees and Tragos leaped off Fotini's back to dash behind the large boulder. He quickly brushed away the cover of leaves and retrieved his sword and Fotini's bow and quiver of arrows.

He held his breath and listened for the approaching men, his mind repeating a chorus of *please go away, please go away.*

"Stop!" Yelled one of the men, prompting the others to pull on their reins. Tragos carefully peered over the cover of the boulder to watch the men.

"Why did we stop?" asked the youngest sounding of the guards.

"This forest is cursed," said an older guard with a gruff voice. "The Cat Sí protects the pannites who live in the forest. She devours any man stupid enough to enter."

How dare he call the Children of Pan 'pannites!' Tragos tightened his grip on his sword as rage coursed through his veins.

The younger man laughed. "You still believe those old fairy stories? There's no such thing as a witch who transforms into a cat monster. You're just an old fool."

The young man tapped his heels against his horse and steered toward the forest at a slow trot.

"Get ready," Tragos whispered to Fotini. She pulled back an arrow as he carefully peaked around the boulder to prepare for a fight.

The young guard stopped, and the blood drained from his already pale face as his wide eyes fixed on something just above the boulder. He must have noticed the fake eyes Tragos nailed into the tree. The man pulled back on his reins and turned around.

"Let's get out of here," he yelled back to the rest of the guards. "We won't be able to catch the pannites in their forest."

The men turned and left, leaving Fotini and Tragos alone. Tragos let out a breath he didn't know he was holding. The best kind of fight is one avoided.

"Looks like my trick wasn't a waste of time after all," he said to Fotini. "You owe me a drink."

"I think they were afraid of her," Fotini said, pointing to the top of the boulder. Tragos turned around and saw a black cat with a small tuft of white fur on its chest sitting on the rock licking its paw clean.

Tragos picked up a rock and threw it, purposely missing the mangy beast, but getting just close enough to scare it off. "Get out of here you wee pest!"

The cat hissed and ran off into the forest.

Fotini smacked his horns with the butt of her bow. "You shouldn't antagonize the cats. For all you know that was the Cat Sí."

"Ah dinnae ken a lot of things, but I ken that is just a cat," Tragos said. "There is no such thing as a witch cat."

Fotini opened her mouth to respond but seemed to think better of it. She was probably as tired of their ongoing argument as Tragos was. Instead, Fotini stripped off the last of her human disguise and Tragos hurriedly looked away from her fully exposed torso. Even after years by each other's side he still did not know if she was comfortable changing in front of him as a seduction technique or because she saw him as a non-sexual entity, like a brother. Tragos hoped for the former but suspected the latter.

Tragos began changing out of his own disguise. The cool air felt wonderful as Tragos peeled away the oversized trousers hiding a thick layer of dark brown fur covering his goat-like legs. He tossed away the baggy plain shirt and replaced it with a green and gold tartan fly plaid and kilt which kept his fur-covered legs from overheating. He strapped his trusted sword to his hip and was finally ready for the long walk back home to the forest village of Coille Sealgair.

Feeling more like himself, Tragos turned back to Fotini. She was also finished with her own transformation and was decked out with practical saddlebags filled with her precious knives, supplies, and even an annoyingly loud salpinx horn was firmly strapped to the smooth chestnut fur of the horse part of her body. A quiver of arrows and a dory spear hung from the tan skin of her humanlike back. A single white cloth was tied around her chest while keeping her tattoo of a crescent moon crossed by an arrow over her navel visible at all times. Tragos once asked her about the tattoo, and immediately regretted it when Fotini started a lecture on the history of the symbol of Artemis.

"You ready?" Fotini asked. Tragos nodded and the pair began their journey through the forest.

The walk through the forest to Coille Sealgair was painfully slow as always. To discourage any humans attempting to find their home there were no trails or visible markers, but Tragos knew he was going in the right direction by the subtle smells of the forest. The distinct aroma of sweet wine, roasting meats, and cat piss wafted from Coille Sealgair and could be identified from miles away.

Fotini was abnormally quiet as they walked. She was probably still mad about Tragos's attitude towards the cats and her goddess. The pair shared many things in common; they both loved roasted venison on a sunny afternoon, enjoyed their job stealing from humans, and were capable of defending themselves if caught, but on the matter of the gods, their beliefs couldn't be more different.

The gods and goddesses of Greece were everything to Fotini. She clung to the traditions of the herd she was stolen from as a young filly by devoting herself to Artemis. When she learned the satyrs and centaurs in Coille Sealgair believed a huntress of their own, the witch Cat Sí, protected the hidden village, she instantly adopted the local rituals along with her own. Each night she left out a saucer of milk for the witch cat and she treated every feral feline with undue respect. She wholeheartedly believed the hundreds of wild cats in the village were there by the command of the Cat Sí. Tragos disagreed.

No one claimed to have seen the Cat Sí in nearly a thousand years. The reason the village was infested by cats was because fools like Fotini kept feeding them. If they stopped leaving out food and milk, the cats would eventually leave and Coille Sealgair would smell infinitely better. Tragos explained this to Fotini hundreds of times, but she kept feeding the beasts. Thinking about it instantly made the heat of Tragos's temper rise.

Tragos caught Fotini's gaze, and her warm brown eyes were like cool refreshing water poured over the burning coals of his temper.

"What are you going to do with your share of our earnings from the idol?" she asked.

Tragos had been trying to decide how he would spend his share of the profits ever since Ailsa told them she had a job paying twenty-five pounds each. They were usually paid a single silver penny for a standard job and two for a particularly difficult or dangerous heist. One day of cheating at jousting was worth years of hard work. It was more money than Tragos ever expected to have.

"I've always dreamed of leaving our smelly little village, but never gave much thought of where I would go," Tragos answered. He took a deep breath and continued. "I was thinking, with this much money we could sail the world. Maybe start by going south around Spain to the Mediterranean. We could stop at the sanctuary you always talk about in Sparta and then continue north to Thessaly."

Fotini stopped in her tracks. "You would help me go home?"

"Of course," Tragos said. "If you would let me come along."

Fotini turned with a smile devoid of any of the anger or sadness normally lingering at the edges of her eyes. She bent her knees low and scooped Tragos up into a giant embrace with his cloven hooves dangling in the air. "Thank you! Of course we can go together. I cannot imagine going anywhere without you!"

Just before Fotini squeezed the last of the air from his lungs, she set Tragos back down on the ground. She enthusiastically listed off all the places from her childhood home, and the land of Tragos's own ancestors, she wanted to show him as they continued through the forest towards Coille Sealgair. Tragos couldn't remember the last time he saw Fotini so excited about anything. She was so happy, she barely shuddered when they finally made it through the forest to the entrance of the hidden village, a dark tunnel at the base of tall cliffs.

Fotini stopped and squeezed Tragos's hand as she stared into the depths of the dark tunnel. "See you on the other side," she said, releasing his hand.

"I'll be waiting."

Tragos watched Fotini turn and trot to a narrow path leading up and over the cliff. The path was only ever used by Fotini since it was a much longer and more difficult path to the village, but it avoided the narrow tunnel barely wide enough for two Children of Pan to pass each other, but not quite wide enough for a centaur to turn around in. Over the years, Tragos watched Fotini fight dozens of men with all manner of weapons, drunken brawls with stallion centaurs twice her size, and even a memorable showdown with a large buck, but the only time he ever saw her truly afraid was when she peered into the shadowy depths of the claustrophobic tunnel.

Tragos slipped into the tunnel as he always did. After a few moments his eyes adjusted to the darkness with the only light coming from the occasional multicolored fae stone sticking out of the rough-cut tunnel walls. A few minutes later, he stepped back into the sunlight in the village of Coille Sealgair.

4

Fotini

No matter how many times Fotini hiked over the mountain, her legs burned with each step up the steep slope. Her lungs practically screamed for her to rest, but it was just another hundred feet before she would reach the summit. It wouldn't be long before she could sit in the shade and let the mountain breeze cool her skin.

Fotini walked to the shade of the only tree at this altitude and curled her legs beneath her to comfortably sit and take in the view of her home in England. The valley was a wide bowl with gentle slopes making a ring of mountains. The sheer cliffs acted as a natural barrier from the world of man, creating a shelter for the Children of Pan. Whenever Fotini looked over the valley, she always thought it looked like a crater created by a god striking the ground with their full might. An image of Artemis sending a celestial arrow to the ground followed by an earth-shattering explosion flashed across Fotini's imagination prompting an amused smile to spread across her face.

After several minutes, Fotini's breathing eased, meaning it was time to head down the slope. Her lethargic legs protested as she forced herself to her feet. Fotini wished she could sit and gaze over the valley for the rest of the day, but if she didn't make it back to Tragos within the next hour, she would be stuck listening to his nonstop complaining about how long he waited for her to join him.

His complaints weren't without a point, the tunnel was far faster than the mountain hike. If Fotini could find the courage to squeeze through the darkness under the mountain, the walk to the hidden village of Coille Sealgair would be hours shorter. She would already have a sack full of silver if she could just push herself to use the tunnel like everyone else. She wished she didn't have to go on this strenuous hike every time she wanted to enter the valley, but the mere thought of the small dark tunnel made her blood run cold.

Her mind lingered on the hole through the mountain as Fotini began her descent. She imagined walking through the dark and both her human and horse hearts started thrumming. She imagined being swallowed by the darkness with no way to move left or right. The stone walls slowly turned to wooden planks and the fleshy bodies of her fellow centaurs. She could feel the ropes binding her legs to the other unfortunate souls captured from the grassy plains of Greece. The centaur to Fotini's left was warm and shook as he sobbed while the centaur to her right was cold, rigid, and unmoving. The ropes binding her and the corpse together pulled into her skin as they held her lifeless neighbor upright. Fotini could smell the sweat and excrement caking all the centaurs' skin and fur after weeks at sea. She felt, heard, and smelled the memories every time she looked at the tunnel, but no images filled her mind because there was no light in the underbelly of the human's ship that stole her away from her home.

Fotini shook away the unpleasant memories as she continued walking down the gentle slope into the valley. With Fotini and Tragos coming into a massive payday, she could finally return to Thessaly, but there was no way home without crossing the sea. She silently prayed Artemis would give her the courage to make the journey when the time came.

Coille Sealgair came into greater focus with each step. From a distance the village appeared like any other, but the closer Fotini trotted the more cramped and thrown together it looked. The residents ran out of space for new buildings several hundred years ago, but they weren't brave enough to settle in the world of men outside the Cat Sí's protection. So new buildings were built on top of the existing structures to give each generation a home. Over time the village grew taller and more precarious with homes slapped together without rhyme or reason. It was cramped, and the smell of sweat, sewage, and while Fotini would never admit it to Tragos, feral cat urine sent shivers through Fotini's stomachs.

She couldn't wait to return to Greece.

Fotini felt the familiar sensation of soft fur brushing against her legs as she walked. She looked down and was greeted by a welcome face meowing for food. The black cat who lived on the mountain path looked up at her expectantly. Years of feeding the creature gave it certain expectations Fotini was too kind to deny.

"Hi there," she said to her wild friend as she crouched low and petted its soft fur. "I saw a cat who looked just like you earlier today, she even had the same crescent tuft of white fur on her chest, but that was miles from here. Do you have a sister? Here, let me give you a treat."

Fotini reached for a strip of jerky from the pouch hanging off her humanlike hip, but her fingers only found her skin. She looked down and patted all over her lower torso where smooth skin transitioned to soft fur, but her belt was missing. She quickly ripped open her saddlebags and frantically rummaged through the leather sacks, but there was no sign of the small pouch. Fotini poured the contents of her saddlebags on the ground in front of the cat who sniffed everything curiously. She had daggers, a blanket, some twine, but the most important item was missing.

The idol of Artemis was gone.

"Malaka!" Fotini swore as she frantically threw everything in her bags and slung them over her back. "Sorry cat, I don't have any treats today."

Fotini took off down the path at a gallop with a fresh surge of energy. The trees and grass blurred as she raced to reach Ailsa's shop before Tragos.

Fotini burst into the village and sprinted round each corner with both pairs of lungs burning. She narrowly avoided stepping on several cats, but knocked a poor satyr to the ground as she barreled down the narrow streets. She told herself the satyr would be fine; she didn't have time to stop and check. Fotini needed to find Tragos before he met with Ailsa. Hopefully, he had the idol so they could avoid Ailsa's wrath.

With a crunch of gravel, Fotini skidded to a halt outside Ailsa's shop, *A Fair Trade*, without meeting Tragos. The shop was on the bottom layer of buildings and stood out from the others with ornate flourishes carved into the colorfully painted wood. Every other building constructed in Coille Sealgair was left untouched in their natural color of wood. No one knew if the building was constructed this way to draw the eye to lure potential customers inside to spend their silver, or if it was Ailsa's style as the only creature in the valley who wasn't a Child of Pan.

After a deep calming breath, Fotini turned the handle and peeked into the brightly lit shop. Her eyes darted across the rows of shelves looking for Tragos. She hoped he was still at a pub somewhere in town drinking his fill, but her stomach dropped when she spotted the familiar dark brown curls with black curved horns.

"Fotini!" Tragos called out across the store.

There was no avoiding Ailsa's wrath now. Fotini trotted past displays of everything from cooking wares to freshly sharpened swords as she made her way across the room to a large countertop where customers paid Ailsa for the things Fotini and Tragos stole. In the center of the massive counter was a tiny desk covered in miniscule papers and ledgers too small to read with the naked eye. Sitting behind the toylike desk was Ailsa, a two-inch-tall pixie with blonde hair sparkling with pixie dust and a matching golden dress which almost looked as if it were woven out of the precious metal. Translucent insect-like wings sprouted from her back and magical dust followed her every movement like enchanted dandruff.

"Hello Fotini," Ailsa said. "I was just telling Tragos how relieved I am that you were able to retrieve the idol from the tournament. This item was requested by a very powerful client with a wild temper. I will send her a letter immediately to let her know the idol has arrived."

Fotini's stomach clenched.

"Here, have a drink and show Ailsa the idol," Tragos said as he handed Fotini a large tankard of ale.

Fotini picked up the drink and poured it down her throat without stopping for breath. The drink was terrible and burned on her parched throat, but she needed the moisture and a little additional courage before addressing Ailsa.

"Before you write your letter, there have been some developments you should be aware of," Fotini said as she wiped the foam from her mouth.

"Tragos already told me. You lost the armor I loaned you," Ailsa said butting in. "I will subtract the cost from your pay to cover a replacement."

Tragos's smile immediately disappeared. "Hey, that armor was a rusted mess that barely held together! We shouldn't have to pay for it. Plus, Fotini had to take several lances to the chest to get your golden trophy, she will probably be sore for a week. You should double her cut and screw the cost of your rusted junk."

"Your contract was already more than generous, and I don't see a scratch on Fotini," Ailsa said as her skin began to take on a reddish glow. "The armor appears to have done its job. I will not renegotiate your contract. You eagerly signed the contract and if you had read the whole document, you would know it specifically states the loaned armor must be returned in working order or you would each be docked five percent."

Tragos also turned red, but without the glow of fae magic. "You think I would be dumb enough to sign a fairy document without reading it first? I ken what it said, but it didnae state we would be facing the royal guard. We weren't prepared for that level of danger!"

"Don't act like you weren't up to the challenge of facing a few humans," Ailsa said calmly as her reddish glow faded into her normally golden light. "Why do you think I requested you two for the job? You are the only thieves I know with a greater than fifty percent likelihood of stealing the idol and returning here in one piece."

"You sent us out with those odds?" Tragos stepped closer to the desk and yelled at Ailsa, face to tiny face, but Fotini placed her hand on his shoulder to calm him and pull him back.

"The price is fine. You can take it out of my cut and leave Tragos's portion," Fotini said.

Tragos calmed knowing he would get his silver.

"That is fine by me," Ailsa said. "So, let's see the idol."

"Tragos," Fotini turned to her friend. "When you cut the armor off me, did you notice my pouch?"

"The one you keep snacks in?" Tragos asked with a confused expression.

"Yes."

Tragos looked goatish. "It was caught on the breastplate and tore off with it. I'll make you a new bag later."

Fotini raised her hand above her head to strike Tragos but decided not to start a fight in Ailsa's shop. She settled on glaring at him while his face shifted with the realization of what had happened. Ailsa was mentally quicker than the satyr and buzzed up into Fotini's face.

"You lost the idol!?!" Ailsa yelled as she fluttered in front of Fotini with sparkling dust trailing behind her. Ailsa's normally golden, glowing complexion gave off a bright red hue as she yelled. "What do you expect me to tell my client? Do you have any idea how important this idol is? Any idea how much trouble we are in?"

"No," Fotini said with an icy calm as she fought the urge to swat Ailsa away. "You never tell us about your clients, so how could we know?"

Ailsa yelled with a volume far exceeding the expected capability of someone so small. "We need to get it now! If not, she will separate our limbs from the rest of our bodies!" Ailsa started pelting Tragos and Fotini with burning sparks of magic to push them outside the shop. She yelled and ranted about how 'she' was going to rip them limb from limb, but never elaborated on who this 'she' was. Client confidentiality was extremely important when purchasing stolen items after all.

Fotini paused outside the shop and flung Tragos onto her back, before taking off down the road at a gallop. Her cheeks burned as she passed a couple of centaurs gawking at her while carrying a satyr, but there was no time to stop. She had to get to the idol if she was ever going to have enough gold to leave this island.

Please let the idol still be there, she silently prayed to her favorite goddess as she ran. *Please help me.*

5

Jaimie

In Jamie's opinion, the worst part of traveling was the moment the journey shifted from a quest toward a destination into the long slog back home. The excitement and adventure of constantly exploring something new, something unknown, only happens in one direction. As Jaimie sat at the front of the cart, he couldn't help but feel a small pang of sadness as he picked out landmarks he noticed on his way to London.

Jaimie did not hate his home at Whitfield, he appreciated what his family's status provided, but it was always the same routine. His studies were interesting, but hearing about faraway lands and peoples would never compare to immersing oneself in the sights, sounds, and tastes of a distant land. It was fine to read about knights going on quests to find godly weapons or face elvish tricks and traps, but it would be another thing entirely to go on a quest himself to see what kind of man he truly was.

This hunger for adventure may partially explain why Jaimie enjoyed his combat lessons with Gorm. Honing his sword fighting abilities with someone who had experienced actual combat across the sea was almost like experiencing it himself. The unarmed skirmishes where he wrestled with the young Viking, pushing and pulling against each other until one of them, usually Gorm, was on top of the other was also very enjoyable. It also helped prepare Jaimie to defend himself if he was ever disarmed, or at least that is what Jaimie told his father.

"So, I couldn't help notice your conversation with Elizabeth was... lacking," Gorm said once the familiar drone of John's snores from the back of the wagon filled the air. Jaimie's father was never one to pass up a nap in the warm sun while others drove the cart.

"That's one interpretation. I tried to connect to her, but she was just so..." Jaimie struggled to find the most tactful way to describe a woman of such few words.

"Boring?" Gorm suggested with a confident smile.

"Yeah, she was definitely boring." Jaimie could not envision himself with Elizabeth or any of the women his father pushed him to consider. While many of them were not as boring as Elizabeth, there was never any spark. Jaimie never felt the desire to move closer to them and never wondered what their lips would feel like against his.

"A handsome man like you can do much better than someone as plain and uninteresting as... What was her name again?" Gorm asked with a sarcastic smirk. "You need someone more fun and adventurous. Someone who can stand by your side as you go on one of those adventures you always talk about."

Jaimie caught Gorm's eye and felt a slight wave of warmth in his chest.

"Someone like..." Jaimie started to say 'someone like you' but stopped when a thin tinge of pink spread across the skin high on Gorm's cheeks above his fair beard. Gorm squirmed uncomfortably in his seat and glanced at Jaimie's still sleeping father.

"So, how were the deliveries?" Jaimie asked to change the subject to something less dangerous. Gorm's smile and easy-going attitude gradually returned as he described his encounters with the merchants and tavern owners in London. While his golden locks had grown out over the years at Whitfield until they nearly covered the tattoos etched into the side of the former Viking's head, the tip of a serpent's head peeking past his sideburns was still visible. His toned arms had no natural covering, so tattoos from his past were clearly visible on warmer days like today when he wore short sleeves. Jaimie held a secret fascination with the curved interlocking patterns and stories of pagan gods and monsters from a world across the sea coating his friend's arms, but he imagined they were quite intimidating to scrawny Englishmen.

Jaimie loved listening to Gorm talk. While his stories about his daily activities weren't nearly as exciting as when Gorm regaled Jaimie with the tales of his homeland, it was nice to just hear his voice. His voice was deep, but soft and comforting like a warm blanket of furs on a winter night.

Gorm was in the middle of describing a merchant so scared he could barely talk, when something seemed to catch his eye. He pulled on the reins tight to stop the horses pulling the cart. He pointed to the road, where nearly a dozen arrows stuck out of the dirt like hedgehog quills. Jamie glanced around at the surrounding wood and spotted additional arrows poking out of the trees lining the road.

"What in hell happened here?" Gorm asked in a low voice more to himself than to Jaimie. He slowly urged the horses to resume walking, but at a significantly slower pace. Gorm scanned the surrounding trees and kept quiet to see if he could hear anything hidden in the shade.

Following Gorm's example, Jaimie sealed his lips and focused his attention on the forest surrounding the road. He spotted more arrows among the trees and flinched at every squirrel or swaying branch. None of the movements ever turned out to be bandits or angry pannites, but off to the side of the road, something reflected the light of the afternoon sun directly into Jaimie's eyes. He pointed out the metallic glint to Gorm, who stopped the horses to investigate.

The reflective item turned out to be most of the top half of a dented breastplate accompanied by a worn leather pouch.

"Looks like a piece of armor," Gorm said. "Wonder why they ditched this?" Gorm said as he opened the pouch. Inside was a broken idol of a woman holding a bow. At first glance, the idol looked like solid gold with silver accents, but the damage showed that it was merely gold-plated hollow ceramic.

"I think this is the trophy from the jousting tournament," Jaimie said. "An old idol of a Roman goddess was the prize, but it was stolen by a centaur during the tournament. They probably left it when they saw it was not actually gold. Looks like the con artists got conned with a worthless trinket."

"Maybe. Or maybe they just dropped it," Gorm said, gesturing to the arrows sticking out of the ground and surrounding trees. Gorm inspected the statue closer and stuck his fingers inside the hollow opening in the top half of the statue. He pulled out an old piece of parchment concealed inside the broken idol.

"What does it say?" Jaimie asked as Gorm unfurled the paper.

"I don't know. I don't recognize these symbols" Gorm handed the slip of paper to Jaimie to examine. Jaimie recognized the alphabet from his tutoring as Greek. John insisted Jaimie be able to read the Bible in all the original texts, so he had a passable knowledge of Latin, Greek, and Hebrew. The words weren't as formal as they were in scripture, the speech was for someone with a close and casual relationship with the writer. It took a few tries, but Jaimie eventually deciphered the letter:

Dear Sister,

I have foreseen you opening a door at the stone of the fae kings with Lugh's crown as the key. The crown is on the trickster's brow in a sapling of Yggdrasil on the island of the fae. You are searching on the wrong island. Please hurry, so you can return home.

Your brother in spirit,
A.

"What does that mean?" Jaimie asked.

"I'm not sure," Gorm replied. "Though I recognize a weird part of it. In the stories from my childhood, there is a tree called Yggdrasil that is so large it holds up our world on its lower branches."

"Pagan nonsense," Jaimie's father said behind them.

Jaimie jumped when John spoke. He was so absorbed in the odd letter he hadn't noticed the sudden lack of snoring coming from the cart. John towered behind the young men with his usual stern expression.

"True," Gorm said in a slight tone of panic. Jaimie noticed his friend always grew nervous whenever anyone mentioned his pagan upbringing around his father. "I was just explaining a word in this letter we found on the side of the road. Jaimie, show your father what we found."

Jaimie showed his father the broken prize and accompanying letter. As Jaimie's father read the letter his slightly irritated expression grew into a deep scowl.

"You found this on the side of the road?" he asked, glancing up from the letter.

"We found it in this." Jaimie handed his father the broken idol of a goddess with a bow and arrow. He looked over the idol for a moment before dropping it unceremoniously into the dirt.

"Well, that clinches it. A false idol is never a good thing, and one with a hidden message is definitely dangerous." Jaimie's father stuffed the letter in his pocket. "I will burn the letter far from here, so the message never makes it to the intended recipient. Let's get moving again, we still have a long journey, and we can't afford to miss the boat."

John turned back to the road and climbed clumsily back into the cart with Gorm dutifully following close behind, but Jaimie lingered in the road. Without any conscious plan or thought, he quickly scooped up the pieces of the idol and slipped them into the leather bag he carried on long journeys. Maybe it was because he appreciated the history and mystery of the object, or maybe it was because it was forbidden, but he wanted to keep it.

Jaimie hopped atop the cart next to Gorm and the group resumed their journey back home to Ireland. It wasn't long before John's snores once again filled the afternoon air, and Jaimie and Gorm were back to chatting and joking as they traveled.

6

The Cat Sí

The Cat Sí was disappointed in Ailsa and Fotini for losing the idol, but not Tragos. Disappointment requires respect, and the Cat Sí could not respect someone who threw rocks to scare away cats, especially since she was often one of the targets. Her cheeks burned at the thought of Tragos almost hitting her with a rock the size of her head. If the Cat Sí was at full strength the satyr would be dead by now. Ribbons of his flesh would be hanging from the tree branches, adding a splash of red to the deep greens of the Cat Sí's kingdom. It was what Tragos deserved, but even if the Cat Sí could harm Tragos she would not. It would break Fotini in a way the Cat Sí could never recover from.

Please let the idol still be there. Fotini's silent prayer reverberated through the Cat Sí's mind as she sprinted through the underbrush towards the edge of the forest. She pushed herself onward, using Fotini's pleas to push past the need for rest. *I beg you, please ensure your idol is safe.*

The Cat Sí remembered what life was like in England before Fotini arrived in Coille Sealgair. Her mind had grown nearly empty in her solitude, only the sense that she was more than merely a stray remained. The Children of Pan told stories of a witch in the form of a cat protecting the forest, but they could no longer recall who she really was or why she protected them from the humans in the fields and cities. As parts of her story faded from the memories of the people, she forgot as well. They called her the Cat Sí, the cat witch, so that was who she became.

She skulked through the streets of Coille Sealgair hunting mice and drinking milk left out by the people who told the few remaining stories about her. The stories were enough to keep her going, to give her enough power to stay tethered to this world, but she was but a shadow of what she felt she once was. She was a witch and a rumor, nothing more.

Then Fotini came.

She would never forget the first night she heard Fotini's voice in her mind. The sound was small, nearly indistinguishable from the sounds of the village. The Cat Sí thought it was just another Child of Pan talking to a friend on the street below, but then she heard an old, yet familiar, name. A powerful name. A name that once meant something to her. Not the title of a nameless witch, but a name with power and tradition. Images of a silver bow and the reflection of a youthful maiden with pale skin untouched by sunlight flashed across her mind as power surged through her for a brief moment reminding her of what she had lost more than providing any answers.

Lady Artemis, please help me through the night. The words echoed through her mind as if they were her own thoughts.

The Cat Sí slunk from her perch atop a leaky roof and headed toward the sound. The voice continued to plead in the night for protection for herself, and for others she feared were eternally lost. The words grew disjointed as their source slipped into the realm of sleep. The Cat Sí rushed through the muddy streets desperate to find the poor soul who knew the old traditions.

As the last words dissipated to the soft sounds of rest, the Cat Sí slipped through a cracked open door and saw a lone centaur asleep on a pile of hay. *"Help me,"* she said in foreign, yet familiar, tongue as she finally drifted to sleep and the Cat Sí heard her with her ears as well as in her mind.

The centaur was covered in dirt, and her chestnut braid was loose and tangled with sticks and leaves. Bruises covered her skin, and deep scratches covered the lower half of her body. Despite all this, the young woman was the most beautiful creature the Cat Sí had seen in many, many years. Beneath the bruises she was strong and wild. She clearly lived as her kind was meant to, free to run over hills of grass and not cramped into a tiny valley with barely enough space to turn around.

The young centaur adjusted herself in her sleep exposing her stomach and a simple tattoo of a crescent bow crossed by an arrow. The Cat Sí silently stepped forward and licked the symbol just beneath the woman's skin and more flashes of the young maiden once again filled her mind. She could feel the smooth warm metal of a bow forged out of light made solid in her hand. She could see a giant boar running through the forest and she remembered drawing back an arrow with thin fingers instead of paws. Were these memories of a life once lived? Was this who the Cat Sí truly was?

Among the snippets of blurred memory, a single image appeared as clear as the young centaur sleeping in the hay. A golden idol of Artemis, the maiden goddess of the hunt and moon. She suddenly burned with the need to locate this idol. She knew it would lead her home, wherever that was.

She looked at the battered centaur and felt compelled to do something, anything to help her. She softly licked the dirt and grime off the creature, and the chestnut fur began to shine in the moonlight. When her tongue passed over a cut or bruise, she was surprised to see them healed by some long-forgotten magic. Just before the sun broke the horizon the Cat Sí stepped back, admired her work, and disappeared into the darkness.

The Cat Sí meowed but otherwise silently cursed her foul luck as she leaped out of the long grass of the meadow and reached the well-worn dirt road on the outskirts of London. She ran toward the city as fast as her four legs could carry her, which was considerably faster than was normal for any other cat. Arrows stuck out of the ground beside the road and she slowed down to search the area. Fresh hoof prints showed how Fotini was chased by several men on horseback a few hours earlier and the Cat Sí knew this would be the most likely spot to find the dropped idol.

She spied a glint of a metal bouncing off a rust spotted breastplate in the thick grass next to the road. The Cat Sí sauntered over and flipped the piece of armor over using her black fur-covered paws fueled by a steady stream of Fotini's prayers. Tangled in the leather straps used to attach the breastplate to a knight was a simple leather pouch smelling of a strange mixture of horsehair and human sweat.

The Cat Sí fumbled with the pouch trying to open it with her small paws. She suspected she would be able to stretch out her paws until they turned into long thin fingers if only another person on this island would send her their prayers. Opening the pouch would be simple with hands and thumbs, but she was stuck with stubby paws. So, instead of taking a more practical form she cursed again in the language of cats and managed to flip open the leather flap closing the bag.

It was disappointingly empty except for a few berries.

She let out an irritated hiss and sniffed the inside of the bag. She easily smelled raspberries and years' worth of squished berry juice, but another scent was present, so faint it was almost the memory of a scent. The Cat Sí drew a long breath through her nose drawing in the scent of summer campfires, olive oil, and the mouthwateringly sweet smell of ambrosia.

The Cat Sí knew this combination of scents, but the full memories still lay just outside her mind. Images of a tall man with a smooth, eternally young face and hair that could have been spun from gold filled her thoughts. She knew she once loved this man as if he were her own brother, but his name still eluded her after all these years. The only thing she could recall clearly was that he was the one who sent her the idol.

A quick look around the grass and roadside was fruitless. While the idol was definitely here earlier, it was long gone now. The Cat Sí pawed in the dirt and sniffed the air. Among the whiffs of men, horses, and one particularly pungent satyr, the Cat Sí could still smell the smallest trace of the idol on the wind from down the road.

The Cat Sí took off following the fragrant traces of her former life. Her heart pounded in her chest with excessive power and speed, and not merely from sprinting mile after mile. Anxiety and excitement coursed through her as her thoughts spun between the prospect of finally finding her prize and the fear of just missing it.

She started to run after the idol but suddenly stopped. In less than an hour Fotini would arrive and learn the idol was gone. Fotini would be devastated,

Ailsa would think she broke her promise, and Tragos would be furious. Two of those outcomes were unacceptable and must be avoided. The Cat Sí looked around and chose a particularly wide silver birch just to the side of the road.

With a single claw extended, the Cat Sí dug into the soft tree bark facing the road and carved a crescent bow crossed by an arrow pointing down the road in the direction of the idol's scent. Most people wouldn't pay the carving a second glance, but the Cat Sí had almost as much faith in Fotini as Fotini had in her.

The Cat Sí purred to herself in satisfaction and raced down the road toward the idol. After a thousand years, she would soon have it in her grasp and be able to return home.

7

Ailsa

Ailsa's fingers were growing numb as she clasped them together with her arms squeezing around one of Tragos's horns. The wind rushed past her ears muffling all the sounds of the forest so the only other sound was the pounding of Fotini's hooves. her stomach lurched as Fotini darted between trees, ducked under low hanging branches, and leaped over the uneven terrain. She had spent years wishing for an adventure outside her clean and predictable store, but now she wished she was back behind her desk writing in her ledger.

When Fotini finally skidded to a stop, Ailsa lurched forward and her skin glowed a faint green as she fought the urge to expel her lunch in Tragos's hair.

"It's... got... to be... here... somewhere...," Fotini said between desperate gasps of air. Ailsa flew to solid unmoving earth and laid down on her back staring up at her larger companions. She noticed Fotini's humanlike chest rapidly rise and fall and the muscles in her horse-like sides tighten and relax in tandem with each breath. Did she have two sets of lungs?

Ailsa expected Tragos to step back and wait for Fotini and her to recover enough to search for the lost idol, but he rose above those admittedly low expectations. Instead, he hopped off Fotini's back and immediately got to work searching for the idol in the tall grass by the side of the road. It was the first time Ailsa had ever seen Tragos outside of A Fair Trade, it was also the first time she watched him work. He was quiet and systematically moved through the grass with intense focus and not a single sarcastic remark. Where was the lazy, uncaring satyr Ailsa tolerated for Fotini's benefit?

"I remember the breastplate with your pouch attached to it landed on this side of the road," Tragos said to Fotini once she had caught her breath enough to join the search. "The damn grass is too hard to see past though. You're taller, maybe you'll have better luck."

Fotini trotted along the road, slowly glancing over the grass. With each passing moment Ailsa grew slightly more panicked. She promised her client, the murderous Cat Sí, she would deliver the idol. She tried not to think about the torment awaiting her if she broke her promise.

The waiting soon surpassed her motion sickness and Ailsa buzzed up into the air. She flew just above the trees and quickly spotted the glint of metal among the green grass. "It's over here!" she yelled as she dived toward the breastplate.

"Thanks for the help," Tragos said as he flipped over the breastplate and pulled off the attached leather bag. He unceremoniously shook the pouch, but only a few raspberries fell out.

"No, no, no!" Ailsa said with her glow turning a dull pale white. The idol had to be here. If it was not here, then it was truly lost, and if it was lost she would never be able to fulfill her promise. As this realization washed over her, pricks of pain began to cover her body, like her blood was growing slightly sharp within her veins.

Tragos leaped deeper into the tall grass. "Maybe it fell out of the pouch, let's keep looking."

A flicker of hope filled Ailsa and the pain receded. She might still keep her promise.

The trio searched the grass and paced up and down the road for nearly an hour. Ailsa buzzed back and forth as Tragos worked silently and Fotini mumbled something under her breath. The pain returned as Ailsa began to accept her fate when Fotini suddenly gasped.

"Look there, at the tree by the road!"

Fotini bounded forward with Tragos and Ailsa following closely behind. "Do you see the idol?" Ailsa asked.

"No," Fotini said with an annoyingly satisfied tone, "but I know where it went."

Ailsa felt a slight burn under her skin and knew she was beginning to glow red. "How could you possibly know that?"

"Artemis left a sign," Fotini said matter-of-factly. The centaur pointed to a freshly cut symbol of a crescent moon crossed by an arrow. "It's my tribe's symbol for the goddess Artemis but inverted. The arrow normally points left as if being fired by a bow shaped like the moon. This carving has the arrow pointing to the right. If we head that way," Fotini pointed down the road, "we will find the idol."

Tragos grunted with a tone to match Ailsa's own feelings. "So, someone carved a couple lines. That disnae mean anything."

"No one on this barbaric island worships Artemis except for me. Who would even know this symbol, let alone carve it?" Fotini asked sternly. "The whole way here I prayed for Artemis to help us find her idol. She is the best tracker among all the gods. She clearly wants us to go this way."

Ailsa looked down the road with a heavy feeling in her tiny stomach. She had no faith in Fotini's deities, but the idol clearly wasn't here. "Where does the road lead?"

"To the docks," Tragos said. "It's a long walk, but there's nothing else but a few farms on this road. Unless it was picked up by one of those farmers, the idol will be headed there."

Fotini suddenly looked less enthusiastic about her plan. "Then I guess we better hurry before the idol ends up on a ship. Get on."

Ailsa landed on Tragos's head between his horns while he hopped onto Fotini's back. Ailsa closed her eyes, took a deep breath, and braced for another bumpy ride.

The sun was setting by the time Tragos, Fotini, and Ailsa approached the end of the road where dry land met the vast open sea. Ailsa thought Fotini must be near collapsing as her entire body heaved with each breath. The centaur trotted shakily off the road, carrying Tragos and Ailsa down a small hill to a nearby riverbank. Tragos, and by extension Ailsa, slid off Fotini's back and she immediately splashed into the water. She bent low and dunked her face underwater seemingly to inhale as much water as possible in a decidedly unfeminine manner. Tragos waded to his ankles and dipped a canteen into the stream to drink with slightly less haste and far more propriety.

"They can't be far off," Ailsa said as she sat on Tragos's head, using his horns to steady herself. "Unless they also sprinted down the road."

"It disnae matter," Tragos said. "They might as well be across the ocean if they've made it out to sea. These boats go all over Europe."

Tragos peaked over the tall grass around the riverbank towards the wooden planks stretching from the sand onto the sea. Large ships swayed at the docks, towering over the humans scurrying up and down ramps to either load or unload cargo. Not a single fae or Child of Pan was in sight, only humans worked these docks.

"Maybe," Ailsa said. "But we need to get that idol, or my client will kill all three of us. I'm going to search."

"Your client will do what!?!" Tragos yelled after Ailsa as she took flight.

Without a response, Ailsa buzzed higher and higher into the air until Tragos and Fotini were only wet specks in a small dirty pond. She made her way above the nearest ship and tried to calm her nerves. Slowly her bright anxious glow faded to a peaceful pale blue. Not the dark blue of fear, but a more pleasant shade reminiscent of the clear sky over a summer picnic. As her color grew peaceful, her light dimmed, and all harshness receded. This light would not be as noticeable as bright reds or yellows. Satisfied, she slowly descended near the mast.

The search was slow. Speeding along out in the open would generate too much light, so Ailsa glided along as if finding the idol meant nothing to her, even though nothing mattered more at the moment. She searched the cargo the best she could. She rummaged through every bag as they were loaded, and even slipped into the packs slung over a few passengers' shoulders, but after an exhaustive search it was clear the idol was not aboard the first ship.

The second and third ships were frustratingly empty of small pagan idols, although the second one contained a disturbingly large assortment of iron weapons, which Ailsa avoided. The fourth vessel Ailsa searched was nearly ready to disembark to Dublin, giving her very little time. As she was about to move on, Ailsa finally spotted a golden glint coming from the top of a young red-haired boy's pack set beneath the bench he was sitting on.

Ailsa landed next to the pack and climbed inside. The interior of the bag was suddenly filled with joyous yellow light as Ailsa saw the golden form of a woman holding a bow. The idol was here! She could keep her promise to the Cat Sí! Ailsa grabbed the arm of the statuette and pulled. The sound of scraping porcelain rang through the pack and Ailsa watched in horror as the idol collapsed into two pieces.

No matter. She would simply have to repair the idol when they got back to Coille Sealgair. Ailsa grabbed the arm of the statuette again and pulled, but she could not lift it. She tried to move the lower half with disappointingly similar results.

As Ailsa pulled, she felt a shudder go through the pack. She slipped out of the opening and noticed the ship rocking back and forth as men used oars to push off from the dock. She dove back into the bag and pulled on the idol, but it was just too heavy.

There was nothing to be done but get Fotini and Tragos. Ailsa flew out of the bag and streamed through the air back to where her colleagues waited.

"Hey!" Ailsa yelled to Fotini and Tragos waiting next to the small pond. "Listen! I found the idol sticking out of a human's pack."

Tragos perked up. "Did you get it?"

"It's three times my size! Can you carry a life size statue of a stallion centaur? It's still on the ship."

"Then let's go!" Tragos said, leaping to his feet.

"Good hustle, but it's too late," Ailsa said. "They just left port to Dublin."

"Well then, I guess we're done," Tragos said, sitting back down. "It's a shame your client will kill you. Can we have your shop when you're dead?"

Ailsa flashed red. "You aren't giving up that easily. My client will hunt us all down if we fail. We cannot abandon it. I said I would get it, so I *have* to get it.

I can fly to the ship and find out where the people with the idol are headed and meet you outside of Dublin."

"How are we getting to Dublin?" Fotini asked. "You know as well as I do, no captain will risk their reputation taking me and Tragos."

Ailsa's light turned a slightly pinkish glow. "I know someone. He leaves England every night at midnight from a hidden dock about a mile south of here. I have an arrangement with him to smuggle fae back and forth to Ireland. I hear he also takes Pannites."

"It's Children of Pan," Tragos snapped.

"In that case, it's Aos Sí, not fae," Ailsa snapped back to hide her embarrassment in calling satyrs and centaurs by the term the humans used. "The point is, if you follow the beach below the cliffs to the south, you can find Captain Harold. Tell him I sent you and to subtract your fare from the money he owes me. I will head to his secret dock in Ireland immediately after I arrive in Dublin."

Without another word, Ailsa flew off into the sky.

8

Tragos

T he ocean roared in the night as Tragos and Fotini walked down the beach with their hooves squishing unpleasantly on the sand. Hills next to the sloping sand dunes rose sharper and more jagged until they became enormous cliffs looming over a small strip of sand and sea. In the dark shadows beneath the cliffs, the night tide swirled and wore away the stone to create a deep sea-cave. Deep in the cave where the moonlight couldn't reach, old and slightly rotted boards covered the jagged rocks. Tragos was perfectly at home with the chaotic terrain, but Fotini held firmly to Tragos's hand. The deeper they delved the tighter she held. She carefully watched each of her nervous and shaky steps. A broken leg spelled death for a centaur. Tragos silently squeezed her hand and helped steady her as they walked. As much as Tragos wanted to think Fotini held his hand out of affection, he knew it was simply out of terror.

At the far end of the dock, Tragos and Fotini found a slightly beat up ship with the name *Harold's Love* in yellow letters painted on the side and an even more worn looking crew leading a stream of fae and a few Children of Pan aboard while Captain Harold watched lazily. Tragos knew the man must be Captain Harold because he was far more well-dressed than the rest of the crew. He was a tall man filled with obvious confidence and swagger, wearing a blue overcoat that faded to a salt bleached white around his shins.

"Room for two more to Ireland?" Tragos asked.

Harold looked at Tragos briefly before sizing up Fotini with a widening smile and addressing her directly. "For a beauty like you? Of course! Two silver coins each. Oh, we also have several fae on board. I assume that won't be a problem?"

"As long as they dinnae have a problem with us," Tragos said as if he were the one addressed by the captain. "I would prefer not to be cursed today. Speaking of Fae, we are on business for Ailsa, the pixie who lives in Coille Sealgair. She said to subtract our fare from her share of the profits from her referrals."

"Of course," Harold's smile disappeared when he addressed Tragos, "but I will charge her a convenience fee on top of the ticket price. As for the fae, they have all promised not to use offensive magic aboard the ship, but in return they ask all weapons to be left above deck."

Harold held out his hand, and Fotini unhooked the spear strapped along her side and held it out. He grabbed the wooden shaft, but Fotini seemed to have difficulty releasing her grip on her weapon. The captain pulled hard to get her to relinquish her spear, bow, and quiver. Tragos didn't enjoy giving up his sword, either, but they couldn't swim to Ireland, so he handed it over without a fuss.

Tragos and Fotini walked up the ramp and were quickly led to a large door with a second rickety decline leading downward into the dark underbelly of the ship. Tragos gazed into the darkness and felt his heart freeze in his chest for Fotini. He turned and looked up into her wide eyes as beads of sweat formed at her temples.

"Let's turn back, we can find another way," she said with a clear note of panic.

"There is no other way." Tragos held her hand gently and tugged slightly to lead her down into the darkness. "Ireland isn't far, we will be there by morning."

"Then we let Ailsa figure things out on her own. We can take a different job. I can't do this."

It was Tragos's turn to be the voice of practicality. "If we abandon Ailsa, there won't be another job, and we will never get enough gold to get you back home to Thessaly. Besides, we live on an island. You will need to get on a ship someday if you are ever going to show me Greece. Think of this as a practice trip."

"What's the holdup?" Harold asked as he stomped up the ramp. "Get below deck. Now!"

"Give us a second!" Tragos turned back to Fotini and clasped both her hands gently. "Everything will be alright. I will be with you the whole way."

Tragos slowly walked backwards into the darkness, never breaking eye contact as Fotini slowly, carefully followed. As soon as they were clear Harold slammed the door shut.

Once Tragos and Fotini were off the ramp and firmly below deck, Tragos looked around to see what exactly they had gotten themselves into. They seemed to be where sailors traditionally stored their cargo, but instead of spices or glittering trinkets, the shipment consisted of squished centaurs, satyrs, and rafters filled to the brim with multicolored fae. Tragos spotted the characteristic glittering wings of pixies and the platinum blonde hair of the elves. All the fae were small. The tallest was probably around two and a half inches, but Tragos was still wary of them. Ailsa was bad enough, but a swarm of magical imps was too much for him.

"Let's get this over with," Tragos said as he attempted to find a place to stand that didn't put his head directly in someone else's rear end. He succeeded by standing behind another satyr and beside the mid-section of a centaur. Fotini took the space on the other side of the two satyrs, and slowly crushed them as the ship rocked in the sea. With the door to the outside closed, the darkness was suffocating, even for Tragos, but it seemed the fae could be useful for something after all. Slowly, small glowing orbs of magic light appeared amongst the fae, giving the ceiling a soft blue glow that almost fully illuminated the non-magically blessed creatures below.

Shortly after the door was secured with a loud click, Tragos heard the crew preparing to launch from the dock and into the sea. Everything swayed and creaked as they pushed off. Tragos closed his eyes tightly and took deep breaths to quell his anxious and tumultuous stomach. He focused on the surrounding sounds to take his mind off of the swaying that would be present for the next few hours. The rest of the Children of Pan seemed to share his feelings toward the sea. He heard many deep breaths and soft groans, but otherwise silence from the normally boisterous bunch. By contrast, the fae seemed downright calm. The elves talked to each other excitedly as they sat in small seats or walked along the network of bridges and railings that crisscrossed the room about a foot below the ceiling. The difference in quality between the accommodations for the fae and

Children of Pan was stark, with no attempts to hide which group the humans preferred, or which they feared more.

It didn't take long to set into a steady stride, sailing on the sea. Whenever the vessel swayed, Fotini slid into Tragos, crushing him into the centaur on his other side. Tragos was the center of a reverse sandwich, where the soft satyr bread was stuck between two slabs of hot centaur meat. He was jealous of Fotini's height; her face wasn't ever pressed into a stranger's naked, sweaty fur. The uncomfortable situation continued for the entire journey, with everyone packed together. After a night of being slowly crushed between two moist horse-like bodies, it was a relief when the ship turned and shifted as it docked at what Tragos assumed was the Irish shore.

9

Jaimie

Jaimie peered over the side of the ship and let his tired mind slip beneath the waves. The shimmering moonlight gave form to the water's surface but did not penetrate the dark of the sea at midnight. Staring into the black void, Jaimie's thoughts were free of distraction, free to linger on things unsaid and what the future could bring if only Jaimie had the confidence to reach out and take it.

His thoughts lingered on the memory of Gorm's expression as he told Jaimie he deserved someone better than the girls his father paraded past him. Someone who would stand by his side and help make his dreams a reality. In the darkness Jaimie could almost hear the part Gorm could not say with words but exclaimed through deep blue eyes, *Someone like me.*

"You see Jörmungandr down there?" Gorm asked, as a way of making his presence known.

"What is Yor-mund-dung..."

"Jörmungandr, the Midgard serpent," Gorm said as he picked up Jaimie's pack, the tip of the golden idol peeking out the top flap, and moved it below the small bench where Jaimie sat. Gorm took the seat beside Jaimie, his body close enough for Jaimie to feel the warmth radiating from the former Viking's skin. "The mighty Odin threw the snake into the ocean shortly after it was born, and it grew and grew until it could wrap itself around the entire world. The Norn say it will someday fight Thor at Ragnarök, the war of the gods at the end of all things."

Jaimie only understood half of what Gorm said, but it didn't matter. He was content just being close, hearing the stories from Gorm's past he would never share openly.

Jaimie thought back to all the times Gorm had told him secret stories of his people's gods and heroes and remembered the difficult to pronounce serpent.

"I remember now. No, I didn't see any legendary snakes, I'm just bored. Do you think we have time for one of your epic tales?"

Gorm quickly glanced around the ship with wide eyes. "I shouldn't have said anything. I am not the man I was before. I shouldn't have mentioned any of that pagan nonsense. I need to forget about the old gods if I am to stay working for your father."

"My dad's asleep," Jaimie said as a matter of fact. "I heard him snoring below deck."

The worry instantly disappeared from Gorm's face, and his whole demeanor relaxed.

"I want to learn more about what you truly believe," Jaimie said. "I know that deep down you're still a Viking."

Gorm thought for a moment and then reached into his shirt and pulled out a pendant at the end of long leather chord. The jewelry was dulled by age but still shone where it rubbed against Gorm's smooth skin. It looked like an upside-down capital T with etched swirls and flourishes.

"Where I come from there are many gods," Gorm said as he handed the necklace to Jaimie. "When Vikings sail to new lands and meet people worshiping unfamiliar gods we do not think we believe in the true gods and theirs are false lies. No, their gods are just as real and watch over them as our gods watch over us.

"While I do believe the things I learned from your father, I also believe in the Æsir, the gods of my homeland."

Jaimie looked at Gorm and understood the trust being given. His father would not understand this, but Jaimie could. He thought about what Gorm said and felt his mind growing with possibilities. There were other ways of being, of thinking. Maybe his life did not need to be what his father always insisted it would be.

"So, what is this?" Jaimie asked, as he held up the unfamiliar pendant wanting to know more.

"This is a representation of Mjölnir, Thor's hammer." Jaimie brushed his thumb over the fine markings etched in silver. "While many Vikings wear this symbol so Thor can hear our prayers for clear skies and strong winds, the people from my village all wear these for another reason."

Jaimie adjusted his position to get comfortable for the coming story.

"Before Thor had his hammer, the world was a much more dangerous place. Monsters roamed the lands of my ancestors devouring every human they set eyes on. The gods fought these beasts the best they could, but one demon scared even the wise Odin and headstrong Thor. A beast much like that one over there," Gorm said pointing to a black cat with a small white tuft of hair on its chest sculking across the ship looking for vermin, "except giant and fur ablaze with the fires of Muspelheimr. This beast came from a faraway land of heat and sand to devour armies of my people and drink their blood leaving only their weapons and armor behind as evidence of the battle. The only way they could prevent the beast from devouring them was to abandon their gods and worship the demon and its half-beast family instead.

"Thor fought this beast many times to drive it off, and each time barely escaped with his life. In their final battle, the trickster god Loki aided Thor by spilling barrels of wine on the battlefield for the creature to drink thinking it was blood. Drunk on blood and wine, the beast struggled to fight, and for once it was the one to flee.

"The gods worried about the demon returning until Loki tricked the dwarves into making weapons powerful enough to destroy the beast once and for all. The most powerful of these weapons is Mjölnir, the hammer of Thor."

Jaimie imagined a Viking god smashing a giant hammer into a giant cat's skull and was more than slightly disturbed by the mental image.

"Unfortunately, Thor never got the chance. Millenia went by and the beast has yet to return. Thor searched every realm, but the monster has remained hidden, no doubt scared of the hammer forged to kill it. My father said that if I ever see the beast, I should raise my pendant to the sky and call Thor down from the heavens."

Jaimie looked at the pendant in his hand. Could Vikings really summon their gods with such a simple piece of silver?

"Why don't Vikings ask Thor to fight alongside them when they raid or go to war? Surely your god on the battlefield would ensure victory?"

Gorm chuckled. "True but summoning a god from one realm to another takes an enormous sacrifice. The Viking who calls Thor will not live to witness the victory, but will instead be rewarded with a seat at Odin's table in Valhalla."

Jaimie winced at the realization that the pendant in his hand was potentially lethal. He quickly handed it back to Gorm who slipped it over his head and tucked it into his shirt away from peering eyes.

"Is Valhalla like heaven to Vikings?" Jaimie asked. Gorm had said the word several times before when telling stories from his heritage, but he never explained what it meant.

"In a way. Valhalla is a part of Asgard where those who die with a weapon in hand go to live with the gods and prepare for the final war at the end of all things. All Vikings hope to die in battle so they can go there."

This sounded a bit different than heaven to Jaimie. "You need to die in battle to go there? Can't you just be a good person? What about thieves and adulterers? Can they go to Valhalla if they die fighting?"

"To fearlessly die in battle is the only thing that matters," Gorm responded. "The gods are beyond caring about the individual goings on in our realm. They need fearless soldiers to fight for a just cause in the last battle. Nothing else matters to them."

"So, no sin?" Jaimie asked. "The pagan gods don't care what we do? What we think?"

"Not really," Gorm said. "They probably would prefer we were happy, but as long as we die valiantly, they will send their Valkyries to collect our souls and bring us to their hall in Valhalla."

Jaimie's world flipped upside down. He had never considered the idea of his personal actions being of little concern to a higher power. The guilt he felt for wanting the things his father told him were sinful would be pointless if that were the case. This thought washed over Jaimie, and he felt a sense of peace he had never known. As if he were finally relaxing parts of his mind that had been clenched for so long, he forgot about the pain they were constantly in.

"I wish I could believe in your old gods," Jaimie said. "It sounds... freeing."

Jaimie caught Gorm's gaze, losing himself in the bright blue reflecting the bouncing moonlight like flashes of lightning. Maybe there was a way he could see those eyes every day without fear. Somewhere far away from his father's judgement.

Gorm returned the gaze, his lips parting slightly.

"Gorm..." Jaimie was unsure exactly what to say next. "Thank you for sharing this with me."

"Of course. I want to share everything with you."

Jaimie stared into Gorm's large blue eyes shining in the moonlight and felt it was only fair to share his secret. The secret he barely acknowledged to himself.

"I feel the same about you." Jaimie moved slightly closer to Gorm till their hips were touching on the ship bench. "You are the best friend I have ever had. I cherish every moment I have with you."

"I cherish our friendship as well," Gorm said with his eyes fixed back on Jaimie's.

"I can't help but want more than just friendship." Jaimie reached up and placed his hand against the side of Gorm's stubble and moved closer. They stared directly into each other's eyes for a moment before Jaimie moved the rest of the distance and placed his lips firmly against Gorm's.

Jaimie's heart sped up, and heat rushed to his cheeks. His whole body seemed to vibrate with anticipation and excitement as the kiss consumed him. Gorm reached his hand up to place it behind Jaimie's head and reciprocated the affection by moving deeper into the kiss for a moment, before abruptly pulling away.

"What are you doing?" Gorm asked with panic rising in his voice. "We can't do this."

"Why not?" Jaimie asked with a note of panic. Did he read Gorm's feelings incorrectly? "Don't you want to be together?"

"Of course I do," Gorm said in a frantic whisper. "But we can't! Your dad would kill me."

"He doesn't need to know!" Jaimie said while simultaneously whispering and yelling. "We can keep it a secret!"

"We would get caught!" Gorm said. "Someone in Whitfield would figure it out and run us out of town!"

"Most people in town are good people who would be discrete to spare us from my father! But if you're so worried we could just leave!" Jaimie pleaded, momentarily losing control of the volume of his voice. "We will pack up and go somewhere else! Maybe we could go to your home!"

Gorm stood up abruptly. "I cannot go home! Don't you get it? I wasn't brave in battle! When faced with defeat I pleaded for life instead of dying as a worthy Viking! There is no place for me with the Vikings or in Valhalla, but maybe I can still hope for a seat in heaven someday if I do as your father says!"

Gorm turned and stomped across the ship and slipped through the door leading below deck. Jaimie collected himself and scrambled after him.

"Wait!" Jaimie yelled as the young Viking began his descent below deck. "Let's talk about it!"

"There is nothing to talk about!" Gorm roared as he turned back to face Jaimie. "I am the kind of man your father wants me to be. I will not betray him to lie with another man!"

Gorm disappeared into the darkness, leaving Jaimie standing utterly alone.

10

Gorm

What just happened? One second Gorm was talking to Jaimie, as he had every day for years, and then Jaimie looked at him in a way Gorm had never seen before but always dreamed of. He leaned forward and their lips brushed for a second before they both dived into the kiss. The wonderful, beautiful, potentially deadly kiss. The kiss that should never have happened and can never happen again.

Gorm paced in the dark recesses of the ship, his mind rocking in a tempest quite unlike the calm sea outside. What was he going to do? Did anyone see? Did John see? Should he flee the second they reach Dublin and disappear forever? He finally felt at home in Ireland after years of being an outsider, but that might all be over now because a handsome idiot didn't comprehend the consequences of his actions.

Footsteps came down the stairs. Gorm held his breath and tried to shrink into the darkness where he couldn't be seen. It was Jaimie following him below deck. A sickening warmth flushed on Gorm's cheeks. He couldn't talk to Jaimie again tonight.

"Gorm? I'm sorry. Let's talk," Jaimie said as he felt around the dark. Gorm stayed hidden and watched as Jaimie looked for him by the moonlight cascading down the stairs. Slowly, his search led him past Gorm's hiding place and deeper into the bowels of the ship. When the sound of footsteps faded and disappeared behind the roar of the waves outside, Gorm finally let out his breath in relief. As much as he loved Jaimie, he could not face him tonight.

Gorm climbed the steep stairs to the deck, emerging into the cold night air with a plan forming in his mind. He would wait out the rest of the night and dive into the water as soon as they were close to shore. He could swim the last stretch to Dublin and disappear with the rising sun before anyone knew he was gone. He finalized his hasty plan as he stepped out onto the deck and saw the last person in any realm he wanted to see.

Standing just outside the stairs was John. His face was twisted into a deep dark scowl and his eyes burned with a hatred Gorm hadn't seen in years. It was the same expression John wore when he pointed his sword at Gorm during the monastery raid two years ago. It was the face that filled Gorm with such fear that he dropped his own sword and abandoned all hope of a death worthy of Valhalla and instead pleaded for his life. John showed him mercy two years ago. Would he again?

"Hello, Lord Whitfield." Gorm tried to disguise his fear, but his voice was a bit too high to be natural. "What brings you out into the cold? I thought you were sleeping below deck."

John's expression grew harsher if possible. "I couldn't sleep with all this rocking, so I went up for some fresh air and found I wasn't the only one awake. I saw something impossible. Do you know what I saw? Gorm?"

Ice beat through Gorm's veins. Did John know? How much did he see? "What did you see, my Lord?"

John put his hand on Gorm's shoulder and looked deep into his eyes. "I saw you push away an attacking fairy. You stood your ground and held on to your morals when that creature attempted to seduce you. A lesser man would have given into the fairy's spell. I am proud of you."

John made no sense, but Gorm appeared to be safe for the moment. "I am glad you are proud of me, but I am confused. I do not remember being attacked by a fairy."

"He did not look like a fairy at the time, but it is clear to me now that a fairy spy is in our midst." John squeezed Gorm's shoulder with a slight tremor of suppressed rage. "Come sit with me and I will explain."

Gorm did as he was told and followed John to the same bench where Jaimie had kissed him less than an hour earlier.

"The fairies have long tormented me and my family. I thought I had finally gotten rid of them through iron and prayer, but they have returned," John's voice choked. "Have I told you how Jaimie's mother died?"

John had never mentioned Jaimie's mother before. "No, my Lord, all I know is that she died a long time ago."

"Indeed, it was a long time ago, and yet it still feels like yesterday. My wife was named Margaret, and she was the most beautiful woman I had ever met. She was a wonderful mother to Jaimie, and she was kind to everyone, from the highest lord to the lowest stray dog. She was even kind to the heathen fairies, despite every warning.

"She considered certain fairies her friends and would often meet them in the castle courtyard on bright sunny days. I foolishly did nothing to stop it. Margaret assured me the rumors of fairies kidnapping children, seducing fair maidens, and cursing humans for fun were nothing but stories. I loved her so much I believed every word."

Gorm had never seen John look so sad, as if decades of emotion were beginning to burst through a dam built to contain them all at once. John took a moment to compose himself before continuing his tale, but his voice still shook and the soft gleam of moisture welled in the corner of his eyes.

"When she was pregnant with our second child, I heard her cry out from the courtyard and found her swarmed by fairies pressing their glowing hands all over her body. I carried her inside and called for a midwife. The baby wasn't supposed to arrive for another month, but something was terribly wrong. There was nothing the midwife could do..."

Gorm put his arm around the older man as he fought back a sob. After a moment of unrepressed grief a slight change came over John. His tears dried as his expression hardened and his voice grew harsh.

"With my wife gone I prayed we could at least save our child, but the thing cut from Margaret's womb was not human. It looked wrong, with wide knowing eyes and not a single cry in the few hours it lived. I knew then that the fairies had indeed bewitched my wife and had attempted to replace my child with a fairy abomination. They must have wanted to take Whitfield Castle, and the surrounding lands, by placing one of their own as my heir.

"I feared they would try to replace Jaimie next." John stood and spoke out to the sea instead of Gorm. "I decreed any fairy seen in Whitfield was to be squashed on site. I drove every single one of those monsters out and made it clear they were not welcome in my lands, but I always wondered if I was too late. What if they had already replaced Jaimie with a changeling and the unnamed abomination was merely a backup plan? No human man would lust after another man in the way Jaimie did tonight. Only fairies are so perverse. They must have taken my real son to Tír na nÓg when he was an infant. He is probably still trapped in that cursed land as the changeling continues its spell."

John broke down and began to weep. Gorm had never seen such a strong, powerful man look so helpless. He awkwardly placed his hand on John's back in a feeble attempt to comfort him, while his own mind raced in fear and confusion. John thought Jaimie was a fairy in disguise simply because he kissed Gorm. What would John think if he knew Gorm secretly wanted to reciprocate that kiss? What would he do?

Memories of John calmly swinging a sword down on the necks of Druids flooded Gorm's mind. Innocent men and women whose only sin was being caught traveling through John's land to worship the fae of the forest. He showed no remorse, no hesitation, as he ended their lives for associating with the fae. If he thought Gorm was a fairy there would be no mercy.

"I'm sorry, I wish there was something I could do," Gorm said to comfort John and to ensure he remained in his good graces. "If it were possible, I would go to the fairy lands myself to free the real Jaimie."

John suddenly stopped sobbing and reached into his pocket. He pulled out an old, crumpled piece of parchment. "Maybe we can save my real son. For centuries people have searched for the doorway to Tír na nÓg, and now, by divine intervention, we find a letter not only telling us where the doorway is, but clues on where the key is. We can save my son, and all the other sons and daughters held captive by the fairy folk."

John handed the parchment to Gorm who looked over the note for the second time since they found it the day before. "When you found this, I heard you say some of the strange words in this message were from your culture. Can you explain?"

"It is just pagan nonsense, my Lord," Gorm said. "I have been striving to put such things out of my mind as you instructed."

"That may have been a mistake," John said. "I am beginning to think this is why I was inspired to show mercy two years ago. If knowledge from your Viking heritage can save my son from the fairy folk, it must be a gift from God. Please tell me all you know."

Gorm had not expected to ever see the day when John would ask him about his heritage and pagan beliefs. "The note says that this Lugh character's crown is the key and that he is hiding in a sapling of Yggdrasil. Every Viking knows of Yggdrasil, a massive tree with all the realms ruled over by the gods resting on its branches or tangled in its roots. Our whole world is but a small place on the lowest branches in the middle of the tree. The gods live in a world propped up at the top. This tree is so massive, that if a sapling were planted it would easily tower over all the other trees."

Gorm's mouth felt dry and uncomfortable. He looked to John to see his reaction expecting a disapproving scowl, but saw that he was giving Gorm his full attention, so he continued. "I think we both know which tree the note is referring to. Everyone in Whitfield can see the tree of the Leprechaun king deep within the forest from our windows. It towers over every other tree I have ever seen, and it is home to the fairies."

The fairy tree in the forest outside of Whitfield was indeed massive. Gorm would often sit with Jaimie on the castle walls watching the bright glow of pixies flying through its branches. On particularly sunny days a glint of green was even visible as the home of the Leprechaun king, the emerald palace, reflected the light of the sun. It was beautiful and terrifying all at once to everyone, except Jaimie, who lived near the castle. His positive outlook was one of the traits Gorm loved about him.

John sighed and crumpled the paper in defeat. "I cannot ask my men to attack the fairies with their magic. No number of swords would be a match for a swarm summoning fire in unison. We need a way to shield ourselves from their flames or we would surely lose."

Gorm looked back at the note. He always thought it was strange how the fairy tree seemed to mimic Yggdrasil. The palace was positioned at the top of the tree just as the god's city of Asgard was in the religion of his people. Now he had confirmation that the tree was indeed a young offspring of the tree that carried all the realms. It couldn't be a coincidence.

Maybe John was right. Maybe they were fated to meet. Gorm failed to be worthy of Valhalla, but through John he may be worthy of heaven by destroying the enemies of John's God.

He swallowed and decided to take his chance of dispelling any doubt John had of his allegiances. "I think I know how to defeat the fae."

John perked up. "What are you proposing?"

Gorm's stomach tightened. It was too late to back out now. "The village I grew up in is across the river from Alfheimr, the lands of beings similar to your fae in every way but size. My people do not fear them because we wear clothing enchanted with a simple spell that protects us from their seiðr magic. A simple belt with a few stitched runes and I believe the fairies would be helpless against us. If our meeting is indeed God's plan, then I believe He would allow this one instance of using the enemy's magic against them."

John thought about it for a moment and then surprised Gorm by nodding in agreement. "God would certainly approve of using his enemy's weapons against them. Still, I only have fifty men I can spare for such a mission. When we arrive in Dublin, I want you to spread the word to all the Danes and Norsemen in town to meet up at Whitfield Castle in three days. They can join us in a raid on the fairy tree and can keep all the treasure rumored to be kept there, except for the crown of the Leprechaun king. We can then march to the Lia Fáil and enter Tír na nÓg to rescue my son."

"I will do as you ask, my lord."

John hugged Gorm for the first time. "Thank you. I may have lost one son, but I believe I gained another."

11

Fotini

Fotini was going to vomit on a stranger's face. The room swayed back and forth through the night, and with every stomach sloshing tilt, Tragos's horns dug into her side. The rocking was not improved by the smell of sweat rising off a dozen Children of Pan squeezed together so tightly it was difficult to determine where one body ended and another began. Fotini always felt Tragos to her right and a fellow centaur pressed against her left side. Something warm and hairy pressed against her backside and her sweaty humanlike torso slid against the slick skin of a shirtless stallion centaur. The air was moist, hot, and pungent below deck.

The uncomfortable traveling arrangement was miserable for everyone trapped in the darkness with only fae lights in the rafters to see by, but it was a special corner of Tartarus for Fotini. She closed her eyes and tried to picture wide open fields, clear star-filled skies, and crisp breezes, but she still felt completely trapped. Memories of the cramped underbelly of the ship that brought her to England flashed over her forced fantasies as the room tilted back and forth. A claustrophobic panic set its claws on Fotini's mind, and both her hearts beat into a rapid hum. Each gasp of sweat-filled air was slow, deliberate, and took all her concentration. She told herself she would soon be in Ireland. She would soon be on solid ground. She would never leave the open skies again.

The ship rocked hard and thudded slightly against something solid. The crew stomped around in a sudden burst of activity until the vessel came to a complete stop. Fotini praised the gods when tiny doors near the rafters slid up and early morning sunlight illuminated the darkness. Her torment was nearly at an end.

"Welcome to Ireland!" Captain Harold called through the small openings. "Fae off first. All elves and pixies are now free to disembark."

A chattering hum wafted from the rafters as the elves left in single file lines along the long wooden walkways near the ceiling, while pixies buzzed through holes accessible only by flying. Fotini heard many remarks of relief that they were finally in the open air away from smelly "pannites."

Once all the fae had disembarked, their small exits closed and the innards of the ship were once again cast into near total darkness. Fotini grew more and more panicked the longer they stayed trapped below deck. When she felt she could no longer stand the frantic feeling of ever shrinking walls closing in, she felt Tragos's rough hand slide across her fur. He stroked her back slowly until Fotini's breathing matched the slow rhythm of his hand. She calmed slightly until the door at the top of the ramp cracked open and Captain Harold stood silhouetted against the morning sunlight.

"Welcome Children of Pan to Ireland! I hope you had a pleasant journey. Come up the ramp in single file, and you may disembark for five silvers each."

The reaction was instantaneous. Every satyr and centaur yelled out some version of 'what do you mean five silvers?' and 'we already paid you two!' Harold put his hand up and waited until the crowd grew quiet.

"The fee to get to Ireland was two silvers," Harold explained, "and I have successfully brought you to Ireland. It is another five silvers to leave the ship."

"But I don't have five silvers!" called out a centaur.

"If you don't have the money, you can work off the debt. One year of work for each piece of silver you're short."

The crowd once again yelled, and a few charged up the ramp. Harold quickly slammed the door shut and a loud click confirmed it was now locked from the outside. The group was once again in near total darkness, but instead of feeling seasick, they were sick with a mix of fear and unbridled rage. Conversations grew among the crowd until it was difficult to hear anyone in particular. Some were offering spare coins, while others pleaded for help, and the rest mumbled to themselves about how unfair this situation was. After a moment, one voice yelling for attention rose over the cacophony of the crowd.

"Hey! Quiet!" yelled one brave satyr with a scar across his cheek whose voice came from the direction of the ramp. After the discussions died down, he continued. "Who here has extra coins? And by how much?"

"I have three extras," said one centaur.

"I can spare two," said another.

Slowly, everyone who had spare silver yelled out the amount and the satyr quickly added it together in his head. After people stopped calling out amounts of unneeded coins, the scarred satyr asked how many people were short, and once again performed mental arithmetic with each response. Unfortunately, the amount they were short far exceeded the amount of available silver. Silence filled the darkness with the collective realization there was not enough silver to go around. Many of the passengers would become indentured servants on some human noble's farm.

"Does anyone have anything we can use as a weapon?" Tragos asked in a hushed voice.

Murmurs spread through the group as they took stock of their possessions. There were even fewer makeshift weapons among the group than extra silver. A few had hammers meant for carpentry, several had knives for wood carving or cooking, and a couple of walking sticks were present.

"Do horns count?" came the low but loud voice of a particularly large satyr with curved horns that curled around his head.

"Yes, they definitely do," Tragos replied. "Okay everyone, prepare to fight."

"Are you crazy?" a large centaur said as he stamped his hooves on the ground. "I have enough silver to pay for my freedom, why should I risk my neck?"

Tragos's expression twisted in anger "Do you think this is the first time these men have done this? How many of our kind have they enslaved? If we dinnae fight today they will just keep on doing this day after day, after day, after day."

The centaur opened his mouth to speak but Fotini wasn't going to let him. "You're the crazy one if you think they are going to let us go. They already lied to us once. What's to stop them from lying again? For all you know they will take your silver and send you to the fields anyways."

The centaur closed his mouth and stepped back into the crowd.

"Alright," Tragos said with a large grin for Fotini. "Let's get ready."

A few hours passed before Harold opened the door again. "Are you all ready to pay?"

"We will pay," Tragos responded and came forward to be the first to hand over his coins. He placed five pieces of silver into Harold's palm and began walking past the rest of the crew, all of whom were holding unsheathed swords.

Fotini followed Tragos up the ramp and into the daylight. The cool sea breeze hit her face, and she filled her lungs with clean air unmarred by moist sweat. Her panic subsided as she trotted across the deck under the open sky. She was finally free of the cramped bowels of the ship, and she vowed to never enter another enclosed space. Death would be preferable to another moment of that torture.

Slowly, more and more Children of Pan paid and walked past the crew. Tragos walked slow enough to give everyone time to get in position, but not slow enough to look suspicious. As he was about to reach the far side of the deck, the deep voice of the large horned satyr filled the air.

"I'm sorry, I don't have any money," the satyr said and immediately smashed his skull against Harold's weaker forehead. All the Children of Pan turned and attacked the nearest crew member using a variety of hidden knives, hammers, and walking sticks. Shouts and the clang of swords filled the air. Fotini pulled a hidden knife out from the tight wrappings around her chest and stabbed it into the forearm of a man who raised a short sword above his head to attack. The man dropped the sword, and she kicked it to Tragos, who leaped into the air and plunged his new weapon through the man's chest.

Adequately armed, Tragos leaped back into the fray. He used his powerful legs to leap high into the air and plunged his sword through an unsuspecting sailor. Most men who fought Tragos spent their last moments with a scared, yet puzzled, expression as they attempted to fight a combatant who fought from the air. He often boasted that most humans did not know how to parry an attack from a leaping satyr. Tragos tossed his former foe's weapon, a short but freshly sharpened sword, to Fotini.

The sword was a massive upgrade from the kitchen knife Fotini was previously using. She joined Tragos in the carnage. Swords were not her preferred weapon, she felt more comfortable with a long spear or bow, but she was familiar with most types of blades. She bucked and spun in circles, slicing at opponents to her front and kicking foes with iron-shoed hooves to her rear.

As Fotini fought she caught glimpses of the rest of the battle raging aboard the ship and it was obvious most of the Children of Pan had no experience in combat. A young satyr who had barely reached adulthood raised a sword with both hands above her head, providing an opening for her opponent to stick his sword into her soft stomach. An older centaur had the tendons of his front legs cut, an injury that would cripple him for life. Screams from men and women of every species cried in fear, rage, and agony as they took their first life or came to the realization theirs was at an abrupt end.

The battle was bloody, but mercifully short. Within minutes, the fighting was over when every human aboard was slain or had abandoned the ship to swim to shore. Tragos cheered in victory, but the rest of the Children of Pan wore blood splattered expressions of relief mixed with horror at what they had just done. Fotini never forgot the first time she was forced to take a life and everyone here today would share a similar memory. They had won this battle, but lost much in the process.

"You can all come out now," Fotini called down into the underside of the ship. One-by-one the formerly trapped Children of Pan who could not fight came out of the dark and stepped into the open air, kicking former Captain Harold's body as they passed and weeping when they found a friend or loved one who did not survive the fight. Fotini spied Tragos as he discreetly approached Harold's body and quickly reached inside the former captain's pockets. He smiled as he found what he was looking for: a large ring of keys. Tragos casually walked over to the captain's quarters, unlocked the door, and slid inside.

Fotini followed the sneaky satyr. She had rarely left Tragos's side in nearly ten years, and she recognized when he was letting greed cloud his judgment. She opened the ship door and saw him standing in a small room with a cluttered desk covered in wrinkled maps and papers, an unmade cot for sleep, a bin filled with all the passengers' confiscated weapons, and a large, locked chest immediately in front of the satyr. A turn of a key and Tragos flipped open the chest, revealing all the silver Harold had collected as payment to smuggle passengers to Ireland.

"What in Artemis's name are you doing?" Fotini asked, taking Tragos by surprise.

"There's enough silver here that we dinnae need to find that damned idol. We can take this and set sail for Greece right here, right now."

Fotini looked at the pile of silver and briefly thought of what that amount of money could do. She remembered running through the fields in Thessaly as a child with her herd and how she had always talked of returning to Greece. Tragos was born north of England and had never been across the sea to the land of their ancestors. She desperately wanted to show him a world where their kind was accepted, or at least tolerated. They could use this money, but she knew it didn't belong to just them, so she silently exited the captain's cabin to address the crowd.

"There's a chest of silver the captain won't be needing anymore!" Fotini yelled. "Come, get a handful as you disembark."

"What are you doing?" Tragos asked with a tone of surprise and rage.

"The right thing. After what we've all been through, we all deserve our money back and a cut of the spoils."

"But we can finally leave these islands. You can show me your home!"

"And I will," Fotini said with a tone of finality. "Once we find the idol, we will get more than enough silver to make the trip."

Fotini saw mental agony on Tragos's expression as passenger after passenger took their share of the silver. Within the hour, the Children of Pan nearly emptied the chest. All that remained for Fotini and Tragos was a modest profit of four pieces of silver each.

12

Ailsa

They say the night is darkest just before dawn. While Ailsa agreed, she thought the saying should mention it is also coldest just before the sun pierces the horizon. She frantically rubbed her exposed legs with her uncovered arms to generate enough heat to stay conscious as the sun finally appeared with promised relief. The sun's warm rays fell on her skin changing it gradually from a light blue hue to the deep red that matched her current feelings of rage but darkened with a hint of fear.

The ship finally docked in Dublin harbor under the rising sun. Even after her frozen sleepless night, Ailsa was alert and ready to seize any opportunity to attack the young Viking, or his master, who plotted the destruction of her people. At first it was entertaining to watch the two young men talk and awkwardly flirt. Even from her hidden perch atop the mast, Ailsa could see the sexual tension between the two men. She struggled to dim her excited glow when they kissed and immediately started fighting. It was more dramatic than anything she saw from the Children of Pan over the past sixty odd years living with them.

Then the older man appeared. The father of the red-haired young man. Ailsa didn't like the look of him when she first saw him milling about in the early evening, but she never expected to hear such slander coming out of his mouth. He ranted about the evil of 'fairies' and how they had killed his wife, kidnapped his son, and replaced him with a changeling. Ailsa always hated the idea of changelings. Horrible rumors vilifying her people while giving human parents an excuse to dispose of unwanted or sick children. Then the old man and the young Viking took their discussion from disgusting and offensive and turned to outright terrifying.

Ailsa's glow turned grey and dim with fear when she heard their plans for her true home in the tree city Crann Na Sióga. Even though she hadn't set foot in the kingdom of the Leprechaun since her banishment, she still loved the emerald tree with its sweet golden apples and constant hum of a thousand songs. If she closed her eyes, she could picture the carved interiors of the tree with flowing knotwork and depictions of the original fae gods, the Tuatha Dé Danann. She could almost smell the wood, like a cross between cedar and eucalyptus, that wafted through the ancient tree. She had nearly twenty years of splendid memories of the city, and only a few unfortunate dark ones.

She could still hear the words of the chanting crowd as the angry Leprechaun king passed judgment on her for attempting to steal from his private vault. With his sword at her throat, she was forced to carry out her own sentence. She would never forget the moment she uttered her last words in Crann Na Sióga; "I, Ailsa daughter of Maewyn, promise to never return to Crann Na Sióga or any other Aos Sí settlement." As soon as she made her promise, the curse of the fae compelled her to leave. To return would mean unbearable pain followed by an agonizing death without a single guard drawing their sword.

Ailsa pulled her mind out of her memories as she watched Gorm, the young Viking at the center of the night's drama, approaching the ship exit to prepare to disembark the moment the crew gave the go ahead.

Ailsa fidgeted as Gorm watched the ramp to the dock being lowered. This was her best chance to stop the young Viking before he could recruit an army to attack the fae. Ailsa gave her wings a flutter and found they had finally warmed enough for flight. She dived off her perch and buzzed toward her target while willing magic into her palms. Sparks popped out of her fingertips and ignited the air into flames as she zoomed towards her target. Ailsa raised her hand to throw a small ball of fire right as the ramp from the ship made contact with the dock.

Burning energy pulsed through Ailsa's veins as if she was struck by lightning. She dropped to the ground mid-flight filled with unbearable searing pain. Memories from the previous evening flooded her mind so the only sound she could hear was her own voice from the previous day.

"I will head to his secret dock in Ireland immediately when I arrive in Dublin," she said right before she left Tragos and Fotini to follow the golden idol. She had officially arrived in Dublin and had to fulfill her promise. The curse of her kind prevented any other actions.

Ailsa stood and turned north towards Harold's secret dock several miles outside of the city. The pain lessened slightly as she faced her promised destination. She flapped her wings and flitted in the direction of Harold's dock with the pain growing softer and softer until it was almost a memory. She turned her head to see the Viking disappear into the crowded city, but was met with another, but smaller, burst of pain, so she continued forward without another look back.

She would have to deal with the Viking another day.

"What took you two so long?" Ailsa asked as she fluttered down from the sky to join her companions. "Harold's ship docked hours ago."

Tragos swatted at the pixie with an open hand, but Ailsa was just beyond his reach. The satyr glared and crouched slightly before springing in the air with his horns directed at Ailsa. Thankfully, she darted out of the way quickly enough to avoid getting hit, but she was not fast enough to avoid the ripples of air created by the sudden burst of speed. She flipped end over end before she was plucked out of the air by Fotini's careful but firm hand.

"What kind of businesses do you run!?!" Tragos shouted his question at Ailsa as she struggled to free herself from Fotini's grasp.

"Thievery and smuggling," Ailsa answered quickly.

"You forgot extortion and trafficking my kind!"

"What? I would never! What happened?"

"Liar!" Tragos unsheathed his sword and turned his gaze to Fotini. "Release her so I can cut the truth out of her."

"No." Fotini pulled Ailsa close to her chest so Tragos couldn't strike the pixie without also injuring his dearest friend. "She cannot lie, remember? Let's hear her out."

Fotini opened her palm, releasing Ailsa. She immediately buzzed a few feet higher in the air beyond her companion's grasp. "So, what happened on Harold's ship?"

Fotini spoke as Tragos fumed in a rage so hot Ailsa wouldn't have been surprised to see steam leak from his ears. "Your business partner locked us below deck and would not release us unless we paid more silver or agreed to years of indentured servitude."

Ailsa's light grew dim and gray. "I'm glad you had the extra silver, but we need to go back right now and tell Harold he can keep my cut to release the rest of the Children of Pan."

"No need," Fotini said flatly.

Ailsa was confused for a moment before she noticed the splatter of blood across Fotini's crescent stomach tattoo. She turned her attention to Tragos and noticed new dark stains in the green plaid of his kilt. A worrying knot grew in the pit of Ailsa's stomach.

"What happened?" Ailsa asked although she felt she already knew.

"Not everyone could pay, and we couldn't leave anyone behind, so we fought," Tragos said flatly. "Harold and his crew won't be extorting or enslaving anyone ever again."

As horrified as she was, Ailsa was impressed that Tragos fought for the rest of the Children of Pan trapped on the ship. She expected selfless heroics from Fotini, but had difficulty imagining Tragos doing anything without being paid. As long as she had known him, money had been his sole driving force.

"Are all the Panni... Children of Pan, okay? You got them all out?"

"No," Tragos said with a grumpy tone. "Eleven brave souls never came ashore, but their sacrifice means the rest are free."

The knot in Ailsa's stomach twisted tighter. "I'm so sorry. I didn't know."

"Well now you know to vet your criminal contacts a bit better," Fotini butted in. "Anyways, where are we going?"

"I hope your weapons are still sharp," Ailsa said in an exasperated tone. "The idol is headed to a castle where an army of humans are gathering to annihilate my people."

"Damn humans," Tragos said as he spat. "Lead the way pixie."

13

The Cat Sí

The Cat Sí's pitch black fur soaked up the sun's horrible rays as she trotted behind the nearly empty cart. Her paws felt slick and squishy with sweat with each step adding an extra layer of discomfort to the irritation of having her idol so close yet clearly out of reach.

As the Cat Sí walked, she imagined herself transforming into the goddess from Fotini's prayers and snatching her prize from the two mortal men. She could almost feel the cool gold plating under her touch after years of searching. The idea was so intoxicating she almost attempted the transformation, but she knew she did not yet have the strength.

Even if she had enough power to transform, she would need to wait until the safety of night. While she still could not recall why she feared the sun, its rays burned into her fur, and she felt like it was endlessly searching for her. The thought of being caught in its gaze undisguised filled her with a fear so palpable it made her taste bile in the back of her throat. It was better to wait until night anyways.

"It feels great to be home, doesn't it?" The young red-haired man, who the Cat Sí remembered being called 'Jaimie', said from the driver's seat of the small wagon. The man undeserving of the title of father, John, merely grunted in response from where he sat in the back of the cart.

The Cat Sí's stomach clenched. She saw and heard everything the night before. When she first snuck aboard the ship to Ireland, she had every intention of grabbing the idol and diving into the sea at the first opportunity, but then she saw Jaimie kiss his friend and the Cat Sí felt something long forgotten.

When Jaimie leaned forward and closed his eyes in nervous anticipation, the Cat Sí couldn't help but remember a woman with smooth pale skin and hair in shades of gold and fire in the same position. The woman's soft lips pursed slightly, and her long lashes closed over her sapphire eyes giving complete trust to the Cat Sí. Her heart quickened as her own harsh mouth melted into another's embrace for the first time. After an age of solitude, the memory was painful yet wonderful, but the vision was shattered when the young men pulled apart violently.

The young man Jaimie called 'Gorm', harshly pushed Jaimie aside. The Cat Sí didn't understand. Gorm had leaned into the brief kiss, had pulled Jaimie in closer for a brief moment before flinging him away like the inedible innards of a fresh kill. Gorm's eyes grew wide and he stepped back, away from the man he clearly desired. The Cat Sí could hear his heart beating fast from the kiss but also intensifying in the aftermath. He looked like the uncounted creatures the Cat Sí hunted just before she sunk her claws into their flesh.

Fire flowed through the Cat Sí's veins. Gorm was afraid, but his fear did not excuse his actions. The Cat Sí wanted to sink her claws into his weak human flesh, wanted to gorge herself on his blood, wanted to hurt him as he hurt Jaimie.

The Cat Sí shook her head violently. Why did she care so much about this human? This boy? She had never cared for a mortal man before. She felt a kinship to young maidens, but men were nothing but a nuisance. They were loud, ugly, and boisterous creatures. So why did she burn in defense of Jaimie?

These questions still haunted the Cat Sí as she stalked through the grass behind Jaimie's cart. She was far too old to feel anything new for the first time, yet her feelings about Jaimie felt foreign.

John grunted in response to another of Jaimie's comments and the Cat Sí felt something all too familiar. Scenes from last night flitted through the Cat Sí's mind whenever she looked at the man. What kind of father plots the death of their child? John's dead eyed glare towards the son he planned to betray felt all too familiar, though the Cat Sí could not recall why.

Jaimie ignored his father's responses and continued the conversation on his own with a forced cheerfulness. "Just over this hill and we will finally be home!"

The Cat Sí stepped over the crest of a small hill and saw what must be Jaimie's home. After witnessing John's pompous and arrogant attitude she was not surprised to see a castle, but it was modest compared to the castles of the undeservedly rich and self-important. There was only one ivy-covered tower attached to a sizable main building with an attached stone wall surrounding what the Cat Sí assumed was probably a courtyard garden. Wooden stables capable of housing over a dozen horses stood just outside the main gate to the castle, and fields of hops and barley encircled the semi-glamorous structure. Beyond the fields to the north was a small village and to the west was a lovely thick forest.

Relief replaced the boiling rage flowing through the Cat Sí. Once they stopped at the castle, she could take her time to finally retrieve her idol. After years of searching she would finally get the answers she searched for.

14

Jaimie

The ride back to Whitfield Castle was long and uncomfortably silent, but at least Jaimie was spared facing Gorm because his father sent him off on an errand in Dublin. Jaimie tried to engage his father in idle chatter about next year's harvest and the goings on in the villages they passed, but his father was in a particularly stoic mood. The day ticked by at a slow, agonizing pace like a fairy with clipped wings making Jaimie feel more and more exhausted. By the time they reached home, Jaimie's need for sleep surpassed his worry over Gorm's rejection and he flopped into bed.

He awoke at dusk when the light streaming through his window was grey, and objects cast few shadows. He stumbled to his bedroom door on a mission to fill his stomach with his first proper meal in days, but it did not budge. He might as well have been pushing against a massive boulder. Jaimie pounded his fists against the thick wood in frustration and panic until his hands were pink and tender.

"Help! The door is stuck!"

Jaimie cried out and yelled long after his throat burned with effort. He was about to give up when he finally heard a voice on the other side of the door.

"Quiet down!" Jaimie's father yelled with uncharacteristic harshness. "Your yelling will do nothing but wake sleeping children out on the farms. Of course, your kind cares little for the wellbeing of our children."

"What do you mean 'your kind'?" His father's words made no sense to Jaimie's newly awakened mind. "It's me, Jaimie! Let me out of my room!"

"I will not fall for your fairy tricks, changeling! Tell me, how long have you been posing as my son? Where have you taken him?"

Fairy tricks? Jaimie's heart hammered in fear and his palms grew sweaty as he pushed against his door. His father hated fairies more than he hated anything else. If he thought Jaimie was mixed up with fairies, the consequences would be dire.

"I don't know what you're talking about! It's me, Jaimie, your son! We just got back from England, where you took me to a jousting tournament! We saw a centaur cheat and steal the prize, remember!?!"

Panic flooded Jaimie. He needed his father to believe him.

"You may claim my son's name and face," Jaimie's father's voice was deep with a slight rumble of barely contained fury. "But only a fairy would attempt to seduce another man. I won't permit your ruse any longer! Tell me where my son is!"

Jaimie's world stopped. His father knew. He knew Jaimie kissed Gorm, but what did that have to do with fairies? Jaimie's thoughts travelled back to his childhood when his mother died. When his brother was replaced by a misshapen fairy changeling.

Oh no.

"I am your son!" Jaimie pleaded and banged against the door with a flurry of fists. He had to convince his father he was his real son. His life depended on it.

"I should have expected more lies. Very well, I will rescue Jaimie myself. I will go to your cursed kingdom and find my son, along with all the children your kind has stolen from us. But before I go, Bishop Fergus will purify your cursed shell with iron and flame so you can never take the form of my son again."

Jaimie vomited. He had heard of the terrible Bishop Fergus, a vile man who used his position of power to punish those he saw as lesser beings. Jaimie had once heard Bishop Moore, who usually presided over Whitfield, say Fergus might know all the stories he preached, but he clearly didn't understand them.

Jaimie's father's footsteps stomped down the stairs as he left. Jaimie slammed his fists against the door and screamed until his throat was too sore to make a sound, but no one answered his pleas. No one would dare cross John Whitfield in his own home.

Jaimie was all alone.

It felt like it took forever for Jaimie to fall asleep. After hours of banging against the door with no answer, Jaimie's hands were raw with red pinpricks of blood along one side. His arms eventually grew so heavy they slumped to the floor and the only sound was his soft sobs. The fear and anguish were so great Jaimie couldn't hold it all in, it seeped out until all that was left was numbness as he finally drifted to sleep with imagination and memory swirling in his mind.

Jaimie's first memory was of his mother gently explaining that he would soon be a big brother. Her smile was warm as she asked Jaimie to speak to his brother or sister through her belly as she held him close. He could not recall what he said, but he would never forget how happy his mother was. When Jaimie thought of his mother he always thought of this moment. It was how he chose to remember her.

His second oldest memory was one he tried to forget. He remembered his mother's screams of pain when his father carried her from the courtyard yelling for a midwife while hundreds of colored lights trailed behind them. Even though he was quickly removed from the room, Jaimie could hear the screams through the night followed by utter silence the next morning. He cried out for his parents, but they never came. Instead, his only comfort were maids who made sure he was warm and fed.

It was three days before Jaimie saw his father.

"Jaimie, come here," Jaimie's father commanded with a low voice as he entered Jaimie's room. "I have something very important to tell you."

Jaimie climbed onto his father's lap and did his best to listen.

"You know the lights you can see in the air circling the tallest tree in the forest?" his father asked as he looked for signs Jaimie understood. "Those are fairies, magical little demons who look pretty, but are very dangerous. Some of those fairies can grow in size and change their form until they look like another person. They usually try to look like babies and take their place."

Jaimie listened carefully, though his toddler mind didn't understand half of what he was hearing.

"A fairy called a changeling snuck into your mother's room while she slept and tried to use magic to switch places with your brother, but because your brother hadn't been born yet, the magic didn't work properly. The fairy went into your mother's tummy and got sick... and its dark magic killed your mother."

This made no sense at all to Jaimie. "Mommy?"

"Mommy is gone."

The only light through Jaimie's tower window for miles in any direction came from a swarm of pixies circling a gigantic tree in the center of the forest north of the castle. Even though his father did his best to instill a fear of fairies in him, Jaimie found comfort in the ethereal beauty of the tree. It was clearly not from the mortal realm since it was easily three times as tall as any other with a wide canopy stretching against the horizon in all directions. Lights of every color blinked around the tree showing the individual emotions of each elf and pixie, while a larger green beacon showed off the emerald palace nestled at the top of the tree. Jaimie often compared it to a lighthouse in a sea of trees.

The first day locked in his room went by slowly for Jaimie with only his thoughts for company. He watched and listened to the world below his window until the sun had fully set, but the night had fewer distractions. He sat by the windowsill watching the fairy lights in the distance while his mind circled the events two nights ago when he kissed Gorm. The look his dear friend had given him as he recoiled was, in some ways, worse than the punishment of being locked in a tower like a young lord in distress. Gorm's normally beautiful sapphire eyes had gone wide with shock and his full lips had curved downward in disgust. It may have been a trick of the moonlight, but Jaimie swore Gorm's short golden stubble bristled like the fur of a cornered beast. He looked more than merely uninterested. He looked afraid.

Jaimie now understood he was right to feel that way.

From the moment he arrived in Whitfield, Gorm spent all his time attempting to prove his worth to Jaimie's father. He dutifully attended every church meeting; despite the glares he often received from people who only saw him as a bloodthirsty Viking. He woke at sunrise and did everything asked of him; from cleaning stables to teaching Jaimie how to properly use a sword. His desire to prove his worth was as striking as his lightning blue eyes. Jaimie's heart sank with the thought Gorm may have lost everything he built because of Jaimie's selfish actions.

Thinking about the changeling purification ritual was the only thing worse than thinking about Gorm's rejection. To ensure a changeling could not continue hiding in the mortal realm, it had to be destroyed, but because of their magic, normal weapons were said to be useless against the fairy folk. Bishop Fergus had long ago learned of the fairies' weakness to iron and fire, but only if the fire burned from deep inside the changeling. To destroy the monster, a glowing hot rod is inserted down the creature's throat until it burns them from the inside out. Then, and only then, could the human child be freed from imprisonment in Tír na nÓg to possibly return home alive.

This was the fate that awaited Jaimie if he did not escape his room. With the door locked and his window four stories from the ground, escape wasn't likely. He realized dying by jumping out a window was likely more pleasant than being burned from the inside. Jaimie leaned out the window several times through the day and imagined the rush of air as he plummeted to the rocks below.

Jaimie searched his room for something, anything, to distract his mind from his misery at the loss of his only friend and the impending death awaiting him. There wasn't much in the room besides his bed, his wardrobe, and a small desk to write at. Unfortunately, Jaimie wasn't much for writing. Usually, he would entertain himself by going through sword drills with Gorm, practicing archery with Gorm, or going horseback riding with Gorm. Everything he liked to do was with Gorm, and he would probably never see him again.

The only thing of any interest available to Jaimie was the broken idol he stuffed in his satchel back in England. The note it once held was gone, but the statue itself remained. He tinkered with the cracked and split gold-plated porcelain as he processed his thoughts and feelings. He wished he had some tree gum or book glue to repair it, but he contented himself by pressing the pieces together and wrapping them with a loose bit of twine he had stashed in his desk drawer. It wasn't the prettiest solution, but he thought it somehow fit with the wild look of the woman it represented.

The tournament prize was supposed to be a golden idol of the Roman goddess Diana found in an old ruin, but Jaimie wasn't confident in its authenticity now that he knew it was merely gold plated. His father never discussed Roman religion with Jaimie, but his history lessons had touched on the basics. He recognized the idol as the goddess of the moon, the hunt, and womanhood, but didn't know much else about her. Pagan beliefs weren't commonly discussed in Whitfield unless they were about how to keep the fairies at bay.

"I wonder how you would judge me," Jaimie said aloud as he looked at the idol. His father clearly found Jaimie's feelings toward Gorm so distasteful he couldn't comprehend they belonged to his very human son. "Would you damn me too? Or would you rescue me? Please, take me far from here if you can."

The statue gave the same answer Jaimie always received from prayerful reflection, complete silence.

15

Gorm

The first time Gorm came to Dublin he wondered if he had found Valhalla on Midgard. After weeks freezing on a damp longboat, it felt amazing to walk on dry land surrounded by an entire city of fellow Vikings. Even though he had never been to Ireland, the city felt like home with the familiar foods, customs, and even architecture. Gorm could easily see himself returning to the city after his raids and settling down. Why go back across the sea when Dublin was so welcoming?

Dublin was not so welcoming these days. Gorm's head was filled with imagined judgements lurking in other people's minds. He walked past an older man with a knotted dragon tattoo snaking around his throat and noticed the man's scorn as his eyes glanced down at him. Panicked thoughts flowed through Gorm's mind. The stranger must know he did not belong anymore, that he had abandoned their ways and chosen to live among their enemies. He was a traitor, and worse, a coward.

Once he was past the older man, Gorm ducked into an alley, placed his palms against the cool stone of an old building and let his head droop low. It felt as if his heart was beating fast enough to burst from his chest. He took a deep breath, then another, and waited for his body to return to normal. He told himself he could handle this mission until he almost believed it.

Gorm was reminded of how he felt when he first arrived in Whitfield. Everyone stared when they saw his tattoos and half shaved skull. Everything from the language to the customs was new and alien to him while seemingly second nature to everyone else. In his early days at Whitfield, he only found comfort in one strange boy who treated Gorm as a friend and not a captive.

While everyone else avoided Gorm whenever possible, Jaimie latched onto him. This strange boy who didn't even speak the same language was constantly by his side introducing him to new foods, games, and patiently showing him how to perform local customs and traditions. Gorm quickly began to see Jaimie as his only friend, and when they were alone, he began to hope for something a bit more than friendship. When he looked into Jaimie's warm brown eyes, he felt a burning in his chest and knew he had made the right decision when he surrendered to John during his first raid.

It didn't take too long for Gorm to learn his feelings for Jaimie would be less welcome than a snake in a chicken coop at Whitfield. Two men in the village surrounding the castle were caught kissing and, as the lord of Whitfield, John showed no mercy in his judgement. Both men were executed the same day their secret was discovered.

"No man could stoop to that level of perversion," John explained to Gorm and Jaimie after the execution. "We cannot permit the fairy folk to infiltrate our community without incurring God's wrath. It is better for those two creatures to die than for all our crops to spoil, our wine to turn to vinegar, and the fairies to continue to steal our children."

Gorm hardened his heart that day. He buried his feelings and resolved he would do what he had to do to be accepted by John and live safely in Whitfield. He would not meet the same fate as those two foolish men.

For years Gorm was successful. He changed his appearance as best as possible to fit in with the people of Whitfield. He took on every task and chore asked of him until he was seen as a dependable presence around the castle and village. After years of work, he finally felt like he belonged, and he wasn't going to throw it all away after one kiss. One kiss could ruin it all, even if it was the one kiss he secretly yearned for above all others.

Gorm caught himself thinking about the previous night and shook his head in frustration. "Snap out of it," he said quietly to himself. Despite his swirling thoughts and emotions, he had a job to do. He just had to convince a bunch of Vikings to go on a raid for treasure. It should be as simple as convincing a wolf to eat a freshly killed deer.

With a final steadying breath, Gorm stood up straight and got to work. He explored the city until he found what he was looking for: a mead hall. He eventually found a large wooden structure in the center of the city with smoke swirling out of a hole in the roof that looked just like the halls he went to as a child. He entered the dark windowless building illuminated only by a large fire in the center of the room and simultaneously felt perfectly at home and as if he were intruding on something sacred.

The room was filled with men and women enjoying strong tankards of mead, a warm meal, and boisterous stories. Gorm got himself a drink and surveyed the room for anyone who looked like they thirsted more for treasure than for the mead they guzzled. Most of the men and women looked to be farmers or traders with only a simple, yet practical, blade hanging from their belts where a sword normally belonged. Finally, Gorm spotted a small group carrying proper weapons and sat down next to them. They hardly glanced at him as he joined the fringe of their group, but the few looks they gave made Gorm feel uneasy. He took a few sips of his drink and told himself there was no way these men could know of his dishonor. He steadied his breathing and waited for the right topic of conversation to come up. Thankfully, he didn't have to wait long.

"Well, this was a wasted trip then," said a large man who smelled strongly of fermented honey. "I sailed all the way here just for the so-called King of Dublin to put a ban on raiding monasteries. What nonsense is this? I say we go up the coast and raid anyway."

"Shut your trap Sigurd, unless you want the rest of the hall to turn on you," said an older man with a few stray grey hairs. "People have built lives here. They want peace with their neighbors, will you put their homes at risk for a few shiny trinkets?"

"I don't know these people," Sigurd said as he took another swig and swayed in his seat. "Why should I care about them?"

"You should care because they are Vikings, just like you," the older man said with a tone leaving no room for discussion. "We will just have to keep sailing, until we find a fresh place to pillage. All the good treasure has already been taken after a hundred years of raiding anyways."

Gorm saw an opening and took it. "I know a place no one has ever raided with enough treasure to make you all kings. The best part is, the men of Ireland will thank you for the raid."

The two men paused and turned to Gorm. "Shut your trap child," the older Viking said. "The only other people on this island are a few Druid camps and they don't have anything of value."

"I never said we would be raiding people," Gorm said calmly but with an attempted air of authority.

"I'm listening," Sigurd said, clearly intrigued. "What do you have in mind?"

Everyone around Gorm fell silent. It felt strange to be the center of attention for once instead of trying to blend into the crowd. "We should raid the fairies of the north forest, west of Whitfield Castle. I'm sure you've heard of the hoarded wealth of the Leprechaun King. Millions of gold coins, towers of silver, and more jewels than have been mined by the hands of man in all of history just waiting for the right men to take. We can claim the Leprechaun's treasure for ourselves and drive the vermin out of Ireland. We would all be richer and more loved than the King himself."

Several men laughed. "You're either crazy or stupid," said a man with an untamed wiry red beard sticking out at all angles like a pile of sticks.

"Or both," said Sigurd.

"No one fights the fairies," said the older Viking. "Not unless they want to be cursed to see visions so horrifying, their mind turns to porridge, and they eat their own flesh thinking it was fresh lamb. Hundreds of Vikings have crept into the cursed fairy forest and not a single one of them has returned alive. It is a fool's quest."

Gorm's cheeks burned red at being brushed aside so easily, but he should have expected such a reaction. He knew the stories of fae magic and how they could twist the mind, burn the flesh, and break a man's will until there was nothing left of who they were before. Of course, the men would be afraid of fairies, they didn't know their weakness.

"How well do you know the stories from the Druids about the fairy folk?"

None of the men responded but glanced around at each other waiting for a reaction.

"The Druids believe the fairies are descendants of their gods, the Tuatha Dé Danann. These mighty gods have tales very similar to our gods. Too similar to be mere coincidence. Their gods fight the same kinds of monsters as ours, like trolls and giants. They decorate their homes in carvings of twisted knots, just like we do. And strangely enough, the Druid stories talk about their gods coming here from across the sea. The fairy gods came to this island to escape another clan of gods led by a powerful ruler with a mighty spear and only one eye... Sound familiar?"

One by one the Vikings nodded. How could they not recognize the one-eyed king of the Æsir? Every Viking knew of Odin the Allfather.

"The fairies are nothing more than a tribe of aelfir from the realm of Alfheimr. Think about it. The aelfir have fair skin, pointed ears, and white hair. The Irish elves have fair skin, pointed ears, and white hair. Some aelfir have insect like wings and attack with magic from above. Pixies have insect-like wings and hurl magic from the air. They are exactly the same."

"Not exactly," interrupted Sigurd. "Aelfir are tall. Not tall like giants, but taller than we are. Elves and pixies are smaller than my hand. Fairies also must be truthful, while aelfir lie with every breath they take."

"True," Gorm admitted. "They are small and seem to be unable to lie, almost as if cursed. I don't know how or when, but I think something happened to them to make them this way. In the old stories of the Druids, they are not described as small but as tall and fair beings who would seduce the people of this island. Only in more recent stories are the fairies described as miniscule tricksters. So, my point stands, they use the same magic as the aelfir."

"So what?" another Viking butted in. "The aelfir are terrifying. Their magic is possibly worse than the fairies. Even if they are only twisted aelfir it does us no good."

Murmurs of agreement filled the hall, but Gorm was prepared for this.

"It does if you know their weakness," Gorm said confidently. "I grew up on the banks of Raumelfr, across the river from where Midgard touches the land of Alfheimr. My clan dealt with the aelfir every day without fear because our clothing was enchanted with runes that make one immune to their magic. These enchantments will protect all of us from the fairies. Making any fight easily won."

Once again, the crowd laughed in Gorm's face while Sigurd acted as their spokesman. "Sure, the mighty fairies with their horrifying magic can be stopped by a few scribbles, yet we haven't heard of it? This is preposterous."

The laughter rang through Gorm's ears until the embarrassment transformed into a burning pocket of anger deep inside his chest. How dare these men laugh at him?

"I'll prove it," Gorm said, barely containing his rage. "Three days from today, at Whitfield Castle, I will show you the power of a few scribbles. I will let a swarm of fairies attack me while wearing enchanted cloth. If I am unscathed, you must follow me and the Lord of Whitfield into the forest to safely raid the vault of the Leprechaun King. If I die, then you will have wasted a day trip but nothing more. What have you got to lose?"

Gorm held out his open palm in front of Sigurd and stared deep into his eyes daring him turn away the offer. Sigurd seemed to reassess Gorm for a moment before grasping his palm. "Alright, I'll give it a go. Worst case, I get to see the buggers burn you alive. It's a deal."

His anger burned into triumph as Gorm held Sigurd's hand as a contract.

One by one the rest of the Vikings stood and shook Gorm's hand agreeing to hear him out in Whitfield. As they all approached, Gorm's remaining insecurities melted away. He would prove they were wrong to laugh at him.

After he shook the last Viking's hand Gorm addressed the crowd a final time. "Spread the word to meet at Whitfield Castle in three days and be prepared to head into the forest the following morning. When you return, we will all be unimaginably wealthy and the fae will either be dead or fleeing this island!"

16

Jaimie

The next day moved by slowly as Jaimie waited to be 'purified'. He continued to stare out his window during the day, watching the clouds circle around the gargantuan tree rising out of the forest like a natural obelisk. At night he stared out the same window, watching pinpricks of light circle the tree as the fairies made their nightly commute from the tree they called home to make mischief in the world of men.

The village just south of the castle was devoid of light as the residents shuttered every window, locked every door, and sealed every crevice a pixie or elf might squeeze through. They feared the fairies would replace their children with enchanted replicas lacking a soul, pluck out their teeth for sustenance, or possibly repair all their shoes. These stories filled the community with fear, but Jaimie hadn't heard anyone claim to witness these events firsthand. It always happened to an acquaintance's cousin, a barely remembered former classmate, or an accusation without evidence. As far as Jaimie could tell, no fairies had come to Whitfield since his father blamed them for the death of his mother.

To Jaimie, the glowing lights of the fairies were simply pretty lights in the distance. More abstract than real. He always imagined what the forest must look like in the glow of thousands of fairies at night. Gorm had promised to sneak out with him to see the lights someday. It didn't look like that "someday" would come now.

Jaimie's melancholy solitude was interrupted by an unfamiliar sound, a rustling and scratching noise just outside his room. He looked outside and couldn't see anything except the distant twinkling of fairy lights, but the sound continued. Jaimie stretched himself slightly over the windowsill and peered down the dizzying drop to the hard earth below. A small black mass was crawling up the side of the ivy-covered tower making scratching sounds as its claws dug into vines and mortar. In the darkness, most of the creature was only visible when it moved, giving it an ever changing yet shapeless appearance. The only consistently visible feature of the creature was its reflective eyes which glowed like polished gold coins. When the creature got close to his room, Jaimie stepped back and prepared to push it out of the window as soon as it clawed onto the windowsill.

With a flurry of claw scrapes, the mass pulled itself up and sat in the moonlight on the windowsill next to the pagan idol which had previously been Jaimie's only companion. Jaimie was prepared for some sort of minor demon or imp, but it was simply a cat. A medium-sized black cat with a small tuft of white fur in the shape of a crescent on its chest and matching white wisps poking out its ears.

Relief washed over Jaimie at the sight of the clearly ordinary creature.

"Here kitty, kitty, kitty," Jaimie gave the universal greeting to cats as he approached his surprise companion with outstretched hands. "What brings you all the way up here?"

Almost as if answering Jaimie's question, the cat swiped at the idol, sending it crashing to the ground. With a thud, the statue of Diana slipped free of the twine bindings and split in two again. The cat leaped to the ground and pawed at the statue. It sniffed and peered into the hollow form of the goddess as if searching for a mouse. After finding the statue empty, the cat hissed and batted a piece of the statue across the floor.

"Hey, what was that for?" Jaimie asked the cat. "What did Diana ever do to you?"

Jaimie picked up the pieces of the idol and once again wrapped them in twine. With the statue somewhat repaired, Jaimie turned back to the cat and spoke to it, mostly because it was something to speak to.

"There, now we won't have any more of that. Promise not to break anything else?"

The cat stared into Jaimie's eyes but did not speak and remained motionless as he approached. Jaimie slowly placed his hand on the top of the cat's head and stroked its thick, soft fur. The animal closed its golden eyes and let out a soft purr while pushing its head against Jaimie's fingers. It was the first kind gesture any creature had given Jaimie in days.

"You're a good kitty, aren't you?" Jaimie scooped up the cat and carried it over to his bed. "You're not afraid of people. Do you belong to someone in the village?"

Jaimie stroked the soft fur behind the cat's ears, and a soft rumble shook from deep within the small creature. The sound brought a small sliver of peace to Jaimie's bruised heart, and he pulled the creature in close.

"I guess you can stay here tonight. The only way out is through the window, or to wait for someone to drop off food sometime tomorrow. I can let you out then."

The cat looked up at Jaimie, and he almost thought it understood what he said, but it likely was responding to the soft tone of his voice as he ran his fingers through its dark fur. Jaimie made himself comfortable, and the cat snuggled up to him purring the whole way.

"Thank you for coming up here, you crazy kitty. I really needed someone to talk to. Can you keep a secret? Of course, you can." Jaimie scratched behind the cat's ears and the vibrating purr increased in volume. "I'm in love with my best friend, but he doesn't love me back. I thought he felt the same, but when I kissed him, he pulled away..."

Jaimie fell silent, and the cat snuggled in closer and licked his cheek.

"Anyway, he rejected me. Worse, my father found out and now he thinks I am a monstrous changeling. Now I'm all alone." Jaimie glanced down at the cat. "Or I was until you got here."

The cat stopped purring, stretched upward, and licked his ear. Jaimie continued to pet the cat and relaxed despite his worries. All the tension and anxiety melted away the longer he ran his fingers over the soft fur. With the cat by his side, Jaimie drifted off into the first deep sleep since his trip to England.

Jaimie fully expected the cat to climb through the window sometime in the night, so he was pleasantly surprised to find it still snuggled against him the following morning.

"Good morning," he said as he scratched behind the creature's ears. The cat responded by pushing its head into Jaimie's hand and purring loudly.

The morning was more enjoyable than the last several days had been now that Jaimie had company. Jaimie spent the morning telling the cat stories of good times with Gorm and Jaimie's father, only occasionally falling into the trap of mentioning their current feelings toward him.

As far as cats go, this one was a good listener. It sat patiently on Jaimie's lap as he ran his fingers through its thick fur. Jaimie determined the cat was female and decided to call it Diana, after the idol it knocked over. The cat seemed to approve, or at least she would look at Jaimie when he said her name.

Around noon a loud knock reverberated through the room and Jaimie's heart sank into his stomach. His daily ration was here, and he could now safely let the cat out of his room.

The door opened and instead of a guard with a drawn sword and a single slice of bread stood Gorm, with a steaming plate of buttered bread, fruit, and a large helping of thick bacon.

"Gorm!" Jaimie rushed to his friend with his arms stretched wide but stopped when he saw Gorm's sour expression. He shook his head slightly and his eyes seemed to scream for Jaimie to stop.

"Sit down," Gorm commanded, in a harsh tone Jaimie had never before heard from his friend.

Jaimie sat on the edge of his bed and Gorm closed the door again. The message was clear; this was not a rescue.

Gorm handed Jaimie the plate of the first real food Jaimie had seen since the morning of the jousting tournament. Jaimie wasted no time in shoving a slice of warm bread into his mouth.

"You really did it this time," Gorm said. "Your father is convinced you are a changeling, and nothing I can say will convince him otherwise."

This was not news to Jaimie, so he continued to eat without slowing down.

"Tomorrow morning you will be executed for the crime of being a changeling."

Jaimie swallowed and thought for a moment before responding.

"You do know I am not a changeling, right?"

"I do," Gorm confirmed.

Finally, someone with some sense!

"Then help me," Jaimie pleaded. "Let me out of here."

"I can't. Downstairs is a room full of Vikings and mercenaries preparing to invade the fairy kingdom in the forest. There is no way I could sneak you out without being caught and getting both of us killed."

Jaimie felt as if he was suddenly plunged into the sea. He wasn't surprised to hear he was being carefully guarded, but he had hoped Gorm cared enough about him to at least try and save him. Something else Gorm said caught Jaimie's attention.

"You're attacking the fairies?" Jaimie lost his appetite and put the plate down on the ground so Diana could eat what was left. She slunk out of the shadows and began nibbling on the bacon.

"Oh, you're a pretty one," Gorm said, noticing the cat for the first time. "Are you one of Freya's? Did she send you to look after our friend." He stooped low and put out a hand to stroke the creature.

Jaimie was not going to let Gorm get distracted. "So, you're attacking the fairies?"

"Yes," Gorm said as the cat stepped away from his outstretched hand. "Your father wants to rescue his real son from the fairy realm, or at least get his revenge on them. I arrived today with a small army of men to take their tree. We leave shortly after your execution."

Jaimie somehow felt worse than he did before.

"Please, there must be something you can do to put a stop to this?" Jaimie pleaded. "Convince my father that I am his real son and the fairy folk aren't involved."

"Why would I do that?" Gorm asked.

Jaimie felt as though time had stopped and his heart along with it. Gorm was his closest friend and confidante, his refusal to help was unimaginable to Jaimie.

"Why... why would you help save my life?" Jaimie asked hoping he misheard.

"Listen, I don't want you to die, especially in such a painful and humiliating way, but this is such a great opportunity for me. I cannot pass it up."

The cat hissed at Gorm, but he continued.

"I thought I had lost everything when I was captured during my first raid all those years ago. I became nothing but a servant with no future in this life or the next, but that all changed when your father saw you kiss me against my will."

"Against your will? You kissed me back!" Jaimie's fear began to turn to anger.

"You lying fairy!" Gorm yelled and glanced back towards the door before turning back to his old friend and lowering his voice. "No one will ever believe you, especially because your father holds me in such high esteem. He said I was like a son to him. When you are gone, he will have no blood heir. Who better to take your place than your closest friend?"

Jaimie clenched his fist and swung at Gorm, but the young Viking caught his wrist, stopping the punch. Gorm pulled back his own fist to strike, but instead let out a pained yell and dropped Jaimie's arm. He turned and Jaimie saw a black mass of fur on Gorm's back, digging it's claws into his neck.

"Damn cat!" Gorm yelled as he pulled the small beast off him and threw it at Jaimie. "I'll make sure that thing is put down too."

Gorm stomped out of the room and slammed the lock down on the other side.

17

Ailsa

Ailsa anxiously vibrated as she stared at the castle through the trees. Three days had passed since she met up with a furious Tragos and Fotini outside of Dublin and they still hadn't retrieved the pesky idol. Finding the castle was easy, Ailsa grew up in this very forest after all, but getting the idol out of the castle was another matter.

"Why dinnae you just fly up there and grab it?" Tragos asked as he sat on a stump at the edge of the forest. She was glad he was finally speaking to her again, but his tone could still use some work. It took Ailsa a moment to realize he could tell she was staring at the tower window where the idol sat glinting in the sunlight taunting her.

"For the same reason I told you yesterday," Ailsa said. "It's too heavy. It would plummet all four stories to the rocks below."

"So?"

"I can't give my client a mangled statue! Think of my reputation!" Ailsa emitted a reddish glow. "We are going to be paid more for this contract than any other ten contracts combined. I will not lose out on that much money because I dropped the statue. Besides I don't see it anymore, it might not even be in the tower."

"Only one way to find out," Tragos said through clenched teeth. "We should just go get it already."

"Will you two stop your bickering?" Fotini asked through tired breaths as she entered the camp from the forest northeast of Whitfield. She had a limp deer draped over her back, slowly dripping blood where an arrow pierced its neck. "Hope you both like venison."

"Dibs on the teeth," Ailsa said as Fotini slid the deer off her back to the ground with a sickening slap as flesh met hard earth.

Ailsa watched in fascination as the centaur kneeled to the ground and effortlessly peeled the skin off the slain deer. The pixie had never seen the violence that preceded a meal before, she usually bought her food from children by leaving a single silver coin under their pillow. The fresh blood and the squelching sound of Fotini's knife cutting into warm flesh disgusted her, but she could not look away from the huntress's gruesome work. Fotini appeared to be in a trancelike state as she transformed the deer from a majestic beast into clean cuts of meat. Her movements were smooth and under her breath she recited rhythmic words in a language Ailsa was unfamiliar with.

"What are you saying?"

Fotini paused at the disruption and looked Ailsa directly in the eyes. "I am thanking Artemis for blessing us with a successful hunt."

"What did she do? You tracked the deer and loosed the arrow."

"True, but she put the deer in my path. She allowed the hunt to take place."

"How?"

"She's the goddess of the hunt, of the wild," Fotini said curtly as she slid her knife through a ribbon of muscle. "Anything that happens on the hunt is because she allows it to happen. If she wanted the hunt to go differently, it would."

"I think you give her too much credit and don't give yourself enough."

Fotini glared, and Ailsa fell silent. She sensed the conversation would only escalate if it didn't abruptly end, so she contented herself with watching Fotini ritualistically prepare the meat for the night's meal. It wasn't long until three large portions of venison and one boiling pot of deer teeth were sizzling in the campfire. As the sun disappeared behind the tree line, the smell of lightly seasoned venison filled the campsite.

Ailsa grabbed a large, boiled tooth and repeatedly smacked it on a rock until it cracked in two. She scooped out the pulpy center of nerves and ate while Tragos eyed her with disgust. For the past six decades, Ailsa lived in Coille Sealgair surrounded by the various races of the Children of Pan, but this last week was the first time she had eaten in front of one. Tragos's obvious disgust reminded her why she usually dined alone.

Tragos reached for the largest and tastiest looking portion of meat and Fotini immediately smacked his wrist with the flat side of her spear. "That's not for you."

"Come on!" Tragos rubbed the back of his hand where Fotini hit him. "Why should the best piece go to waste? I'm tired of throwing out a third of our food."

"Who's it for?" Ailsa asked. It just occurred to her that there were three cuts of meat, but only two people who would eat it.

"It's for Artemis," Fotini said, grabbing the piece of meat and carefully placing it on a large flat stone.

Ailsa watched but did not understand. "Is she coming here? Your goddess? Is that why she blessed the hunt? For her dinner?"

"No," Tragos answered before Fotini could. "She never comes because she's not real. We just waste the best food after every hunt for no damn reason."

"It doesn't matter if she comes and eats it or not," Fotini said barely disguising her rising rage. "It will be here if she ever graces us with her presence. I would hate to be unprepared for a visit from a goddess. They can be quite unforgiving if crossed."

Ailsa watched Tragos roll his eyes in the firelight while Fotini kneeled next to the fire, looking smug. Neither spoke again and Ailsa felt the awkwardness of an ongoing argument. The tension was thicker than campfire smoke and just as hard on the eyes. Ailsa decided to abruptly change topics before either of them decided to escalate the discussion.

"There's another group," Ailsa said between bites. Groups of armed men started arriving at the castle just before lunch. After arriving, all the men set up tents in an empty field just outside the castle walls. In the early afternoon, there were only a handful of tents, but it gradually grew to dozens of small camps. Ailsa was beginning to think she was out of time to delay going to Crann Na Sióga to warn the other fae. The Viking's army was already gathering.

"We can't wait much longer. I need to know when and how they are going to attack." Ailsa took off out of the woods and soared high into the sky, hoping no one would look up. She zipped past the tower, where the idol previously sat on a fourth-floor windowsill and continued over the walls where she could see inside the large inner courtyard and garden.

Ailsa dropped into the courtyard and fluttered through tree canopies, bushes, and behind anything that would block her light from prying eyes. She made a dizzying trail peeking in windows, looking for any signs of a large gathering, but mostly finding dusty rooms with dark and unsettling décor showing fae and Children of Pan as grotesque monsters. At the north end of the garden, Ailsa finally found what she was looking for when she peered through a window and saw a massive group of hulking men and a spattering of intimidating women seated at a large table eating, drinking, and laughing merrily with a somewhat sinister undertone.

At the far end of the room Ailsa noticed something that made her blood boil and skin burn with a scarlet glow. A large object concealed under a blood red cloth stood at the far end of the room. Hundreds of small points of light too dim for human eyes to notice, twinkled from within the structure. Deep red and pale sickly yellow lights told Ailsa exactly what was hidden from the crowd. Hundreds of elves and pixies were trapped in an enclosure about the size of a horse stall. Despite her anger and disgust, Ailsa took a deep breath and focused on relaxing her emotions to a neutral unnoticeable light and prepared to spy on her enemies' plans.

18

Gorm

"This will work," Gorm told himself as he synched a black sash with gold embroidered runes around his waist. "You will be fine. Fairy magic is the same as aelfir magic. It can't hurt you with the protective belt."

It was easy for Gorm to confidently say he could render fairy magic useless with a simple enchantment, but it was much harder to prove it. Gorm had stopped at every pub, tavern, inn, and mead hall from Dublin to Whitfield castle enlisting Vikings and mercenaries to join the raid on the Leprechaun's kingdom. He convinced over a hundred men and women to come to Whitfield where he would prove his enchanted belts would protect the raiders from the horrors of a legion of magical imps.

Looking in the mirror, the enchanted belt looked stylish, but not very magical. Most people would scoff at the idea of something so simple being so powerful. The belts were simple strips of cloth with stitched symbols with no remembered meanings. They were not soaked in sacrificial blood, whispered over in a moonlit ceremony, or made by anyone with any magical prowess. The crates of belts were all stitched by the seamstresses in Whitfield under Gorm's direction earlier that day. Gorm himself had a hard time believing this would be enough to protect him, but it was too late to back out now.

"The crowd is ready for you," John said as he stepped through the door from the dining hall. John glanced back with an unconcealed scowl. Gorm never would have expected John to host over a hundred Vikings in the same hall where visiting holy men regularly met. By the look on the old man's face, Gorm figured John never envisioned this day either.

Gorm took a final deep breath and nodded. He grabbed a simple wire push broom and a large, folded fan. "I'm ready."

John tenderly placed a hand on Gorm's shoulder. "Thank you for this, for trying to bring my son back. You truly are a loyal man and a pillar of light for this community."

"Thank you, sir," Gorm said with a nod of gratitude.

"Before you go out there, I want to tell you something important," John said. "For your part in rescuing my son you will have earned a reward. When we return to the castle, I will hold your penance for your upbringing fulfilled and declare you a son of Ireland. You will be given land and titles befitting your service to the people here. While your plan to face the fairies is surely blessed by God, I know better than most not to underestimate the tricky bastards. I accept there is a real possibility they will kill Jaimie before releasing him from their wretched realm. If the worst happens, I am without an heir."

Gorm held his breath. Was John saying what Gorm hoped he was saying?

"If our calling is merely to destroy the fairies, and there is no hope for the stolen children, then I will leave the care of Whitfield Castle in your capable hands. I have no other children or even any nephews to carry on my legacy. You may not have been born here, but you are more of a true Irishman than any I know. I would be proud to call you my son."

The ever-present fear and shame Gorm carried seemed to fade away into the air. He was home. He belonged here. Despite his best-efforts tears swelled in his eyes as he embraced John. "Thank you, my lord."

"Thank you." John returned Gorm's embrace and firmly wrapped his arms around him. "Now go show these Vikings how to destroy the fairies!"

Gorm and John released each other and they both wiped tears from their eyes.

Gorm shook out his nerves, took a calming breath, and opened the door. He stepped into the great feast hall of Whitfield Castle feeling like he could face a hundred men. He looked over the sea of people and felt truly at home for the first time since leaving his village on the banks of Raumelfr. Gorm almost felt like he was in the village longhouse for a feast after a victorious raid. The sounds of rambunctious laughter, the smell of cooked lamb and spilled liquor, and the warm dim glow from torches and candles transported Gorm through time and space to his childhood with his mother and father. He felt a surge of confidence and knew his plan would work. He walked across the hall to a large object concealed by a crimson sheet and turned toward the crowd.

"Attention everyone!" John said in his loud authoritative voice. The room fell quiet at the host's words, and all eyes fell on John and Gorm. "Thank you all for coming here. I know our people have not always been on the best of terms. We come from different lands, speak different languages, and believe in different gods, but there is one thing that unites all of us, a deep hatred of the fairies who plague these lands!" The crowd cheered and John paused to soak up their boisterous energy. When the cheering waned, he continued, "for far too long these pests have cursed our crops, seduced our women, and even stolen our children. We finally have a chance to drive the fairies from our shores and even rescue all the children they have taken from us and replaced by changeling spies."

The crowd grew completely silent as John paused and closed his eyes in a feeble attempt to hold back his emotions. Firelight reflected off a new moist shine on his cheeks as he resumed his speech. "The fairies took my son and heir and replaced him with one of their kind, but we have been blessed with a way to rescue him and get our revenge on the cursed fairy folk."

John raised his hand above his head clutching an old piece of parchment. "Gorm, a man I have grown to trust more than any other, found these ancient instructions on how to reach the home of the fairies, Tír na nÓg! The door to the cursed realm is beneath the coronation stone of the Irish kings, the Lia Fáil, and the key to the door lies on the head of the Leprechaun king. For your help rescuing my son, you can keep all the plunder from the Leprechaun's vault and the fairy realm save one piece of treasure. I only require the crown of the wicked king to open the door to their vile realm!"

The crowd exploded in cheers. The wealth of the Leprechaun was legendary; a small portion of his treasure would make anyone in the room wealthy enough to buy their own castle.

John raised his hand, and the crowd fell silent once again. "Small treasures are often jealously guarded, and the Leprechaun's hoard of gold is the most well protected collection of wealth in the world. Armies have tried to invade numerous times only to be utterly destroyed. Swords are no match against magic and only a fool would dare attack the fairies in their own kingdom. Once again, the blessed Gorm has the information we need to be victorious."

John stepped aside and all eyes focused solely on Gorm. This was the moment these warriors travelled to Whitfield to see. They would either gain the secret to defeating the fairies or watch in glee as Gorm burned alive. Gorm took a deep breath and began the presentation that would lead to his glory or demise.

"Thank you, Lord Whitfield, and thank you all for coming this evening! As I mentioned to you all when we met in mead halls and taverns along the Irish coast, I was raised on the banks of Raumelfr, across the river from where Midgard touches the land of Alfheimr. The aelfir from Alfheimr are a race of elves similar to Irish fairies, though much, much taller and infinitely more powerful. They used to plague our lands until we learned the weakness of all magical beings, something as simple as the written word can stop them. Probably why the fairy folk did not allow the Druids to have a written language, so they could not revolt against them."

Gorm lifted the ends of the black sash tied around his waist. "These enchanted belts are inscribed with ancient symbols that completely protect the wearer from magic. While wearing this sash I cannot be burned by fairy fire, stopped by invisible walls, or driven mad by illusions in the mind. Now, you may all be thinking I am full of shit, that something so simple will surely fail to protect me from something as potent and terrifying as magic. There is no need to worry, I will prove to you this will indeed work or die for your amusement."

In a single swift motion Gorm pulled the crimson sheet aside, revealing a large wire cage with two chambers separated by a wall of iron wire and a similarly crafted pair of doors. The first section of the cage was mostly empty except for two small lumpy pouches. The other chamber was filled with hundreds of pixies and elves flashing various shades of angry red. The crowd gasped and shifted in their seats debating on staying or fleeing from the hall for their safety.

"Don't worry, this cage is made of an iron mesh that burns the skin of fairy folk as if it were sitting in a fire for hours. With powerful magic comes easily exploited weakness. As flimsy as the cage may appear, it is quite impenetrable to fairies."

The crowd relaxed slightly, but they were still uneasy. Everyone seemed prepared to run at a moment's notice if the demonstration went horribly wrong.

"I will now show the protective power of the enchanted belt and a few weapons I think will be more effective than trying to hit such small and speedy targets with a sword."

Gorm took a final breath, opened the first door of the cage, and stepped inside with a false mask of calm confidence. "Safety first, no need to risk the buggers escaping since you are not yet wearing any protection." Gorm closed the first door and opened the second.

The reaction was instantaneous. Hundreds of sparks ignited the tiny hands of the elves and pixies who wasted no time throwing fistfuls of fire at Gorm. The flames hit their target, and the young Viking was fully engulfed in a man-shaped inferno. The small iron bars of the cage began to glow and the people closest to the cage felt as if their faces were being singed. After a few long seconds the fairies stopped their attack, and the flames dissipated.

Gorm was untouched. He stood in the center of the cage without any indication of pain or injury. He laughed in relief and with an overwhelming feeling of power. He was right. It worked! Drinking in the feelings of invincible ecstasy he snatched a pixie out of the air and slammed it into the iron bars of the cage. The fairy screamed and writhed as its flesh burned where it made contact with iron.

"As you can see, I am completely fine! These simple symbols stitched on an ordinary piece of cloth completely protected me from the fairy's magic. I could stand her all day and be perfectly... OUCH!" Gorm's demonstration was interrupted by a sharp pinching sensation on his calf. He reached down and plucked an elf off the top of his boot and pulled a tiny needle like sword out of his leg. A wicked grin spread across Gorm's face as he took the sword and slowly pressed it through the elf's chest until it stopped screaming.

"I should thank my former assistant here for demonstrating the importance of the next part of the demonstration." Gorm tossed the elf's lifeless body aside and wiped its emerald blood off his hands on his tunic. "The belt will protect us all from magic, but not from mortal weapons. So, we should still be prepared to fight."

The pixies in the cage suddenly darted at Gorm as they realized they could still hurt him as a swarm. Gorm ducked down and grabbed the large fan he brought with him and began waving it around in swift motions. The pixies tumbled back through the air on the sudden gusts of wind. They readjusted their flight and tried again only to be hit with a second, stronger gust. Several pixies fell against the iron bars and screamed in agony as their wings ignited on contact with iron. The remaining pixies landed to avoid the wind and the attack ceased.

"Pixies are easily pushed aside by a little gust of wind, and it looks like this lot are thoroughly terrified enough to stop attacking. The royal guard of the Leprechaun will likely be a bit more resilient than these simple fairies caught stealing grain from nearby farms. I would expect the elves to attempt to swarm by the ground as well, but they are also easily dealt with."

Gorm grabbed his push broom and began sweeping the floor of the cage. Elves and pixies were pushed into a corner of the cage with a few unlucky souls being pushed against the bars with a scream and a flash of flame.

"Now, there won't be iron bars to sweep the fairies into once we are in the forest, but there are other ways to exterminate pests." Gorm stomped his foot down on a few fairies with a sickening crunch. "You will also be given another simple weapon courtesy of the Whitfield blacksmiths." Gorm picked up one of the small pouches in the corner of the cage and pulled out a handful of what appeared to be metallic sand.

"Fairy dust has long been a potent weapon of the fairy folk. Why shouldn't we make them fear twinkling dust as well? You will all be given a pouch of iron shavings."

At the mention of iron shavings, the remaining fairies began to scream. Gorm sprinkled the dust on his victims until the screaming ceased and all that remained of the captured fairies was a smoldering pile of tiny bodies. Gorm exited the cage and was immediately met by John who pulled him into a firm embrace.

"Absolutely fantastic," John said, hugging the former Viking. "I couldn't be prouder if you were my true flesh and blood."

Gorm returned John's embrace and felt something he hadn't realized he was missing since his mother and father died many years ago, the love of a parent.

John released Gorm and turned to the crowd. "Tomorrow we will start the day with the execution of the changeling spy who dared assume the face of my son, then we march to the fairy tree!"

The crowd stood, clapped, and cheered. Gorm could sense the dangerous mixture of greed, bloodlust, and the desire for revenge in the mob's boisterous cheers. They would finally get rid of the creatures that plagued their nightmares, and they could do so with little risk of bodily harm. For once, the fae would feel powerless in the presence of humans.

Through the cheering a sharp ringing seeped into the dining hall from the courtyard. The people nearest the door grew quiet and the ringing grew more noticeable. Someone was ringing an emergency bell.

"What's going on!?!" John shouted above the ringing as he ran beside Gorm outside of the dining hall.

"There's a fire in the stables!" came a reply from the young man ringing the bell. The men burst into action and rushed outside to save their precious steeds.

19

Tragos

The fur on Tragos's legs bristled as he peered into the dark sky searching for a moving twinkle of light amongst the static tapestry of stars. Where was Ailsa? It had been nearly an hour, and Tragos hadn't seen, heard, or smelled any change coming from the castle. Twisted knots tightened in his stomach as he scanned the unchanging sky.

"I'm sure she's fine," Fotini said as she trotted up to Tragos. "She's resourceful, and humans are terrified of the fae. They would probably... What's wrong?"

Tragos interrupted Fotini with a raised finger to his lips. His sensitive ears twitched pinpointing a sound from far away. A hundred small voices were screaming, and the sounds were growing quieter and quieter, as if voices were being removed from the wailing chorus. Tragos was no stranger to screams. Humans often screamed whenever they spotted him walking through the forest. He knew the difference between the sound of someone being startled and the sound of true fear. The sound from the castle was the sound of pain, despair, and the horror of knowing death was imminent. Worse than the screams, was the boisterous human laughter joining the cacophony.

"Do you hear the screams?" Tragos asked.

Fotini paused and a look of concentration fell over her face, but everything above her waist was decidedly human, including her less sensitive ears. She shook her head.

"Fae are screaming in terror inside the castle while humans laugh," Tragos added.

Fotini grew pale and grabbed her bow. Tragos unsheathed his sword and the pair of them sprinted to the castle as quickly and quietly as possible. Before they made it to the gate the last scream was extinguished.

"I'll never be able to get in unseen," Fotini said between deep gulps of air. "I'll cause a distraction so you can sneak in."

Without waiting for a response Fotini galloped to the left, away from the castle gate towards a large wooden stable. Tragos dove behind a row of bushes outside the gate and waited. It wasn't long before unbridled horses burst out of the stable into the fields of barley surrounding the castle. Smoke soon joined the panicked beasts streaming from the building followed shortly by a man screaming about a fire. The man ran past Tragos, through the gate, and into the center courtyard where he started furiously ringing a bell. Fotini did say she would make a distraction.

With everyone's attention on the bell and the fire, Tragos quickly slipped through the gate and ran up a small flight of stairs where he could watch and wait for the opportunity to sneak deeper into the castle unnoticed.

Over a hundred human men and women flooded into the courtyard from a large structure against the far wall. Upon hearing their horses were in danger they all rushed past Tragos's hiding place and outside the castle into the surrounding fields. Tragos anxiously waited until all the men left the courtyard before leaping off the stairs toward the building where the humans were previously gathered. He was about halfway across the open courtyard when he heard the most wonderful sound in the world; a high-pitched buzz accompanied by the silvery ring of fairy dust particles bouncing off one another.

Tragos looked skyward and saw a red and gold light diving from the sky. Ailsa stopped just in front of his face and frantically whispered so quickly Tragos struggled to keep up. "We have to warn the fae in Crann Na Sióga! The men have enchanted belts that protect them from fae magic! They leave to attack the tree city tomorrow!"

Before Tragos could ask her to repeat herself, Ailsa zoomed across the courtyard toward the castle exit without further explanation. Tragos scrambled after the pixie; he had never seen her so scared. Angry, yes, but not scared. For once Tragos didn't question Ailsa's orders but obediently followed after her.

As they reached the exit, Ailsa's lights suddenly went out and she dropped to the ground with a hard thud. Tragos's heart sped to a frantic hum as he scooped up the pixie and held her up to investigate. "Are you okay? What happened?"

Ailsa struggled to her feet but did not take flight. "I forgot about the idol. I cannot leave here without it, no matter the reason."

"Then let's get it," Tragos said. He gently picked up Ailsa and held her in just one palm. She felt so small and fragile in his hands, like a porcelain figurine. As he held her, Tragos felt his fear of pixies fall away.

Ailsa's light blinked and Tragos leaped into action. He ran up the stairs leading to the castle tower with Ailsa in his hands and burst through the door at the top without regard for who, or what, was on the other side. Thankfully the room was empty. "Okay, we're in the tower, now how do we go higher?"

Tragos looked around the room but couldn't see much at first in the darkness. He carefully trotted around as his eyes adjusted, but the growing sight raised the hair on his arms and set his blood aflame.

A large painting hung on the wall illuminated slightly by Ailsa's presence in the room. The art, as the humans no doubt regarded it, depicted a holy man robed in green with a golden staff pointing to the sea before a crowd of snakes and Children of Pan. The centaurs and satyrs were painted with red eyes and long fangs protruding from twisted grins. The sea was filled with their bodies splashing about as they died.

Tragos suddenly remembered why there were no Children of Pan settlements in Ireland and his hatred for the people here reignited.

"This way," Ailsa interrupted Tragos's silent fuming with a weak voice. She weakly flitted from his hand and through an open archway to a spiral staircase. Tragos turned his back on the painting and marched up the stairs with the images smoldering in his mind.

At the very top of the stairway was a small landing and a large wooden door. Tragos pulled on the handle with all his strength, but it didn't budge. He pounded his fists against the smooth wood with no returning answer, but a faint shuffling sound on the other side let Tragos know the room was not as deserted as the rest of the tower.

"Let us in!" Tragos yelled through the door as he repeatedly smashed his fists against it. "I can hear you in there!"

"Go away!" A scared voice yelled from the other side.

"If you let us in, I promise not to kill you," Tragos said in a forcefully calm voice. He wasn't certain if he was making a promise he could keep, but he wasn't a pixie so lying didn't bother him.

"I cannot let you in," the voice responded. "Even if I wanted to, I am locked in here."

Tragos stepped back and looked at the door again. Sure enough, a large iron latch with a large padlock kept the door closed.

A smile spread over Tragos's lips. He rarely had the opportunity to really use his horns. Few things were as satisfying as the crunch of breaking wood under hard curved bone. Tragos lowered his head, shot forward, and felt the wood bend and snap under the force of the impact. After two more charges, the wood splintered, and the door swung open with a bang.

Tragos stepped into the room with Ailsa hovering next to him. Inside was a human with a mop of red hair and the scraggly whiskers of a man not fully grown. Flashes of the painting downstairs filled Tragos's mind, and he raised his sword. He would relish this particular fight.

20

The Cat Sí

The smell of goat sweat left little doubt in the Cat Sí's mind on who was hammering against the door, but seeing the cat tormenter standing by the splintered remains of said door still made a rageful heat spread throughout her body.

"Give me the idol," Tragos commanded in an extra gravelly voice as he drew his sword and waved it around theatrically.

Was his performance supposed to be intimidating?

The Cat Sí turned her attention to Jaimie, whose eyes seemed to scream in submission while the rest of him moved in conscious defiance. He grabbed a worn training sword from his desk and pulled it from the scabbard in a single, swift motion.

"I don't want to fight you," Jaimie said with a quiver, "but I will not let you rob me."

Maybe the Cat Sí hadn't spent enough time in the company of mortals, but this was only the second time one earned her respect in untold millennia.

"Are you willing to die for some trinket?" Tragos yelled. He made slight adjustments to his stance, clearly preparing to strike.

"Why not? I have nothing else to die for."

Tragos leaped forward and swung his sword. Jaimie stepped to the side and blocked the attack with apparent ease. The Cat Sí was impressed, the mortal clearly knew how to use a sword.

Ailsa dived at Jaimie's face, throwing fistfuls of pixie dust which burst into flashes of flame on contact. Jaimie swung his sword wildly in Tragos's direction while striking out with his free hand towards Ailsa. With a lucky swing, he swatted her away, sending her crashing onto the desk in the corner.

The top of the desk flashed a series of colors before settling on a burning red light.

Ailsa being hurt seemed to send Tragos into a rage. He slammed his sword against Jaimie's with enough force to push the fighting across the room to the windowsill where the idol sat. Jaimie glanced at the gold-plated statuette and stepped directly between Tragos and the graven image.

"Give up!" Tragos snarled.

"No!"

Tragos pressed the attack, and the Cat Sí saw a shift in his eyes. Instead of the determined focus of a fighter, he had the manic expression of someone not only determined to defeat his opponent, but wanting to destroy them. Jamie blocked Tragos's next strike, but the satyr punched him in the nose with his unarmed fist. Jaimie stumbled backward with blood dripping off his lip while Tragos swept his leg, sending him crashing to the floor.

The Cat Sí could not remember if she had ever come to the defense of a human before, but as Tragos plunged his sword down toward Jaimie's chest she did not hesitate. She felt the combined power of Fotini's prayers course through her veins alongside a new equally powerful voice. Jaimie's desperate pleas spoken to the idol in darkness filled the Cat Sí with another source of magic to draw from.

She leaped forward with an outstretched paw that grew and stretched as she reached Tragos. Long slender fingers replaced short toes, but retained the curved claws, and wrapped around the sword. Golden blood seeped out of fresh cuts where she gripped the blade soaking into the black fur still covering her hands. The fur faded halfway up her forearm and transitioned into warm bronze skin. Her vision rose higher as she grew to match Tragos in height. She dug the claws from her uninjured hand into his shoulder as she felt her snout recede into her face while long humanlike hair sprouted from her head.

Tragos yelled and fell to the ground with his eyes growing wide in shock. The Cat Sí pushed the satyr onto his back and opened her mouth wide enough to expose a mouthful of needle-like teeth. Tragos screamed and lost all bravery as he stared into the Cat Sí's gold flecked eyes. "Please dinnae eat me! I wasn't going to kill the lad! Please! Please! Please!"

The Cat Sí did not listen. She was finally going to avenge every cat Tragos had ever shooed away. She could almost taste the sweet warmth of still pumping blood as she pressed her fangs against the satyr's scruffy throat.

"Stop!" Jaimie yelled. "Don't kill him!"

The Cat Sí paused, a flicker of familiarity burning deep within her.

"Why not?" she asked, hearing her own feminine voice for the first time in uncounted years. "He aimed to harm you. What is he to you?"

"He isn't anything to me," Jaimie said, "but he doesn't deserve to die."

The Cat Sí looked into Jaimie's eyes and was transported through time where a soft voice flowed into her mind from the deepest recesses of her memory. She could almost see the hazy figure of a woman standing before her with a calm, yet firm command: "stop, don't kill them. They have done nothing to deserve this."

With the faint memory ringing in her mind, the Cat Sí looked down at Tragos pleading for his life and momentarily remembered pinning down a young man in the snow in a similar way long, long ago. Her rage and thirst for blood subsided slightly and the Cat Sí was once again in Jaimie's room.

Ailsa fluttered down and landed on Tragos's forehead and put both hands in the air in an attempt to push away the Cat Sí.

"Stop!"

The Cat Sí released her prey and stood. She stretched her muscles as she reacquainted herself with her own body. It felt amazing to be free of her feline shape, but it wasn't quite the form she pictured while listening to Fotini's prayers. She still retained many aspects of a black cat instead of the fully human form of a maiden goddess.

As the Cat Sí mentally grappled with her identity, Tragos scrambled to his feet and stared at her in horror. His eyes darted from her catlike claws to her fur-covered ears across her body to her tail. As he seemed to realize he was not about to die, his eyes roved away from the catlike portions of the Cat Sí's anatomy and widened as they took in the rest of her form. The Cat Sí noticed a change in his demeanor and followed his gaze as it flitted from her face lower down her body. She glanced down at her humanlike form, naked save for a jagged crescent necklace dangling between her breasts and felt the familiar burn of righteous anger return.

The Cat Sí shot forward and gripped the collar of Tragos's tunic to pull him so close his face took up her entire vision. "I am choosing to spare you for Jaimie. Avert your eyes or my limited mercy ends."

With a light shove, the Cat Sí released Tragos, who lowered his gaze to the floor where he could only see the Cat Sí's fur-covered clawed toes. "As you command."

"Why do you put up with this... male?" The Cat Sí asked Ailsa.

"He works for me. I sent him to retrieve the idol for you," Ailsa said as she fluttered above Tragos. "I assume you are the one who left the contract for its acquisition? The Cat Sí?"

"I am," the Cat Sí said, "but you're a bit late. As you can see, the idol is already within my reach."

"Please," Ailsa said with a slight tremble, "I promised you I would get you the idol, and as a pixie, I must keep my promises."

The Cat Sí sighed and fought the urge to roll her eyes. *Fae really complicate everything.* She placed the idol on the floor between Tragos and her clawed feet. Ailsa landed beside it and motioned towards it with a bow as if she were presenting a grand prize.

"Please, Queen of the forest and all felines, the great Cat Sí, I present to you the golden idol of the huntress Diana as promised. I hope you find it satisfactory."

The Cat Sí nodded, ending the transaction.

Satisfied, Ailsa fluttered up to the level of the Cat Sí's eyes. "With the contract fulfilled I would like to make a new one. I have terrible news concerning the lord of this castle and a plot against my people. I would like to hire you to help us warn the fae in the forest, and defend them if necessary. I will pay whatever you ask of me. Please, I'm desperate."

The Cat Sí had the idol, what else could the pixie possibly give her? She was about to decline when she glanced behind the pixie at Jaimie. The pesky foreign emotions plaguing her since she met him bubbled in the pit of her stomach.

There was a long silence before the Cat Sí responded. "I will hear you out, but not here." The Cat Sí walked over to Jaimie's wardrobe in the corner of the room and flung open the doors. She grabbed a tunic, cloak, gloves, and boots and ran a claw lightly over them. Darkness spread from her touch until they were all dyed a black so deep it was as if light were afraid to touch them. "We are too exposed. Go back to your camp with young Jaimie and I will meet you within the hour. If he is harmed, I will eat each one of you one-by-one while the others watch."

"Wait, we're not bringing the kid!" Tragos said, suddenly finding his voice again.

The Cat Sí turned her gaze on him, and he winced in fear. "Did I sound like I was asking? You will bring him, or I will not help you."

Tragos thought for a moment before responding in frustration. "Fine, he can come, but I'm taking his sword. I won't let him stab me as soon as we are out of here."

Jaimie handed over his sword to the grumpy satyr. "Deal, for now."

"With that settled," the Cat Sí said, placing a foot on the windowsill, "I will meet you at your camp in one hour." The Cat Sí leaped into the moonlight outside the tower window.

21

The Cat Sí

The cool night air rushed over the Cat Sí's body as she ran through waist high fields of barley toward the tree line. She marveled at the refreshing touch of wind as it passed over her smooth skin. It was colder than she imagined, but not unpleasant, and the barley tickled her legs as she moved through the field. Without a protective layer of fur, the world felt closer, unrestrained, in every way 'more' than it was before.

The Cat Sí quickly crossed the fields outside Whitfield Castle and reached the pond at the edge of the forest. She carefully set aside the cloak and tunic she took from Jaimie and gracefully stepped onto a half-submerged stone, careful not to disturb the clear still water. With a deep breath, the Cat Sí leaned forward to gaze at her reflection for the first time in memory.

A beautiful, otherworldly face stared back at her from the glasslike surface. Her striking features were almost too perfect and symmetrical to be real and her unblemished skin and pronounced cheekbones gave her the look of youth and regal power, untouched by the harsh elements of the world. She appeared almost ageless, most of her features made her appear as a young maiden having just entered adulthood without the creases of time, but her almond-shaped eyes gazed back at her with the wise stare of an ancient being. As she long expected, she looked like a goddess in the flesh, but not the goddess she expected.

When Fotini's prayers first floated into the Cat Sí's mind her memories showed an eternally young goddess with piercing brown eyes, warm brown hair, and pale ethereal skin untouched by the sun. The face in the reflection had glowing golden eyes, deep black hair, and a warm complexion that would look at home under the warm summer sun.

More surprising than her coloration was the features she retained from her catlike form. The most obvious inhuman feature was her glowing golden eyes with slit-shaped pupils. She also kept her tail, though it had grown in length to match her current size. Fur-covered triangles protruded through the dark curtains of her hair, and her hands and feet were human shaped, but retained the fur and claws she had all those years as a feline. She also wore a strange pearlescent white pendant shaped like the white tuft of fur on the chest of her cat form and seemed to be the only thing that stayed with her when she transformed. At first glance the pendant appeared to be a crescent moon, but closer inspection showed an incomplete symbol ending at the inner curved edge, which was jagged as if the pendant was a piece of a broken circle.

As she inspected herself, she couldn't help but wonder if she really was the goddess Artemis. Maybe she had lived as a cat so long she was cursed to remain tainted by its form? Or was she someone else, and her memories were simply Fotini's imagination seeping into her mind?

"Who am I?" The Cat Sí asked to no one in particular.

Visions similar to the ones she experienced when Fotini first prayed to her flashed through her mind as if in response to her question. She once again saw the silver bow in her hand, but this time it was gripped through a golden glove. She remembered running through the forest after a large boar with a group of young huntresses by her side, but this time the edges of her vision were blocked by the white cloth of a soft hood that hid her unique ears. Her memories seemed to be changing as she slowly remembered more about who she was.

The familiar, but now clearer visions of life as the goddess who hunted by moonlight were soon joined by new memories previously out of reach. She saw a tall golden-haired man with a radiant smile standing next to her at twilight in a grove of trees. Instead of the blurred fragments of memory, she clearly saw his handsome features, so clear and perfect as if they were carved out of stone by a master artist. His white chiton with gold embroidered trim looked soft and the Cat Sí could smell his scented oils and the remnants of ambrosia on his breath.

"Your father is royally pissed at me this time, Apollo," the Cat Sí heard her own voice say in the newly recovered memory.

Apollo looked around the grove with a temporary flash of worry across his face. "You mean *our* father is pissed. Though for all the trouble he put us through over the years you think he could overlook your first and only real blunder."

The Cat Sí snorted. "If only I had just given birth to a small army of demigods to wreak havoc in the mortal world, instead I let a relic of Olympus get stolen by those new gods across the sea."

"That would have been easier to deal with," Apollo said with a light smile. "At least that wouldn't run the risk of the Tuatha Dé Danann invading our home, though I wouldn't fret too much if I were you."

A flicker of hope surged through the Cat Sí. "Do you say that to be encouraging, or as the god of prophecy?"

Apollo's smile grew wider exposing his gleaming teeth.

"Both. I saw that you will successfully retrieve the hide of the Calydonian Boar, but your journey will be very, very long. I daresay it will be the longest quest of any Olympian."

If Apollo was trying to comfort her, he wasn't doing a very good job. "Thanks, *brother*, for having such faith in me. Maybe it would go faster if I could take my bow?"

"Sorry, *sis*, but you know what *Father* said. You are not to take any other relics of Olympus with you because they will surely be stolen by yet another pantheon, and the rest of us are forbidden from helping you as part of your punishment."

"But you'll still help me, right?" The Cat Sí said with a sly smile. Apollo looked at her and shook his head, so she quickly changed shape into a small black cat with oversized pleading eyes looking out from a pile of white cloth.

Apollo looked at the cat and sighed. "Fine, I'll help you." The Cat Sí transformed back into her more human form. "I'll see what I can divine and send you a message hidden in a small idol that looks like you, or at least what the human's think you look like," Apollo flicked aside the Cat Sí's hood exposing her catlike ears. "I'll send it with a band of Roman satyrs and centaurs, Father never pays attention to what they are up to so the message should reach you just fine."

The Cat Sí wrapped her arms around Apollo and the memory melted away leaving the Cat Sí alone once again staring at her own reflection.

22

Fotini

Both sets of Fotini's lungs burned as she ran through fields of barley with a herd of frightened horses on her tail. She only wanted to distract the humans inside the castle by releasing their steeds, she had no intention of terrorizing dozens of the poor creatures by starting a fire.

A few minutes earlier, after leaving Tragos's side, Fotini slipped into the stables outside the castle and frantically started opening the short gates keeping the poor horses imprisoned instead of free to run along the countryside. After successfully freeing three of her less human relations, a shuffling noise from a pile of hay in the corner startled her. A young man sat up in the hay with errant bits of straw sticking out of his uncombed hair.

"What are you doing?" the man asked groggily as he shook himself awake. He stood and grabbed a lantern hanging from a post to get a clearer look at Fotini. His eyes grew wide in surprise as they wandered down Fotini's torso to the chestnut fur of her mare body.

Without a second thought, Fotini whirled around and pointed her spear at his chest before he could reach for a weapon. "Go to the empty stall," Fotini said as she directed the young human with her spear.

Unfortunately, the young man was either too brave, or too stupid, for his own good. He attacked the second his neck did not have a blade pressed against it by charging at Fotini with a small construction hammer in one hand and his lantern in the other. He roared as he lunged forward, probably in an attempt to appear intimidating, but it reminded Fotini more of a child throwing a tantrum.

Fotini shifted the sharp point of her spear away from the young man until the blunt end of the weapon swung into the side of his head with a sickening crack. The yell stopped abruptly as the man crumpled to the floor, momentarily dazed. As he fell, he released the lantern in his hand and it shattered open on the ground, spilling oil and flame across mud, dirt, and hay.

In a panic, Fotini leaped into the flames and attempted to stamp them out before they could spread, but her attempts were in vain. The dry hay ignited, and the flames spread around the stables at an ever-accelerating pace.

Fotini abandoned her vain attempts to stop the blaze and hastily resumed her mission of opening all the stalls to release the horses. She no longer cared about creating a distraction or stealing a golden idol. She simply wanted all the horses to get through another night alive and unburnt. She focused on the stalls closest to the flames and moved outward to ensure every creature made it out.

The fire grew until it licked the outer walls of the stable and filled the windows with a raging glow. Fotini charged and smashed into the stable doors, breaking them open with her hooves releasing a stream of horses out of the inferno and into the cool, dark fields. The human fool gathered his senses and ran screaming from the stables toward the castle while Fotini followed the herd of terrified horses, it wouldn't be long before the area was swarming with men.

Fotini circled the horses as she ran to get their attention while periodically letting out a sound that wasn't quite a neigh or a human yell but had elements of both. The horses understood the call and fell in line behind their natural leader and followed the centaur through the fields, away from the castle and the burning stables.

A mile or so later, when the glow of the flaming stables was out of view, Fotini stopped at a river where the horses could drink and calm their nerves. The men from the castle would eventually find the horses, but Fotini, Tragos, and Ailsa should be far away by then. Fotini trotted among the noble creatures, letting out a low hum to assure the animals of their safety and command them not to follow her any longer. Confident she wasn't being followed, she snuck away in a wide arch near the tree line to make her way back to camp.

Fotini raced through the forest, silently praying her companions would be there unscathed, but when she reached the camp, Tragos and Ailsa were nowhere to be seen, yet the camp was not empty. Sitting on a large stone was a figure draped in a black hooded cloak with its face hidden in shadow, except for reflective eyes that almost seemed to glow in the dim light. The only other thing Fotini could clearly see was a jagged crescent moon hanging off the end of a cord around the stranger's neck and a hastily made bow by their side.

"Who are you?" Fotini asked the unwelcome stranger. "What are you doing here?"

The reflective orbs under the hood shifted slightly towards Fotini, and the person answered in a feminine voice, "eating."

The stranger picked up a cut of venison and took a large bite. Heat rose into Fotini's cheeks as she realized the blasphemy taking place in front of her.

"Hey! Put that down, that's an offering to Artemis." Fotini drew her bow and aimed at the darkness beneath the cloaked figure's hood. "I'm warning you; another bite and you die."

The stranger sunk her teeth into the meat and ripped off another large chunk. Fotini released her grip on the bowstring and the arrow shot straight toward the dark recesses of the blasphemer's hood, but she ducked to the side just in time to avoid getting hit.

Fotini pulled out another arrow, and the stranger shoved the last chunk of venison in her mouth, grabbed her own makeshift bow, and nocked an arrow in the same amount of time it took Fotini to prepare another shot. Fotini hesitated as the precariousness of her situation dawned on her. Was it worth risking injury or death to punish someone for desecrating Artemis's offering? Without further hesitation, Fotini released the bowstring.

The arrow shot forward in a blur, but was prevented from reaching the intended target when another arrow slammed into it, sending them both spinning off into the forest. Fotini loosed another arrow, but it was also deflected by a defensive shot from the stranger.

"Malaka!" Fotini cursed, dropped her bow, and switched to her spear before charging the desecrator. She jabbed the iron spear tip at the stranger but missed as the figure leaned to the side. Fotini pulled back her arm and swung the spear in an arc, only to have the stranger leap high into the air over the weapon with the grace of a lion.

"Stop!" The angry red glow of an irritated pixie descended from above the trees. "What are you doing?"

Ailsa had finally returned.

"She was eating the offering to Artemis! I cannot let such blasphemy slide!" Fotini responded while taking another unsuccessful swing at the stranger.

"You can and you will! She is the Cat Sí, immortal witch, and guardian of Coille Sealgair! I think your goddess would allow such a mighty huntress a meal in her stead."

Fotini stopped attacking for the moment but did not take her eyes off the supposed protector of the Children of Pan. "Is this true? Are you the guardian of the forest, the Cat Sí?"

"That is what your people call me," the Cat Sí said.

Fotini hastily dropped her weapon, bent her knees, and bowed as low as a centaur could. Shame heated her cheeks and chest in the chill night air. She had attacked a huntress so revered she was almost a lesser goddess. "Forgive me, I was unaware I was in the presence of one so mighty."

Fotini braced herself for the Cat Sí's verbal assault but was surprised to hear laughter instead.

"Well, I never thought I would see you, of all people, bow to anyone," Tragos said with a laugh as he entered the clearing in the trees leading a scared looking human at the point of his sword. "Why dinnae you ever bow to me?"

Fotini stood up with embarrassed heat pounding in her cheeks. "I bow when I meet someone deserving of respect. She is perhaps the only being I will allow to eat the offering to Artemis, in the goddess's stead."

"What did Artemis ever do to deserve such devotion?" the Cat Sí asked from the darkness beneath her hood as she took another bite.

Fotini stood tall in disbelief. She had never been asked such a ridiculous question. "What hasn't she done? She leads the beasts of the forest into the open and guides the arrows of all hunters. She protected me when I was a young woman alone in a foreign land. She commands the moon itself to shine. She deserves everyone's devotion."

Even beneath the dark hood, Fotini swore she saw the Cat Sí smirk. "You give the goddess too much credit. I have watched over the forest back home for as long as I can remember, and never once have I seen a god or goddess do anything to deserve such devotion."

Blasphemy! The respect Fotini had freely given instantly dissipated. She grabbed her spear to resume her attack when Ailsa once again intervened.

"If you swing that spear at the Cat Sí I will never hire you again!" The fairy threatened Fotini mere inches from her face. "I need her to help fight the humans. She is the only one powerful enough to stop them from destroying Crann Na Sióga."

Fotini seemed to have missed a thing or two while she created a distraction at the stables. "Okay, what exactly happened at the castle? Why is the Cat Sí here? And why do you have a human with you, of all things?"

"This is Jaimie, and he is my guest," The Cat Sí answered before Ailsa could respond. "And I am here because you all couldn't steal a simple trinket for me."

The Cat Sí was really trying Fotini's patience. "We successfully stole the idol from the tournament and then…"

"And then you dropped it to be picked up by travelers about to set sail to a different island," the Cat Sí said with undisguised judgement.

Fotini stammered not knowing how to respond, so Tragos stepped in. "We nearly had it back," Tragos said. "You needn't have traveled all the way out here for it."

"After I learned you lost the idol once, how was I supposed to trust you to succeed?" the Cat Sí asked as she began pacing the edge of the camp in a large circle around the rest of the group.

Ailsa flushed red once again and even Tragos shut up.

Fotini felt uneasy about the newest addition to the group. The Cat Sí was supposedly a guardian who watched over the Children of Pan, but this creature didn't seem like she was protecting anyone. She seemed dangerous. Fotini recognized the circular stalking of a predator and knew the beast could strike if they made the wrong move.

"So, did you get the idol?" Fotini asked Tragos to break the tension.

"It's right here." The human, Jaimie, dared to address Fotini and handed the idol to the Cat Sí. Even by the dark firelight, Fotini could see the once pristine form of Artemis was cracked and split in half, held together by clumsily tied twine.

"When I reached your room the idol was already broken with a hollow cavity. Was there anything inside when you found it?" the Cat Sí asked, turning to Jaimie as she inspected the statuette.

"Yes," Jaimie said meekly. "It had a message inside."

"And where is the message now?" The Cat Sí asked softly. She seemed far more patient with the human than with Fotini or her companions.

"My father probably burned it," Jaimie said.

The Cat Sí cursed in an unfamiliar tongue and threw the idol to the ground, sending it rolling to Fotini's feet. Fotini tightened her grip on her spear and prepared to defend her companions.

"But I remember the message," Jaimie said with a shaky voice. "I can pass it along to you if you'd like."

The sides of the hood hiding the Cat Sí's face shifted slightly, like large ears were struggling to rise in excitement. "What did it say?"

"The message was for the writer's sister. It said the door to the fairy realm is at the Lia Fáil, and the key to the door is a crown in a sapling of Yggdrasil, which is some sort of giant tree. My friend said it has to be the fairy tree deep in this forest."

"Your friend is probably right," Ailsa interjected. "I grew up in Crann Na Sióga, below the canopy of the tallest tree in the world. My parents said the tree was brought to this realm a thousand years ago when the Aos Sí became the fae." Ailsa directed her attention to the Cat Sí. "Does this mean you are going to Crann Na Sióga anyways?"

"If the key is indeed in Crann Na Sióga I have no choice," said the Cat Sí. "So, yes, I will need to go to the tree city."

"So, will you help defend the fae from the humans? You will be in the city anyways," Ailsa asked with a note of hope in her voice.

"The fae will be fine," the Cat Sí said as she stopped circling the camp. "Hundreds of armies of men have tried to invade Crann Na Sióga to claim the Leprechaun's horded gold. Hundreds have failed."

Ailsa's glow turned bright red. The pixie took a deep breath to calm herself and responded. "One of the humans knows some sort of rune magic that protects them from fae magic. He single-handedly killed dozens of elves and pixies in a demonstration and none of their magic could touch him."

"None of their magic?" the Cat Sí asked, a hint of surprise in her tone.

"None. The fae engulfed him in flame and not even his hair was singed."

This revelation disturbed the entire group. Like most Children of Pan, Fotini was usually wary around fae in large numbers. The rumors of them swarming solitary travelers and burning them, paralyzing them, or leaving them tied up naked on the roadside were enough to warrant at least an ounce of caution. Worse still, they were next to impossible to hit with a spear or arrow.

"So, they are well defended, but how do they plan on attacking?" the Cat Sí asked. "I've heard the tree is nearly impenetrable."

"They have several weapons they are planning on using to kill fae in large numbers, but I don't know how they plan on scaling the tree. The fae have never had to fight an enemy immune to our magic. At least not since Tír na nÓg..."

Ailsa grew suddenly silent. Fotini didn't understand what she meant, but the Cat Sí seemed to.

"Fine. I will help defend the fae, but I have conditions," The Cat Sí said as she resumed her pacing. "First, you must help me steal the crown."

Fotini had never seen Ailsa look so flustered when making a deal. It was refreshing to see her struggle to get what she wanted for once.

"Thousands of elves and pixies will die, and you have conditions?"

"Yes," the Cat Sí said. "Also, Jaimie will come with us."

It was Tragos's turn to turn red. "The hell he will! I am not traveling with a human!"

"Then you are free to leave," the Cat Sí said as she turned to Tragos and looked into his eyes with an unblinking reflective stare.

"Don't I get a say in this?" Jaimie interrupted the staring contest Tragos would certainly lose. "Maybe I don't want to travel with a smelly satyr."

The Cat Sí softened slightly. "Do you want to go back where they plan to execute you with a hot rod slid down your throat? Or do you want to come with us?"

"I want to go back to the way things were before," Jaimie said.

"We both know that's not possible."

Jaimie looked at the castle and then back at the Cat Sí. "Then I want to try and help the fae."

"Then count me out!" Tragos yelled.

The Cat Sí turned her attention back to Tragos and any gentleness in her voice disappeared. "You can leave, or you can come with us and help the fae." She paused for a moment and then added, "The very wealthy fae who may be very thankful for the warning."

"Wealthy?" Tragos asked, his voice suddenly containing a note of excitement.

"Remember, this is the tree of the Leprechaun King," the Cat Sí said. "I am sure you have heard of his penchant for gold?"

"Fine, the boy can stay," Tragos said. Fotini could almost hear the greed in his voice. He was no doubt already thinking of ways to sneak into the Leprechaun's vault.

"So, it's all settled? Jaimie is coming and you will all help me get the crown?" the Cat Sí asked as the group nodded. "You should leave at first light; I will meet you there. I have some things I must see to in the forest before approaching Crann Na Sióga. Get some rest, you have a long walk ahead of you tomorrow."

23

Jaimie

The stars and moon shone brighter than any other night in recent memory. The celestial objects were the only source of light at the campsite where Jaimie and his reluctant companions slept. The campfire had long cooled into black lumps with specks of red and did little to warm the young man, making him almost miss his comfy bed. He was free from his room for the first time since the night he kissed Gorm. The threat of being ritualistically killed as a misidentified changeling no longer filled Jaimie's mind with paralyzing dread. He was safe. He should feel as light and free as the stars overhead, but his thoughts still swirled with a new set of worries.

The uncomfortable moist feeling of the inner heat and sweat that came with an anxious mind washed over Jaimie as he waded through fresh worries. He was so preoccupied with saving his life, he jumped at the chance to follow the Cat Sí without thinking about what this new life would be like. Now the weight of that decision was nearly crushing. He could never go home again. He would never see his father again. He would never see Gorm again.

Jaimie gazed around the campsite at the strange creatures, which were now the closest thing he had to friends, regardless of whether they liked him or merely tolerated his presence. The satyr was asleep and silent for the first time. He wasn't yelling, scowling, or swinging a sword. Instead, he was breathing steadily and kicking his foot as he dreamed. It was oddly similar to an old hunting dog dreaming of chasing rabbits.

The centaur slept in the opposite manner. Her four legs were bent beneath her with her human half upright, her arms crossed, and her head bowed. She looked like a woman kneeling in prayer and Jaimie supposed she probably was praying when she drifted off to sleep. The broken statue of Diana, or Artemis as the centaur called her, stood directly in front of her on the hard earth, giving validity to this notion.

Even the pixie slept soundly, her soft glow emanated from a saddle bag draped over the sleeping centaur. It must have been warm, bundled up in a satchel strapped to a friend's body. Definitely warmer than the simple shirt and pants Jaimie threw on as he left his home. The only other thing he had was a slightly dull sword, and that was in Tragos's possession. As he shivered, he wished he had at least brought a blanket. Clear nights were always the coldest, no matter the season.

Sleep wasn't going to come soon, so Jaimie stretched and stood up. Walking between the trees would warm his muscles and possibly allow him to glimpse his home one last time. It didn't take long for Jaimie to reach the tree line where Whitfield Castle was still clearly visible. Smoke swirled off the charred stables in the moonlight, the glow of embers fading away to darkness. His father's room was the only light in the entire castle still burning. His own room was nothing but a dark hole in the tower wall.

"Couldn't sleep?" Jaimie jumped at the feminine voice coming from the darkness of the trees above him. The Cat Sí dropped silently to the ground next to him. The deep black cloth completely covered her as before, but up close in the moonlight Jaimie noticed silver angular swirls sewn at the hem of the sleeves which weren't present when they belonged to him. A dark hood and cape still cast her face in shadow except for her golden reflective eyes. The same reflective eyes from the small black cat that curled up beside Jaimie a few hours earlier.

"No," Jaimie responded. "Figured I would stretch my legs a bit. You can't sleep either?"

"I never sleep when the moon is out," the Cat Sí said with an accent unlike any Jaimie had ever heard. She turned her face toward the heavens, her face finally visible in the bright moonlight. Jaimie was still surprised to see youthful bronze skin instead of dark fur and whiskers. The Cat Sí's formerly wild hair was styled in a braid similar to the styles Jaimie saw in the Norse and Danish settlements around Ireland. It seemed somewhat out of place with the rest of the Cat Sí's appearance.

"Earlier, in my room, you were a cat..." Jamie said, fumbling over his words. He never knew how to start awkward conversations.

"So? They call me the Cat Sí for a reason." The Cat Sí pulled back her hood, exposing her less than human features. Instead of the rounded ears of a human, the Cat Sí had the same fur-covered triangles she had as a cat poking through her shiny black hair.

"True, but the thing about cats is they don't talk..."

"They do when they have something to say. They talk to me all the time. Some of them never shut up."

"Well, they don't talk to me, they..."

"Of course, they talk to you," the Cat Sí interrupted. "Humans just don't know how to listen. Or maybe it's your ears. How do you hear anything with those things?" The Cat Sí grabbed Jaimie's ear and pinched.

Jaimie rubbed his ear when the Cat Sí let go. "What I mean," he continued, "Is that people say things around cats because they assume the cat won't be repeating it."

"Also, not true. I know a tabby in Northumbria whose human companion is having multiple affairs, and he never shuts up about it. All the cats in the area are keeping up with the drama."

"Okay, so I don't know much about cats." Jaimie was growing flustered at the tangents. He was starting to prefer it when the Cat Sí was just a cat. "What I mean is, are you going to tell anyone what I told you?"

The Cat Sí cocked her head to the side and stared at Jaimie. "Tell them what?"

"That I like men." Jaimie had never said these words out loud. The sudden stark admission was equal parts terrifying and freeing. It felt as if Jaimie released his breath after holding it so long, he forgot what it was like to breathe.

The Cat Sí didn't move but stared ahead blankly in confusion.

"That I am in love with my best friend who just so happens to be another man..."

"Oh," the Cat Sí said. "Well, unlike cats, I don't gossip about other people's private business. But why should anyone care about that?"

Jaimie didn't immediately answer. He had never had to explain why he would want to keep his sexuality a secret. It was a taboo subject at best, a reason to fear for your life at worst.

"Because it's wrong. My father always said it was unnatural and a grave sin that would incur the wrath of God. He was about to have me killed because he found out."

The darkness beneath the Cat Sí's hood seemed to grow darker, almost like the moonlight had dimmed, but the sky was still clear. "While I have never met this God your father worships, I have spent enough time in these Isles to hear stories of his kind and loving nature. If he is truly a loving God, would he be angry because of who you cared for? It seems to me your father may be passing off his own feelings as the words of your God."

Jaimie reflected on the Cat Sí's words. Were his feelings toward Gorm inherently wrong? Or was his guilt just the fear of his father?

"You shouldn't be ashamed of who you are or how you feel," the Cat Sí said. "Do you think I'm a monster because I only love women?"

Jaimie was surprised with how easily the Cat Sí discussed her sexuality, but he couldn't help but notice her pointed teeth and razor-sharp claws. "Not because you like women..."

The Cat Sí lightly pushed Jaimie's shoulder. "The point is, you should not be ashamed of who you are or how you feel. I won't tell anyone anything you don't want shared, but you shouldn't need to feel like you need to hide."

"Thank you." Jaimie felt another weight lifted off his shoulders. He wasn't sure why, but he felt he could trust this odd creature even though they had only met the night before. She treated him as if they were family, which was absurd. They couldn't look less related.

"Why did you save me from Tragos?" Jaimie asked suddenly. "Why are you helping me?"

The Cat Sí had a puzzled look on her abnormally expressive face. "I don't know... I hadn't even spoken to a human in an age and am usually irritated by the mere presence of men, but something about you made me remember someone..."

Jaimie stayed silent as he watched the Cat Sí process her emotions. He learned a long time ago the best way to get an answer is to wait. "I think it's because you asked me to spare Tragos, even though he was your enemy. You sounded just like someone I think I used to love. She also asked me to show mercy. When I looked at you, I saw her and felt something I didn't know I could still feel."

Jaimie didn't know what to say. He always felt awkward when people shared their intimate thoughts, so he broke the tension. "I hope I don't remind you of her too much, because I think we've established you're not my type."

The Cat Sí laughed more than the joke warranted. "Don't worry, we've established you're not my type either. Though I do think that would be the easiest way to annoy the satyr."

The Cat Sí playfully smacked Jaimie's back and rose to her feet. "Let's go back to camp. You probably forgot any travel gear when we left. You can use this as a blanket to stay warm until morning, but I will need it back at first light." The Cat Sí pulled off the hood and cape she previously stole from Jaimie and handed it back to him.

Jaimie swung the cape across his shoulders and pulled the hood over his head. The cloth was still warm from the Cat Sí's body heat. Without her hood, cape, and angry demeanor the Cat Sí looked far less mysterious and intimidating. Instead of making her appear as a formidable huntress, the catlike features made her look like a cute fluffy pet. Otherwise, she looked like a normal young woman wearing a simple black tunic and necklace with a crescent dangling from the end.

"Thank you. I was freezing earlier. Are you sure you don't need it?" Jaimie asked as he felt the soft material.

"I can keep myself warm just fine," the Cat Sí said. "Just leave it in the shade of the trees near the campsite when you leave in the morning, and I will retrieve it."

24

Tragos

"**K**eep moving," Tragos barked as he smacked the human lightly across the back with his own sheathed sword. He couldn't believe he was stuck trudging through the forest with such a creature. He silently hoped the thing would turn around and attack so he would have an excuse to hit it a few times, but unfortunately it took the abuse in stride.

"Be careful," Ailsa said from between Tragos's horns, her gentle glow lighting the shadows in front of him. "Remember the Cat Sí's conditions? If we harm the human, she won't help us save the fae."

"It was barely a tap," Tragos grumbled. "Why exactly do you want to help the fae in Crann Na Sióga? Didnae they banish you or something?"

There were many rumors back home in Coille Sealgair about Ailsa as the only fae in town. Some Children of Pan feared going near her shop because they heard she once murdered other fae, while others saw her sympathetically as someone who did something terrible out of desperation, but all the stories agreed she was no longer welcome in the fae kingdoms.

"I was," Ailsa confirmed. "But that doesn't mean all the fae in the city are bad."

Tragos kept quiet but didn't know if he agreed. Nearly all his dealings with the fae had turned out poorly. He once traded a newly carved reed flute he spent weeks making to an elf for a barrel of wine, only to find the barrel almost empty. It technically was a barrel containing wine, but Tragos forgot to specify it needed to be a full and unopened barrel. He tried to retrieve his flute, but the elf disappeared with it before he could react.

Another time a pixie promised him all the gold he could carry from his underground vault in exchange for a day's hard labor mining fae stones. Tragos inspected the vault before signing any contracts and found it full of columns of gold and silver, but the pixie had a different trick up his sleeve. When Tragos entered the vault, exhausted by the day's work, and covered in sweat and grime, he tried to fill his pockets, but the sneaky pixie bewitched the weight of the gold. Tragos could barely lift a single small coin and carry it outside. He only took ten more steps before he had to abandon his pitiful payment in the middle of the path because it grew heavier with each step.

The fae never lied, but most still found ways avoid the truth.

"Is it just me, or are the trees getting closer together?" Fotini asked as she squeezed her much wider hips between a pair of tall but thin trees.

"The forest is bewitched to keep out invaders," Ailsa said. "You big folk have a hard time fitting between the trees in large numbers. King Lugh used his magic to plant this forest and make it grow to maturity in a single day to protect Crann Na Sióga."

"I didnae ken fae could use magic to grow forests overnight," Tragos said as he drew his sword and began hacking away at the trees in front of the group.

"We can't anymore," Ailsa said with a tinge of sadness.

Tragos couldn't see Ailsa on her perch between his horns, but the shadows grew hazy, and the trees blended together more in the darkness as her normally bright light dimmed.

"Why not?" Tragos asked to break the silence enveloping the group. He had worked with Ailsa for years but couldn't say he really knew anything about her or the rest of the fae. She was the only pixie living in Coille Sealgair after all.

The silence lingered a while before Ailsa fluttered off Tragos's head to where she could speak to him face-to-face and answered. "Most fae wouldn't want me to tell any of you big folk, but we barely have any magic left. Our ancestors were once called the Aos Sí, and they overflowed with magic. They could grow forests, summon the tide, and grant others the ability to fly, but my ancestors must have done something to anger our gods. The door to Tír na nÓg was abruptly sealed and the Aos Sí traveling in the human realm were cut off from their magic.

To add further insult, the Aos Sí grew small and so weak even a lie or broken promise would cause unbearable agony. From that moment forward they ceased to be the Aos Sí and became the fae."

"So that's why you cannae lie?" Tragos asked.

"Yes."

Tragos always assumed the fae told the truth out of principle or a strict moral code. He looked at Ailsa and instead of seeing someone with a brutally honest, stubborn streak, he saw sadness and anger.

"Wait," the human interrupted the conversation, speaking for the first time since the Cat Sí left. "Fae barely have any magic? Then what about the stories of changelings?"

Ailsa immediately took on a bright red glow. "It's a slanderous lie. You humans blame us when your small children don't act the way you think they should. Then you feel less guilty about getting rid of them because you can say it was a 'fairy' child."

Jaimie stopped walking and Tragos nearly ran into him.

"Fairies don't kidnap children?" He asked.

"No, why would we?" Ailsa answered.

"To trade places with them? Maybe eat them?" Jaimie said quietly.

It was hard to tell in the dim light, but Tragos swore she saw Ailsa roll her eyes.

"That's the dumbest thing I've ever heard. Babies don't even have teeth." Ailsa shook her head.

"Well, that's what I always heard," the human said.

"Bet you heard a lot of things that aren't true." Tragos whacked Jaimie in the back with the flat side of his confiscated sword. "Like how all us satyrs are alcoholics with insatiable sexual appetites."

The young human's embarrassed expression was enough confirmation for Tragos.

"Yeah, I kent you must believe that one after seeing the 'art' in your castle," Tragos said in a biting tone. "I especially like the one showing my kind being forced out of Ireland to drown in the sea."

The human stepped forward, he seemed to be regaining some of the courage he showed the night before. "I had nothing to do with that wretched painting. I've never agreed with my father and his hatred of fairies and pannites."

Tragos pointed his sword at the human's throat as Ailsa quietly egged him on from between his horns. "How dare you call us that! One more word and I'll give you a reason to fear the Children of Pan."

"Enough!" Fotini stepped between Tragos and the human. "We get it! Everyone's species is garbage, but save the fighting for if the raiders' attack. There's no point in killing each other before the battle."

Tragos lowered his sword. If the human died fighting his own kind, he wouldn't shed a tear.

Everyone walked in awkward silence as the forest grew ever darker. The trees were now so close together they were always touching a tree with some part of their body as they weaved through the brambles. Tragos stepped in front of Fotini and hacked away smaller plants to make sure she could fit. It made the journey painfully slow, but there was no space to stop and set up camp, so they pressed on in the midday darkness.

The human groaned and mumbled as he squeezed between tree after tree. "Can I please have my sword to cut a path?"

"Absolutely not." Tragos wasn't stupid enough to arm a human.

"Fine," the human huffed, "but you will need to keep cutting me free then. Your arms must be getting tired."

Tragos's arms were burning with exhaustion, but he was as stubborn as any goat.

"You obviously dinnae ken much about satyrs if you think I am getting tired. I can do this for days." Tragos hacked away at another group of thin stalks in their path.

"We are getting... close," Ailsa said from between Tragos's horns. Her voice was quiet and strained.

"Are you okay up there?" Tragos asked.

"No," Ailsa said with a wince. "I was caught stealing when I was young and as punishment, I was forced to promise never to return to Crann Na Sióga, and now I am actively breaking my promise. The closer we get, the more it hurts."

Ailsa let out a small groan and her light illuminating the trees flickered.

"Then let's stop. I can go warn the fae and you can stay here." Tragos said, surprising himself. He wasn't usually the type to volunteer for anything, especially if it concerned the fae.

"They won't trust you. *You* can lie. We just need to get outside the city to warn them, so I'll be fine. It's not like I will have to actually break my promise by going inside."

A short while later, Tragos pushed through a pair of trees and was suddenly in a much wider section of forest. The trees were still dense, but not unnaturally so. Miniscule lights filled the canopy, and when he focused, Tragos could see small bridges connecting the branches and buildings carved into the tree trunks. Whispers followed the group as they walked beneath the structures, and they could hear singing reverberating through the dim light.

As the fae buildings in the trees grew more common, the trees grew even further apart, but in a more organized fashion. With the canopy thinned, light from the afternoon sun filtered through the leaves, illuminating the treetop suburbs. The detail and craftsmanship of every small structure impressed Tragos; the fae had a penchant for beauty that the Children of Pan seemed to lack. Carved swirls and knot patterns embellished everything from house frames to bridge railings. The entire community was made as a work of art, not just as a practical place to live.

The forest ended abruptly in a uniform line, allowing sunlight to shine through in a large circle around the tallest tree Tragos had ever imagined. The tree was wider than any castle tower and at least thrice as tall. It overwhelmed Tragos's mind. Nothing this large could be natural.

While the tree was unfathomably large, the intricate arch and doorway carved into the base of the tree was very small. It barely reached Tragos's waist, but to the elves walking through the door it must have seemed massive.

"I present to you the entrance to Crann Na Sióga," Ailsa said from her perch between Tragos's horns. "Please put me down on the ground, I don't think I can fly right now."

Tragos scooped Ailsa off his head and carefully placed her on the ground in front of the door. She shakily walked to an elf wearing all green and holding a miniscule silver spear standing in the center of the entrance watching everyone who entered. The elf looked at each member of the party with slight confusion before addressing Ailsa with a glare.

"What brings such an... eclectic group to Crann Na Sióga?"

"We need to pass a message to Lugh, King of the fae," Ailsa said.

"The king is very busy," the elf said, exasperated. "He will not meet with every traveler who comes to our city. Who are you? What makes you worthy to meet with the king?"

"Who I am isn't... important." Ailsa struggled to speak and had to pause frequently. "We have a warning for the king that... enemies are on their way."

Instead of acting alarmed, the elf seemed suspicious. "Are you okay? You are sweating profusely. Are you... lying?"

"I am not lying," Ailsa said before bending over and vomiting on the elf's shoes,

"It certainly looks like you are," The elf said as he shook off the vomit. "What are you trying to pull? Are you trying to cause a panic? Why did you bring such creatures to our door?"

Tragos reached for the sword secured at his hip, but Fotini placed her hand on his shoulder. He released his grip and tried to force himself to let Ailsa take care of things.

"I am telling the truth... please you need to listen to me," Ailsa pleaded.

"I do not. In fact, I will not. I will not hear another word you say," the elf decreed.

Ailsa wailed and begged but the elf ignored her, almost as if he could not hear her at all. Tragos suspected he couldn't.

"I dinnae think that is going to work," Tragos said. "Should I squash him?"

The elf may not have been able to hear Ailsa, but he certainly heard Tragos's threat.

"How dare you threaten a guard of the Leprechaun's kingdom! You will pay for this!" The guard pounded the end of his spear on the ground three times, sending echoes through the trees. A slow rumble started small but grew in intensity as thousands of elves wearing the same green and gold uniforms streamed out of the main door to the city and dozens of previously hidden doors beneath the tree roots.

Tragos unsheathed his sword in panic as one of his worst nightmares unfolded in front of his eyes. The hoard of elves pointed their needle-sharp spears toward Tragos, Fotini, and the human while hundreds of pixies descended from above with outstretched hands holding small fireballs.

"Non-fae are not welcome in the city. Go back to the forest or burn," the first elf guard said.

Tragos slowly picked up Ailsa, placed her gently on top of his head, and carefully stepped backwards away from the angry fae. Fotini and the human followed suit until they were all out of range. The moment they felt it was safe, all three ran back to the forest.

"So that's it? We're just out of luck? How do we warn them now?" Ailsa asked in a small camp they set up just inside the thick growth of trees.

"We did what we set out for," Tragos said, more than ready to abandon this quest and head home. "Theres nothing else any of us can do."

"That's not good enough," Ailsa said. She seemed to have more strength now she wasn't actively heading toward the city.

The group was silent. Tragos didn't think there was any choice but to give up. They couldn't fight past the guards, and even if they could, no one would listen.

"I need to speak with the Leprechaun directly," Ailsa said softly. "I will have to go to the palace."

This was the last thing Tragos expected. Ailsa was banished; she shouldn't feel the need to sacrifice herself on their behalf.

"No, no way!" Tragos yelled. "You promised you would never go to the city again. You were sick just going to the door, it will be too painful for you to actually go inside."

"It will be painful beyond imagining," Ailsa said. "But I can do it."

"You cannnae do it," Tragos said. "You already did all you could, why die for people who banished you?"

"Lugh the Leprechaun banished me," Ailsa said. "Why should thousands of innocent fae die because of a grudge against their king? Would you condemn satyr children to death because you didn't like Pan?"

Tragos hadn't thought of it that way. He knew he couldn't let his own people die if the roles were reversed.

"I can do this," Ailsa said to herself more than to anyone else. "I have to do this. I will do this."

With that, Ailsa buzzed toward Crann Na Sióga leaving the rest of the group to worry from the safety of the tree line.

25

Ailsa

Ailsa flew straight towards the mighty tree city feeling more and more queasy the closer she got. She landed a few feet away from the entrance and heaved, but her stomach was already empty from the last time she was so close to breaking her promise never to return. She gathered her strength, marched to the door, and stopped at the line where the dirt road transitioned into the golden tile floor of the tree city.

One more step and Ailsa would break her promise, and what was a broken promise, but a lie deferred? The doors to Crann Na Sióga were wide open to allow the passage of elves and pixies making their daily excursions in and out of the city. Several silver-haired elves brushed past Ailsa as she stood just outside the thin golden line marking the threshold of the city. The elves may have thought it was odd to see anyone standing still in the middle of the road, especially a pixie who could easily hover out of traffic, but if they did, they kept their opinions to themselves. Elves had manners after all.

Ailsa stalled by staring into the entrance to the city for the first time in sixty years. The tree hadn't changed. It was the same hollow structure with a circular hole in the center of each floor, where pixies fluttered between sections of the city with ease. The flightless elves had the joy of climbing circular staircases winding around the perimeter of the hollow trunk when they wanted to reach a higher floor. As with all fae architecture, every banister, wall, and staircase was a work of art. Swirling Celtic knots decorated every surface while the walls acted as large murals, telling stories of the age of the ancient fae, the Aos Sí, and their gods, the Tuatha Dé Danann. The most prominent figure in the carvings was Lugh, king of the gods and rumored ancestor of the Leprechaun who shares his name. Carvings depicting his war with the gods from across the sea circled the large ground floor. One large panel showed him fighting the one-eyed Balor with his bloodthirsty spear Areadbhair he stole from the Northmen, while another carving showed him healing wounded soldiers using the enchanted pig skin he stole from the Greeks. Most of the stories involved Lugh stealing something, yet his descendant jealousy hoarded his wealth and punished any theft with banishment or death.

There was no more use in stalling. Ailsa took a deep breath, braced herself, lifted her left foot, and stepped forward.

The pain was immediate. Blinding. All-encompassing. It felt as if Ailsa's blood boiled as lightning surged through her veins. She screamed, fell forward, and the world went black.

Ailsa woke with a circle of elves standing around her. The pain of remaining in the city was still excruciating, but after the initial shock, she could form the occasional coherent thought. She had to get up. She had to warn the king. Lugh. The Leprechaun.

"Are you okay, miss?" asked an elf woman with a kind face standing over Ailsa, her sparkling blue eyes brimming with concern. "Should we get you a healer?"

"No," Ailsa said through clenched teeth.

"Did you eat a rotten tooth?" asked the elf. "Human children have such a penchant for sweets. My husband forgot to carve away a cavity before dinner and had stomach cramps for a month. Let me help you home."

The elf grabbed Ailsa, pulled her up, and draped the pixie's arm over her shoulder for balance. "Where are you from?"

Another wave of heat and pain hit Ailsa. She winced and looked up. "I grew up near the palace." It wasn't a lie, so it did not increase Ailsa's pain, but it wasn't an answer to the elf's real question.

"Oh dear." The elf gave a resigned sigh. "Well, good thing I didn't have any plans for the afternoon. The stairs will take hours. Can you fly? It will be much faster."

Ailsa fell to her knees and wretched until she managed to spit out a mouthful of bile.

"Guess not."

The elf slowly helped Ailsa limp across the main square at the base of the tree. Each step was agony. While Ailsa's shoes were elf made, and therefore of the highest quality, the soft soles felt as if imbued with shards of glass. The kind elf's arm around Ailsa's shoulder gave off a burning heat instead of the usual comforting warmth of a friendly touch.

The silvery light coming from the elf turned dim and gray whenever she looked at Ailsa. "Your light is so faint... so colorless. We really should take you to a healer."

"No," Ailsa barely uttered the word. "No time. Have to get to the palace."

The elf helped Ailsa up another step. "Why the palace? Didn't you say you lived near the palace?"

"Have to speak to the Leprechaun." Ailsa blacked out again.

Ailsa opened her eyes and saw a bright white orb surrounded by darkness. The orb looked familiar, but it was difficult to focus on it. Ailsa blinked herself further into consciousness. The orb was the moon. Ailsa was outside but still filled with burning pain, so she was still within the city boundaries.

The moon seemed to sway back and forth in a rhythmic motion. Ailsa turned her head and found she was being carried by two elves holding each end of a blanket. The blanket swung slightly with each step across a wide grassy field held in place by the large branches of the tree city of Crann Na Sióga. The elves were carrying Ailsa toward the emerald palace at the top of the tree canopy. The palace was massive by fae standards and carved out of a single giant emerald mined from the earth by the god Lugh himself. The spires and central dome sparkled in the moonlight and normally would have inspired awe in Ailsa as a lover of treasure, but at the moment she only felt relief that she was nearly at her goal.

"You carried me all the way up here?" Ailsa asked.

The elf woman panted as she forced herself to continue walking. "Oh good, you're awake." She lowered Ailsa's feet to the ground. "If you are determined enough to seek the king through all that pain, then it must be important. We're almost there."

The pair of elves helped Ailsa to her feet and steadied her as she slowly made her way to the palace. She stepped through the open doors carved out of the massive emerald for the second time in her life, the first being for her trial before the king. Somehow, her second trip to the palace was worse, and she wasn't being led by the end of a spear this time.

One short, yet grueling, hallway march and Ailsa was inside the throne room with vaulted ceilings and chandeliers illuminated by golden fae stones. At the far end of the room was an ornate emerald throne made of the same piece of gemstone as the floor and walls. Sitting on a golden pillow was Lugh, the Leprechaun King.

Lugh lounged sideways on the throne with his legs propped over one arm, his feet dangling to the side. He had shoulder length orange hair sticking out from underneath a circlet woven out of strange white metal that shimmered with every color imaginable. His eternally youthful face was framed by a well-groomed beard the same fiery shade as his hair. His clothes were of the highest quality, a green tunic with golden flourishes and gemstone accents. A golden cape draped off his shoulders and pooled onto the emerald floor. His entire countenance exuded an air of wealth and confidence, but it all paled in comparison to the king's beloved shoes.

The Leprechaun was famous for his deep love of footwear. He was regarded as the most talented cobbler known to men or fae. No other elf could dream of matching his skill, so his own shoes had to showcase his abilities. Today, he wore golden sandals with straps that wound up his legs. The gold shone brightly but moved like leather and looked softer than lambskin. As a signature of sorts, the sandals had enchanted solid gold wings protruding from the heel that slowly flapped as the king moved.

"Who do we have here?" Lugh asked in a clear voice, with only the faintest hint of interest.

"I do not know her name," said the kind elf. "My name is Niamh of Clover. I found this pixie collapsed from eating a rotten tooth in the main square at the base of the city. She was determined to speak to you. She kept muttering in her sleep about Vikings."

Lugh seemed intrigued. He stood up from his throne and walked across the hall to see Ailsa more clearly. The Leprechaun was nearly three times as tall as the average elf or pixie, further distinguishing himself as something else entirely, something regal and unique. The descendant of the fabled gods of old. He bent down to face Ailsa once he reached her and the elves.

A dark look of recognition fell over Lugh's face. "I know you," Lugh said in a harsh tone. "Ailsa, daughter of Mauve. Ailsa the merchant. Ailsa the thief."

Ailsa heaved, but her stomach was still empty. She regained her composure and faced the king. "I need to warn you. An army of men are coming to Crann Na Sióga."

Lugh once again stood straight. "I know. My lookouts spotted them worming their way between the trees. They will arrive within the next hour and die a few moments later. What I don't know is why a banished thief would return to my kingdom on such a pointless errand."

"They have enchanted belts," Ailsa said slowly. She could feel her mind slipping into darkness but forced herself to stay conscious. "Magic won't work. Fly. Run."

Lugh studied Ailsa a moment before speaking. "I don't believe you."

"What?" Ailsa had never known what it was like to be distrusted by anyone except Tragos.

"I don't believe you," Lugh repeated. "You are clearly experiencing the effects of lying. You are already breaking your word by returning to the city. Another lie would be nothing compared to the pain you are undoubtedly already feeling."

"I'm not lying."

Lugh ignored her. "Getting us to evacuate would make it easier for your companions to loot my vaults. I know you are accompanied by your faithful half breed thieves and worse, a human. I cannot say I am surprised; you tried breaking into my vault once before, why not again?"

Ailsa tried to respond, but between the scorching waves of pain and Lugh's accusation, she didn't know what to say.

"I expected a better plan from you. A fae should be an elegant thief, not a brutish plunderer attempting a war as cover. Oh well, now that you have broken your vow of banishment, the only thing left to do is carry out your execution. Guards!"

Ten pixies in the matching green and silver tunics of the royal guard descended from a circular walkway around the perimeter of the throne room near the ceiling. They rushed down and grabbed Ailsa so she couldn't flee. A redundant show of force given Ailsa's condition.

"Take her to the palace lawn and ring the bells. I want everyone to see what happens when the banished break their oath."

The royal guard dragged Ailsa out of the palace and across the carefully manicured lawn. Each blade of grass raked across Ailsa's back, the tips like daggers against her thin translucent wings. The only relief came when the guards arrived at the center of the field under the soft moonlight.

Ailsa summoned her remaining strength and flipped her arm across her body. If she could turn over, maybe she could crawl away. She had to get away.

"Oh, no you don't!" A guard slammed his heel into Ailsa's wrist, pinning it to the ground.

Ailsa screamed.

Bells rang out from the palace; the reverberations bounced between every part of Ailsa's being. A second sound slowly replaced the sharp clangs of bells as thousands of tiny feet responded and marched toward the palace. The unbearable buzz of a thousand wings filled the air. The sky brightened with every pixie in the forest answering the Leprechaun's signal.

"People of Crann Na Sióga hear me!" Lugh said in a loud and clear voice. "To be fae is to be honest, but this pixie is beyond deceptive. Many years ago,

Ailsa chose banishment over death for attempting to steal gold from my vaults. Today she has broken her vow, and worse, brought an army of humans to our door. Since I cannot trust her word, I have no choice but to show you all what damage a lie can cause."

"I only returned to warn you all!" Ailsa said as loudly as she could manage. "The horde of men marching towards the city is not with me or my friends! They wear enchanted belts that protect them from our magic! We cannot fight them!"

"Behold, she cannot help but lie!" Lugh said as he unsheathed his silver sword. "If the humans knew of such magic, they would have used it a thousand years ago when we were at our weakest! When we were first cut off from our true home in the realm of twilight!"

"I'm not..."

"Ailsa, daughter of Mauve, I hereby sentence you to death by deception! Instead of dying by the sword, you will perish slowly and painfully by the consequence of your own actions."

Ailsa sobbed but her tears brought no relief, instead it felt like acid burning her cheeks.

"I ask all fae to bear witness to Ailsa's pain and death. What will happen to each of us if we tell an untruth or break our oaths. This is the consequence we shoulder from the curse of our ancestors' deceit."

Lugh raised his arms and beckoned the crowd forward to walk past Ailsa as she squirmed and moaned in agony. Thousands of elves and pixies walked forward and formed an orderly line so they all could walk past Ailsa in a slow procession. Each elf gasped as they passed, but the first pixie in line spat at Ailsa for bringing such disgrace to the flying fae. After that, everyone spat as they passed.

The pain was still unbearable, but a new feeling climbed from the depths of Ailsa's heart and rose as a burning in her chest and behind her cheeks. As flecks of moisture dampened her skin and soaked into her clothes, Ailsa felt ashamed. She once again felt the hatred and disapproval of the city she grew up in, and in some ways, it was worse than the physical pain she was feeling.

Ailsa tried to escape the glares of the crowd by once again rolling to her stomach to face the ground, but she was stopped by the same guard as before.

"No, you will face them all," the guard said.

Ailsa squirmed and writhed but could do little else while pinned to the ground on her back. Each fairy had a look on their face of utter disdain for Ailsa as they walked past and spat. Their expressions were nearly as unbearable as the excruciating pain of the fae curse. Ailsa closed her eyes and gave into the pain flowing through her and passed into unconsciousness.

26

Fotini

Fotini slowly let the air out of her lungs and held her arms perfectly still. She focused on her barely visible target until it took up her entire vision and released the bow string. With a quiet snap, the arrow was propelled between the trees until it slammed into a specific knot in a specific tree's bark.

"Nice shot," Tragos said as Fotini nocked another arrow. It was a nice shot, but not a perfect one. The arrow was off by several inches. Fotini meant to hit the center of the tree knot, but she misread the wind slightly.

"I missed," Fotini said, raising her bow again. She pulled back on the string, steadied her aim, and released another arrow. This arrow flew down the path and struck the same tree as before, but several inches to the left of the previous arrow. "Better."

Tragos squinted at the target, straining his rectangular pupils to see the arrows. "They both hit the same target."

"Yes," Fotini replied, "but one hit the center of the knot."

"Both are better shots than I can make," Tragos admitted.

Fotini's chest burned with pride. Tragos was the most boastful and competitive satyr she had ever met. He rarely admitted when someone was better than him at anything.

"Can I have a go?" Tragos asked.

Fotini handed her bow and an arrow over to the satyr. He stood firm and pulled the arrow back with good, but not perfect, technique. His breathing was heavy and erratic, causing his arms to shift with each breath. He released the string, sending the arrow whizzing through the forest, past the target, and into the distance.

Tragos cursed and raised the bow above his head to slam it down into the dirt in frustration, but Fotini was thankfully close enough to pluck her weapon from his grasp. He wasn't as good of a shot as Fotini, but he was usually a good enough shot to at least hit the tree he was aiming for. "Are you okay?" Fotini asked.

"I'm fine." Tragos held out his hand asking to try again, but Fotini wasn't about to risk him breaking her bow when he missed another shot.

"Sure, you are." Fotini quickly raised her bow, pulled back the string, and fired another arrow into the tree knot in a single swift motion. "That's why you can't hit the tree."

"I'm just tired," Tragos explained.

"After walking through the forest all day, we are all tired." Fotini fired another arrow into the knot. "That's why the Cat Sí's human pet is snoring in the grass. But you're always tired, and I've never seen you this distracted."

"I'm not distracted," Tragos huffed.

Fotini shot another arrow without speaking. She knew Tragos wouldn't be able to stand the silence very long and she was proven right while positioning her next arrow.

"I'm worried about Ailsa," Tragos said, breaking the silence.

"Ailsa is tough, she will get through this." Fotini pulled back and released her arrow for another bullseye. "Since when do you worry about her? The only feeling I've seen you express about her is annoyance."

"I've never needed to worry about her before. Normally she stays behind in her shop counting coins half her size while we go do the dangerous shit."

Tragos had a point. Over the past decade they had taken hundreds of dangerous jobs from Ailsa and not once had the pixie budged from her shop. Fotini couldn't recall ever seeing Ailsa outside the store. She was never at the market or the pub, and it would be hard to miss the only glowing fairy in town.

"And this mission of hers is suicide." Tragos continued verbally processing his thoughts. "The closer we came to the tree the sicker she got. When we started walking through the forest this morning her light was so bright, I could feel her heat from where she sat between my horns, like I had a tiny star resting on my head. By the time we got within sight of the tree she was cold and dark."

"That's the fae's curse for you." Fotini slung her bow across her back. "She promised never to come back to Crann Na Sióga, breaking a promise is agony for her kind, but she knew this before she asked us to come here."

"Then she shouldn't have come here in the first place. She should have let the fae who banished her rot for what they did to her."

"You're being a bit harsh," Fotini said. "Wouldn't you warn the Children of Pan back home if you heard of an army of humans marching towards them? Even if it meant pain or even death?"

Tragos glared. "Of course I would, but I wasn't banished and abandoned by everyone back home. It's different."

"Ailsa wasn't banished by everyone; she was banished by the king. It's not that different and you know it." Tragos opened his mouth to protest but Fotini stopped him. "You two are not that different. I've always admired your willingness to help others when it really matters, and Ailsa has that exact quality. You might be different in size, shape, and talents, but you are the same in stubbornness and recklessness."

Tragos thought for a moment and bowed his head. "She is stubborn... I think that's why I'm worried. She's stubborn enough to keep going when it's pointless, and there's nothing we can do down here to save her."

Fotini patted Tragos on the back. "Then we help the rest of the fae for her. Let's get some food and rest while we can before the humans catch up to us."

Tragos followed Fotini as she retrieved her arrows, except for the one Tragos lost with his poor aim. He stopped talking about Ailsa, but Fotini could see he was still struggling to clear his mind. Fotini was also worried about her friend, but clearly not as much as Tragos. Why did he suddenly care so much?

When the pair made it back to the clearing where they left their packs, they found the human, Jaimie, awake stuffing his face with cakes.

"Hey, hand one over," Tragos said as he plopped next to Jaimie in the soft green grass. Jaimie handed a cake to Fotini and Tragos, both of whom shoved the desserts into their mouths and ate them in a single bite. Jaimie pulled a few more cakes out of a bag and passed them around.

The cake was some of the best food Fotini had ever tasted. Most of the food she ate consisted of raw vegetables, unseasoned meat, and as an occasional treat, oats mixed with honey and raisins. Centaurs and satyrs were not known for their baking. Only humans and fae made such complicated delicacies, so her opportunity to try it was limited. Now that Fotini had tried the food, she didn't ever want to eat anything else. It was good enough to make bringing a human along almost worth it... almost.

"This is fantastic," Tragos said. "I guess there is a perk to bringing a human. What else did you bring from that castle of yours?"

"I didn't bring these," Jaimie said between bites. "I found them in one of your bags. I could smell them when I woke up from my nap."

Fotini spit out the cake in her mouth and looked at the spongy lump in her hand half expecting black poison to be dripping from the center. She didn't bring any food like this. She took another deep look, but it appeared to be a normal cake, or at least it looked like what Fotini imagined a cake would look like, with thick sugar crystals and multicolored flecks inside.

"We didn't bring these either," Fotini said. "Which bag were they in?"

Jaimie pointed to a cloth sack sitting atop her saddlebags. The cloth was bright white and too clean to have been carried through the forest and shoved between the thick wall of trees surrounding the fae kingdom. The top of the bag was trimmed in green with golden swirls that glowed in the setting sun.

"You idiot, it's fae food," Tragos said horrified. "Do either of you feel weird? Sick? Wings growing anywhere?"

The three companions patted themselves down and didn't feel any strange growths, and no one felt sick. The cakes seemed to be perfectly fine.

Jaimie picked up a cake and inspected it closely. "Maybe Ailsa was successful in warning the fae and they gave us the food as a thank you?"

"If that were the case why sneak it into our camp when no one was looking," Fotini said. "No, this is a trick of some sort."

Fotini walked away from the packs and started trotting towards the fae tree. She would get an explanation from the little monsters by the time the sun had fully set.

At the edge of the clearing Fotini stopped suddenly when something hard slammed into her face. She grabbed her smashed nose and swore loudly with her eyes closed in shock and pain. After pausing for a few seconds to collect her wits, Fotini opened her eyes and saw... nothing. She looked up, down, left, and right but all she could see was the last bit of the open clearing. Did someone throw something at her?

Fotini stepped forward and once again felt her face meet something hard in her path. She looked around and saw a large rock the size of her head lying in the grass. "Who threw this?" she yelled, but there was no answer.

Fotini slowly walked forward, and this time her face gently met a solid surface. She kept her eyes open and could not see anything blocking her path, but she could feel an impossibly smooth and completely transparent wall in front of her. She took a step back, unhooked her bow, and drew an arrow. She aimed directly at the fae tree looming above them and fired. The arrow shot forward at incredible speed and splintered apart when it met the invisible wall.

"Ouch!" Jaimie was rubbing his head twenty feet to Fotini's right. At his feet there was a large stone just like the one in front of Fotini. She looked around and spotted more stones every few feet making a wide circle around the edge of the clearing.

Tragos ran his fingers across the barriers, stepped back, and launched himself forward only to smack into the wall. Even his horns were no match for this magic.

Fotini yelled in the direction of the great fae tree. "What is the meaning of this?"

A low hum like a hundred tiny feet pattering over soft earth rose in answer. Elves appeared from behind nearly every stone. Like the elf at the entrance of Crann Na Sióga, the elves all wore the matching green and silver tunics of the kingdom's guard.

"Haven't you heard never to eat fae food? I thought it was well known even among your kind that to eat our food traps a person in our realm," one of the elves said with a laugh. "Good thing pannites are almost as stupid as humans. Now you can never leave."

Tragos rammed the air in front of the elf with little effect. "We aren't trying to leave your 'realm,' we cannae even fit into your cursed kingdom!"

"That's because these desserts were enchanted to keep you inside this circle of stones. You three are a huge threat to the city, we couldn't let you wander around so close to our homes. As long as the circle remains unbroken you are trapped here. Now we can rest assured that we are safe from you as you slowly starve to death or are killed by the Vikings marching through the forest."

Tragos drew his sword and began wildly hacking at the air, but the barrier held. Fotini took her spear and plunged it into the earth in front of the nearest stone and leaned on the long pole as a lever to push the stone away, but the stone did not budge.

"Silly pannite, don't you think we would have thought of that? The barrier is impenetrable, and the stones cannot be moved from inside the circle. If I were you, I would enjoy more of the delicious food we left for you and accept my fate. There really isn't any more you can do." With that the elf hopped down from the stone and began marching back to the city with the rest of the elves following behind him.

"What do we do now?" Jaimie asked.

"We wait and pray," Fotini said, turning her back on the city to face the dense forest. "Your father and his men will be here soon enough."

27

Jaimie

Jaimie always wondered what war was like. Gorm would ramble on about feeling full of jittery energy before his first, and only, raid. He said all the Vikings bounced in the longboat fueled by bloodlust with no space to work out their excess energy. The anticipation and excitement before the attack were better in Gorm's opinion than the raid itself. All the excitement, with none of the risk and danger.

Jaimie disagreed. He couldn't help but compare waiting for war to waiting for execution. True, the likelihood of death was not quite as high as it was when he was waiting in his room for his executioner to arrive and shove a burning rod down his esophagus, but it was just as boring and free from distraction. The small field had nothing to occupy Jaimie's mind as he waited and listened for the approaching army. Every sound, from Tragos sharpening his blade to some distant elves singing, was an impending army to Jaimie's ears.

This was not what Jaimie expected before his first proper battle. He always pictured himself standing next to Gorm at the back of a large battalion, and not next to a small assortment of unnatural creatures as the only line of defense. He certainly never expected to be waiting to fight Gorm as a member of the attacking force.

How could he fight Gorm? How could he fight his father or the men of Whitfield? He knew some of these men. Jaimie felt a hot burning sensation bubbling up from his stomach into his throat. He couldn't kill them, but he couldn't let them pass either. As the taste of bile crept into the back of his mouth, Jaimie swallowed and made the only decision he could live with. He would fight as he did every day as he sparred with Gorm, to defeat his opponent but not kill them. A disarmed, or injured, man was little more of a threat than a dead one. At least that is what Jaimie told himself.

His heart thrummed as it always did before sparring with Gorm, but in dread instead of excited anticipation. He felt the energetic jitters, but with none of the associated joy. He knew he was facing hundreds of experienced fighters, and while his companions may be skilled, they weren't gods of war who could lay waste to multitudes. It would be a miracle for him to see the sunrise in just a few scant hours.

Jaimie's companions seemed less worried, or at least outwardly calmer. Fotini stood silently to Jaimie's left, holding her spear tightly as she gazed into the darkness with unmatched focus. Her chest rose and fell slowly, but steadily, as she made her own mental preparations. Jaimie pitied anyone who wove between the trees directly in front of the centaur. If they avoided being impaled by her spear, they would surely receive broken bones if kicked by her powerful legs.

To Jaimie's right, Tragos prepared for war in his own way. He scraped a whetstone over his sword in steady motions, methodically sharpening the blade. He scowled and was silent for the first conscious moment since Jaimie met him. Jaimie found himself wishing the normally loud satyr would say something to break up the silence, even if it was to insult him.

Jaimie glanced around the forest but could not spot the Cat Sí or Ailsa. The pixie had not returned from her quest to warn the fae and the witch still hadn't finished whatever it was she was doing. Jaimie wished she would hurry up. Ailsa was convinced the Cat Sí would be able to help stop the marching army, and after witnessing the tail end of her scuffle with Fotini, Jaimie was inclined to agree. Fotini was absolutely terrifying with her spear, but the Cat Sí seemed to be toying with her in their fight.

After hours of torturous silent waiting, a distant twig snapped. The sound of wood splintering quickly joined it as a sword or ax split a small tree apart. Slowly, the sounds of the approaching force grew louder and more frequent.

"Please give me my sword," Jaimie said to Tragos for the tenth time.

"So you can betray us?" Tragos asked.

"So I can defend myself and fight alongside you! These men are here because I found the idol! They are here because my father and all those men think I am a changeling. My father will kill me, you, and all the fae in this forest because he thinks it is the only way to save a version of me that doesn't exist. Let me help save as many lives from my mistake as I can."

Tragos stood firm holding Jaimie's sword and scabbard tightly in his grasp. He stared into Jaimie's eyes as if trying to determine if he was sincere. Jaimie mentally pleaded for the satyr to give him his sword but could see the deep distrust written on his face.

"For the god's sake, give him his sword," Fotini said as she firmly tapped the back of Tragos's head with the flat side of her spear tip. "If he dies because of our negligence, that cursed cat will kill us both. I hate to admit it, but neither of us is a match for her."

With Fotini's prompting, Tragos handed over Jaimie's sword. Jaimie squeezed the warm familiar grip, and a wave of relief washed over him. He had used this sword daily for years to spar against Gorm and he knew this blade as if it were an extension of himself. Jaimie suddenly felt hope that he would survive the night.

The sound of splintering wood grew louder from the wall of trees just outside the magical barrier trapping Jaimie and his companions in the wide circle of stones. Men's voices joined the growing sounds of the advancing army, and within the span of a few minutes Jaimie could hear what they were saying. The thin trees at the edge of the fae kingdom shuddered as something in the dark forest hit them from behind. With a loud crack the dull grey iron of an axe blade sliced through the magically grown wall of trees.

Jaimie held his sword with both hands and adjusted his stance. He took a deep breath as the first man broke through the forest wall and stepped into the open meadow. The man looked confused as he stood just outside the ring of stones. He clearly did not expect anyone who wasn't fae to be waiting inside the fae kingdom. The confusion didn't last long though. The man let out an angry yell and charged over the circle of stones toward Tragos. The satyr held up his sword to block the oncoming swing of the man's axe, but the man fell over dead with an arrow sticking through his neck long before he could complete his swing. Tragos caught Fotini's eye and nodded in silent gratitude for her perfect shot.

Yells erupted from inside the dark shade of the forest and more men hacked through the trees. Several Vikings burst out of the forest with swords drawn ready for combat. Fotini fought two men at once using her long spear to keep them at a safe distance. Tragos clashed swords with a third who took his complete attention, while a fourth man targeted Jaimie.

The man standing before Jaimie was not from Whitfield. He was a tall, well-built man who looked confused to see a human fighting in defense of the fae. The confusion did little to dissuade the man from attacking as he rushed forward to strike. Jaimie stepped to the side and met the man's sword with his own blade. Practicing with Gorm for the past two years was finally paying off.

Jaimie hooked his sword around his opponent's weapon and pulled him in close enough to smash his fist into the man's jaw. This angered Jaimie's opponent more than it injured him. He kicked Jaimie in the chest, knocking him to the ground. The man swung his sword down towards Jaimie, but he rolled to the side and stabbed upwards, careful to avoid anything vital. He felt his blade pierce through the man's feeble leather armor and into his shoulder. The stranger dropped his own sword as he slid down Jaimie's blade under the weight of his massive frame. Jaimie pushed the man to the side, stood, and retrieved his sword. The man struggled on the ground, but in a fit of rage Jaimie smacked the hilt of his sword against the man's skull, knocking him unconscious. A pool of blood began to form beneath the man's shoulder and Jaimie silently prayed to any god who would listen that the man would live.

In all his years of practicing, Jaimie had never seen his sword coated in blood. Fighting had always been a make-believe game of sorts. The aim was to defeat your opponent, and at most give them a bruise or shallow scratch. This was something else, something horrifyingly real.

An arrow whizzed past Jaimie's head and hit a man running at him from the forest. The man collapsed to the ground mere feet from where he stood reflecting on the realness of the battle.

"Pay attention to the tree line!" Fotini yelled as she loosed another arrow.

Jaimie followed her directions and rushed toward another mercenary emerging from the dense wood. He swung his sword and stabbed when possible, blocked when necessary, and dodged whenever he had the opportunity, but he could not bring himself to land a blow he knew would be fatal. His arms and legs burned with effort as he fought man after man. He was skilled enough to hold his own against most opponents, and whenever he faced a foe surpassing him in skill, an arrow blurred past piercing his enemy's flesh.

Whenever he wasn't about to be stabbed, Jaimie checked on his new companions. He was correct in his earlier assessment of Fotini. Out of the corner of his vision, Jaimie caught the occasional blur of a spear as the centaur struck down her foes with remarkable accuracy long before they could hope to reach her with their swords or axes.

The first glimpse of Tragos fighting surprised him to the point he nearly lost focus on the battle. Jaimie was about to engage a large man holding a sword in one hand and a shield in the other, when Tragos seemingly dropped from the sky driving his sword through the man's shoulder deep into his torso. The satyr used his weight to force his weapon through flesh and bone until it pierced the heart or lungs. The man died with a shocked expression since he never saw what had killed him. Renewed fear of Tragos's constant threats flowed through Jaimie, he wouldn't take them so lightly from now on.

Jaimie turned his attention back on the tree line just in time to avoid the slash of a sword whistling past his throat. The momentum of the swing turned the man's body exposing his back for a brief moment. Jaimie grabbed the neck of his shirt and pulled him to the ground. He kicked him in the face, and the man went limp.

"Good instincts," Tragos said.

Jaimie turned to the voice and saw the satyr pulling his sword out of a fallen foe. A frenzy of movement caught Jaimie's attention as he saw a man with blood pouring from his shoulder charge haphazardly at Tragos with a dagger in his good hand. Jaimie yelled in warning, but it was too late. He swung the dagger as he stumbled towards his target and plunged his blade into the fur-covered flesh of Tragos's thigh.

Tragos yelled and collapsed under the man. Without thinking, Jaimie leaped toward Tragos and his attacker to stop a killing blow. Jaimie took advantage of the man's focus on Tragos and smashed the pommel of his sword into his face, knocking him unconscious.

"Thanks," Tragos said as he tried and failed to get to his feet. The wound on his leg was bleeding freely, and he could not stand. "Finish him before he wakes."

"I can't do that," Jaimie said in a shaky voice.

"What do you mean you cannae do it?" Tragos said gritting his teeth in anger and pain. "Have you been leaving them alive?"

Shame and anger fought deep within Jaimie. "They may be doing something horrendous, but they are still my people."

Tragos yelled furiously. "No, they aren't. They stopped being your people when they sentenced you to die. Now finish him before he wakes up and kills us both." Tragos used the last of his energy on his anger and collapsed fully onto his back from the pain of his injury.

Jaimie ignored Tragos's demands and grabbed him by his arms to drag him as carefully as possible to the far edge of the stone circle away from the tree line. Hopefully he would go unnoticed in the tall grass.

"Rest now," Jaimie said. "I'll make sure no one comes near."

Tragos said something crude but not unexpected.

Jaimie stayed close to Tragos as he fought. Unfortunately, there were too many attackers to stop them from slipping past their feeble line of defense. With clear paths cut through the dense wall of plant life, Irish and Viking mercenaries streamed past. Most ignored Jaimie, Tragos, and Fotini and ran straight past the magical barrier as if it didn't exist. Fotini attempted to chase down a few of them, but she slammed into the invisible wall as if it were made of solid stone. Even her arrows glanced off the magical barrier instead of hitting their targets. The invaders were the only ones making it through. They hadn't eaten any of the fae's food and were untouched by the Leprechaun king's magic.

Once the Vikings and mercenaries passed the feeble defense of a single human and two Children of Pan there was nothing to stop them from massacring the fae. The men quickly got to work chipping out chunks of wood from the base of the giant tree with their axes. Thousands of elves swarmed out of the main door to Crann Na Sióga and small hidden doors under the tree's roots, while hundreds of pixies descended from the tree canopy. The collective fae summoned thousands of tiny flames and flung them at the men as they chopped down the tree, but the fire bounced off them harmlessly. The enchanted belts successfully stopped fae magic from harming the men, but the tree had no such protection. As the protective tree bark was hacked away the soft wood underneath ignited under the barrage of flame.

The fae switched tactics and charged at their attackers with tiny swords drawn, but a line of men began sweeping the elves aside while other men stomped them flat. Some men waved large fans creating small bursts of wind to knock the pixies off course in the sky, while other men ran around sprinkling handfuls of iron shavings on groups of fae who screamed and burned from touching the forbidden metal.

"Jaimie?" a familiar voice caught Jaimie's attention and pulled it away from the battle between men and fae. Gorm stood just outside the splintered wall of thin trees. "What are you doing here? You can't be here!"

It was the first time Jaimie had seen Gorm since leaving Whitfield. He expected him to look angry or disgusted with Jaimie for siding with inhuman creatures, but he mostly looked concerned.

"Leave here," Gorm said. "If you run away now you might be able to live. Just leave before your father sees you."

"No," Jaimie said. "I can't let the fae die because of my father's feelings toward me. They haven't done anything, and you know it. Tell him that I am really his son and call off the attack!" Despite everything, Jaimie still hoped Gorm would do the right thing.

Gorm's concern turned into a slow simmer of anger. "No. Your father will never accept that you are his son. I beg you, leave or he will kill you."

Jaimie's thoughts flickered back to the last time he heard his father's voice. The harsh tone of scorn and revulsion without the slightest sign of love. He knew Gorm was right, his father would stubbornly insist Jaimie was a changeling instead of accepting who he is and who he loves.

"Then come with me," Jaimie pleaded. "Help me stop this and then come with me where we can both be free together. My new friend, the Cat Sí, will help us find sanctuary. We can be free to be ourselves, to be with each other."

Gorm stepped toward Jaimie, his sword pointed downward but held firmly in his hand. "Your father has given me a second chance at greatness. I lost my chance for Valhalla, but by driving the fae from Ireland I can secure a home by your father's side, and maybe even a place in heaven. I will not fail again. Please step aside or I will be forced to hurt you."

Jaimie's heart sank. Had Gorm truly sided with Jaimie's father? Had he really turned against him after years by his side?

Gorm readied his sword.

Jaimie hesitantly raised his own weapon in response.

Gorm stuck hard and fast, but Jaimie expected the attack. The first thing the Viking ever taught him was to always attack first and attack aggressively. The two men stood face to face, both pushing against the other, each hoping to gain the upper hand. The last time they were this close, Jaimie reached in for a kiss, but this time Gorm was the first one to make a move, to smash his head into Jaimie's face.

Blood spurted from Jaimie's nose onto his boots and the trampled grass and dirt. Jaimie stumbles to the ground, and his sword clattered against a nearby stone.

Gorm pointed his sword at Jaimie's throat. Jaimie looked up at the man he loved and saw only hate returned. "Leave now or..."

Jaimie didn't hear what would happen if he didn't leave. A distant roar tore through the air shaking the trees and sending the birds in their branches skyward. The sound felt ancient, primal, and powerful, but did not fill Jaimie with fear. Instead, it gave him hope.

As the roar faded it was replaced by another sound. A low rumble like a small army crashing through the trees. Jaimie looked toward the forest and saw a small herd of deer burst through the barrier surrounding Crann Na Sióga using paths cleared by Viking axes. The majestic beasts leaped past Jaimie and Gorm, lowered their antlers, and charged at the men still hacking at the tree. The first few men were caught unawares, only noticing the deer once they were being gored. Their screams alerted the rest of the men who swung their swords and shot arrows at the deer, but the creatures were far too numerous.

"Retreat!" One of the more seasoned looking men yelled. The Vikings and mercenaries abandoned the tree and ran into the forest, but the damage was done. The interior of Crann Na Sióga was visible through holes hacked by the men, the flames already spreading through the inside of the great tree.

With Gorm distracted, Jaimie took his chance and attempted to scramble to his feet, but Gorm's attention snapped back to him with the sudden movement. Gorm swung his sword and caught Jaimie's back with the tip of the blade leaving a shallow slash.

Jaimie cried out and fell back to the ground with a thud. Part of him still could not believe his dearest friend was trying to kill him. Gorm stood above him and raised his sword with an expression of sadness mixed with determination. He was about to swing when a dark mass of cloth and hair pounced on him, bringing him crashing to the ground.

It was the second time the Cat Sí had stopped Jaimie from losing a duel, but it was somehow more terrifying than the first. The Cat Sí roared, letting loose the same deep thundering sound that drove the deer toward Crann Na Sióga. All fighting ceased for a moment as everyone froze in terror. The roar was the sound of a creature filled with ancient rage and power that burned like the searing desert sun.

"How dare you!?!" The Cat Sí yelled in a jarringly human voice, her oversized teeth inches from Gorm's face. "You would kill someone who cares so deeply for you? Have you no honor?"

Gorm sputtered, all courage gone. He kicked his legs wildly as he attempted to worm free from the Cat Sí's clutches.

The Cat Sí raised one hand in the air and prepared to strike.

"Wait! Don't kill him!" Jaime called out, blood still flowing from his broken nose. "Give him just one more chance."

The Cat Sí turned to Jaimie, her yellow eyes reflecting moonlight from beneath her cloak. She lowered her hand and pushed herself to her feet, releasing Gorm from her clutches.

"This is the only time I will stay my hand," she said as she slowly retracted her claws.

Gorm scrambled to his feet and fled toward the forest. Jaimie hoped it would be the last time he saw Gorm, for his sake.

"Took you long enough," Tragos said as he and Fotini joined Jaimie and the Cat Sí at the edge of the circle of stones. He sat on Fotini's back with a hastily torn strip of his tartan wrapped tightly around his leg. "Where have you been?"

"I've been herding reinforcements," the Cat Sí said gesturing to the deer still circling the giant tree. "What have you been up to? Eating fae snacks I see." The Cat Sí lifted a few stones and tossed them aside making a break in the stone circle to remove the magical barrier. "Where's Ailsa? Did you get the crown?"

"Ailsa is still in Crann Na Sióga," Jaimie said before Tragos could butt in with a passive aggressive response. "She went into the tree hours ago to try and warn the Leprechaun King. We haven't seen her since."

"She what!?!" The Cat Sí wasted no time as she sprinted to the tree, yanking off her boots as she ran. As she approached the base of the tree, she leaped over the growing flames and dug her sharp claws into the tree bark. She quickly scurried up the tree and disappeared into the canopy.

28

Ailsa

The loudest sound ever heard in Ireland ripped Ailsa into consciousness. A feral roar from some monster hung in the air as she collected her thoughts and remembered where she was. She expected to wake up to the continuous procession of the citizens of Crann Na Sióga spitting or kicking her as they passed, but the sounds of shuffling feet and buzzing wings from a crowd of fae were eerily absent, replaced by distant screams and the crackle of fire. She slowly pushed herself up into a sitting position to search for her tormentors.

The field was almost entirely abandoned. Every elf and pixie had vanished leaving only Ailsa and Lugh the Leprechaun King behind. Lugh stood at the edge of the field where the grass met the open sky watching as thousands of pixie lights twinkled in the distance. Ailsa carefully stood and limped forward, each step feeling like she was walking on shards of glass. She eventually reached the edge, though she stayed far away from Lugh, and peered over the side.

Chaos had erupted in the world below. The tree was on fire and through the smoke she could see the distant shape of men fighting what appeared to be deer. The wild animals were winning, and the men began retreating into the forest to avoid being gored to death.

The popping sound of fire and the cracking of wood filled the air as a backdrop to the fighting below. The ground beneath Ailsa's feet shuddered and swayed in the wind as the base of the tree slowly turned to ash. Ailsa attempted to fly away, but her wings were beaten, bent, and bruised.

Ailsa turned to Lugh who stood watching the mayhem with the glistening shine of tears running down his cheeks.

"Please, help me?" She begged, though with little hope.

"Why should I?" Lugh said. "I sentenced you to die earlier this very evening. Why should I care if you die by my hand or burn as the city falls."

"Because I tried to warn you... I wasn't lying..."

Lugh turned away from the scene below and faced Ailsa with his golden gaze. "I simply don't care. Your kind are so far beneath me it is laughable I am even speaking to you. Live, die, it doesn't matter. Just do it out of my sight." Lugh turned back and continued to watch his kingdom burn.

Ailsa wasn't going to let Lugh pity himself in peace. "Just because you are a king doesn't mean..."

"I am so much more than a mere king!" Lugh yelled releasing his pent-up rage as he once again faced Ailsa. "This city might have been a shining beacon of beauty in this realm, but it is nothing compared to the kingdoms I once ruled! Yet even this small shred of glory is being taken from me! Die and give me a moment's peace!"

The tree groaned and shuddered as the lower floors of the city were consumed by flames. Ailsa felt a slight bit of relief as the city burned away. As it disappeared so did her promise to never return. As the pain receded it was quickly replaced by anger.

"How dare you speak to *me* like this," she said with a calm yet burning rage. "I tried to help you, tried to prevent all of this, and you wouldn't listen. You think *I* am beneath you, but you speak of lost glory while your people die. Do you even care for them? Or only for the power they gave you?"

In less time than it took to blink, Lugh moved toward Ailsa and punched her in the stomach. She wanted to curl up on the ground in pain, but she was not going to give Lugh the satisfaction of standing over her again. She leaped into the air and swung at Lugh's perfect, smug face. Pain shot through her fist as it connected with his jaw. Ailsa landed and examined her hand. She could barely move her fingers and small specks of green blood dotted her knuckles. Meanwhile, Lugh appeared untouched.

Lugh smirked. "You might not be entirely mortal, but you are still nothing compared to me. I am not named after Lugh Longarm, King of the fae gods. I am Lugh Longarm, and so, so much more."

Lugh shoved Ailsa to the ground.

"I came to the fae realms and was crowned king by your lesser Celtic gods." He kicked Ailsa in the face, sending viridian blood spraying across the grass. "They saw my potential, unlike the rest of my fellow Olympians, and gave me a crown. Yet, a lowly pixie dares look down on me?" Lugh kicked Ailsa with such force she was sent tumbling across the grass.

The tree shuddered again as if hit by something hard. Lugh stumbled and fell but Ailsa no longer had the strength to move, let alone flee. She lay on her back and gazed up at the moon. She didn't know why, but she felt comforted by the glowing sphere.

Please help me, she thought as if speaking to the moon. *Please make it quick and painless.*

The tree shuddered again and again in an almost rhythmic pattern. Lugh climbed to his feet and dusted himself off in quick uncontrolled movements. He drew a magnificent emerald encrusted sword with a pair of snakes twisted around the grip and stepped toward Ailsa. "I'm tired of this chatter. I was going to let you attempt to save yourself, but now I just want you dead."

29

The Cat Sí

The wood gave way under the Cat Sí's claws as she propelled herself upward. Any semblance of stealth was abandoned in favor of speed as she frantically climbed. She had to make it to Ailsa before it was too late.

Please help me, Ailsa's silent prayer flooded the space between the Cat Sí's ears. Ailsa's scared inner voice filled her with equal parts fear and strength. She could feel the trust and belief flow through her limbs, making her move faster.

The Cat Sí reached the top of the tree and leaped high into the air. She unslung her bow and nocked an arrow as she scanned the canopy for her friend. It only took a fraction of a second to spot Ailsa in the nearly deserted grassy lawn. The pixie was on the ground, pleading for her life, as an abnormally large fae towered over her with a sword raised to strike. There was something oddly familiar about the fae's red hair and the golden glint of his shoes, but there wasn't time to waste wondering who he was. The Cat Sí took aim.

One moment the arrow was nocked on the Cat Sí's bowstring and the next it slammed through the large fae's cape, pinning him to the ground. The Cat Sí landed, drew back another arrow, and loosed it. Sparks flew through the air as the iron tip of the arrow met the polished ceremonial sword, knocking it free from the fae's grasp.

The Cat Sí crossed the palace lawn in two easy steps and scooped up Ailsa in her soft fur-covered hands. "Are you okay?"

Ailsa nodded but barely stayed conscious. She was stark white except for the deep green of fae bruises and she let off a faint sickly glow. The Cat Sí gently licked the pixie, her tongue covering the majority of her body all at once, and the bruises started to fade.

"You're safe now," the Cat Sí said as she gently tucked Ailsa beneath the folds of her tunic where she would stay warm against her skin. A small drop of relief flowed through her, she made it in time to save Ailsa, but her work was far from over.

With Ailsa safe, the Cat Sí's countenance changed. Her fur bristled as she stood, and she turned her attention to the fae pinned by her arrow. She caught his eye and bared her teeth exposing a mouthful of fangs.

"You must be Lugh, the Leprechaun King," the Cat Sí snarled.

Lugh removed his cape and stood free once again. He stepped towards the Cat Sí and an all too familiar smirk spread across his lips. The Cat Sí felt she recognized something about the fae's arrogant expression and how it failed to mask the envious hunger in his golden eyes.

"Do you no longer recognize me, sister? It's only been fifteen hundred years since we last saw one another," the Leprechaun said with a sneer. "Though you have also changed since we last met. Are those claws why I never saw you without gloves before?"

The Cat Sí pulled on her hood to make sure it was firmly in place to hide her ears. She focused on the Leprechaun and felt she knew him, but she had barely had any contact with the fae and never met the fabled Tuatha Dé Danann. The Leprechaun stepped towards the Cat Sí, prompting her to glance down and notice his winged sandals.

Faint memories of a smirking god with similar sandals flitted through her mind.

"Hermes?" The Cat Sí's tone changed from anger to confusion. "Why are you masquerading as a fae?"

The Leprechaun glowed redder than his beard. "I am not masquerading as anything. It is no secret I wasn't always what I am today. The Tuatha Dé Danann welcomed me into their pantheon, saw my promise, and named me their king. The King of the Celtic pantheon. They saw my true value as more than a pet messenger. So, I renounced my name and so-called family. I am now Lugh Longarm, Leprechaun King, and the last of the Tuatha Dé Danann."

Lugh paused for a moment, and his smirk grew into a slimy grin. "Of course, you of all people should understand reinvention and trading one family for another."

"What is that supposed to mean?" All amusement left the Cat Sí's voice and the dark fur on her hands and wrists bristled. What did he know?

"You know what I mean. I did some reading a while back from a loose end of yours. What was the author's name? Herodote? Herseus?... Herodotus." Lugh looked more like a predator staring down trapped prey than the literal cat he was talking to. "He wrote all about how he saw you turn into a cat and run to the desert. You should have paid more attention to what mortals put in their libraries. Don't worry, dear sister, if you leave now and go home to *my* family, I will let you continue your little charade."

She pounced at Lugh but caught only air. One second, he was standing in front of her and the next he was behind her.

"Come now, why so hostile?" Lugh taunted.

"You know who I am!?!" The Cat Sí roared. "Tell me!"

Lugh's smile grew slimier as something seemed to click deep within his mischievous mind.

"Oh, this is too good!" Lugh danced over to the Cat Sí. "You've been here too long, cut off from the prayers of your worshipers back home. The people here must not revere you for you to be so diminished. Why don't you go home to Olympus where prayer and ambrosia flow freely?"

The Cat Sí swiped at Lugh but he was fast enough to stay just out of reach of her claws. "I can't go home until I retrieve the boar skin you stole from me. Give me your crown so I can retrieve it from your cursed fairy realm."

Lugh laughed. "I won't tell you what you want or give you the key to Tír na nÓg, not for all the gold in Ireland."

"Then what do you want?" The Cat Sí asked.

"You can't give me what I want." Lugh paced around the Cat Sí. "When they cursed the fae to only speak the truth, the Æsir cursed me as well. They stole my divinity. They made me a mere immortal, without a drop of ichor in my veins. Without the blood of a god, the key to Tír na nÓg is useless, so I cannot undo the curse. With how few worshipers you have in this part of the world, I doubt you have the power to break it either."

After Ailsa's prayer to the moon, the number of prayers the Cat Sí had recently heard only came from three people. At this point she could barely call herself a goddess.

"I can try."

Lugh paused to think.

"Come on, take a gamble on me," the Cat Sí said with the grin of someone sharing a private joke. "I may not have the power I once had, but I bet I can still break your curse if I had the key to Tír na nÓg. Take my bet. If I win, we will both get what we want. I will get the boar skin you stole from me, and you will have your curse removed."

"And if you fail?" Lugh asked.

"I won't."

"But if you do, I will tell everyone in Olympus of your lies so you can face their wrath," Lugh said. "When they find out who you really are, your punishment will be so much worse than anyone who crossed Olympus before."

Lugh stared into the Cat Sí's eyes for a moment and held out his hand to shake on it. The Cat Sí hesitated. She knew what happened to those punished by the gods. Prometheus chained to a rock, screaming as an eagle devoured his liver each day. The beautiful Medusa punished with a twisted form and an eternity of loneliness because she had the audacity to be raped in the wrong goddess's temple. The talented Arachne turned into a terrifying insect. Who was she that her punishment would be worse? What had she done?

Still, she needed his crown.

The Cat Sí nodded in agreement to his terms and stepped forward to shake his hand. As she approached Lugh her weight, light as she was, tipped the balance of the ever-weakening tree. The sound of splintering wood split the air, and the entire field tilted to one side. The Cat Sí ran across the field uphill as Lugh sped alongside her, propelled by the flapping wings of his shoes. As fast as they moved, the tree began to tilt at a faster pace. The Cat Sí stopped and dug her claws into the ground to hold on as the tree fell. Lugh took to the air but was hit by a spire from the emerald palace and dropped alongside the Cat Sí and Ailsa to the earth below.

The Cat Sí awoke on her back with a deep throbbing pain coursing through her entire body. Her head pounded and the whole world had a golden tint. She groaned and wiped her fingers across her eyes until her vision cleared, and the only gold was the warm sticky ichor coating her hands.

She sat up and took in her surroundings. Branches as thick as houses lay splintered on the ground with normal sized trees crushed and sticking out beneath them looking like twigs. The emerald palace had shattered against the earth releasing shards of green gemstone and the contents of the Leprechaun's famous vault throughout the underbrush. Nothing but ruin remained of the once glorious fae kingdom.

A small noise from within the folds of her tunic brought the Cat Sí out of her daze. She reached inside her shirt and removed the pixie. Ailsa was still warm and breathing, actually she appeared far healthier now that she was outside of Crann Na Sióga. Some color had returned to her skin, and her glow was strong enough to illuminate the wreckage surrounding them. "Oh good, you're alive," the Cat Sí said softly as Ailsa began to stir.

"Thanks to you," Ailsa responded. She opened her eyes, and her face fell as she saw the remains of the place of her birth. "Looks like I failed."

"No, I did," the Cat Sí said. "You did all you could."

Ailsa looked up at the Cat Sí as if to respond and her expression shifted from distraught to surprised as she glanced at the golden liquid still seeping from the Cat Sí's wounds.

"Are you... hurt?" Ailsa asked. "Is that your blood?"

The Cat Sí wiped away the warm golden liquid. "How much did you hear?"

"You mean, did I hear Lugh proclaim himself a god and refer to you as his sister?" Ailsa asked with only the smallest bit of snark in her tone.

"Please don't tell the others," the Cat Sí said as her cuts closed. "I've been away from Greece so long I had forgotten where I came from until Fotini and Jaimie's prayers gave me the strength to remember. I'm still too weak to remember much more than the name the Greeks gave me."

Ailsa stared at the Cat Sí with an expression of pure puzzlement, but she nodded in agreement.

"Thank you. With that settled, let's find Lugh."

The Cat Sí got to her feet and Ailsa fluttered to the top of her head shining a light on the ruined clearing. They looked in all directions, but Lugh was nowhere in sight.

"Figures he would run away without giving me the crown," the Cat Sí said as she paced around the remnants of the emerald palace. "Running away and breaking promises was always his specialty."

"Maybe once, but he has the curse of the fae now," Ailsa reminded the Cat Sí. "He shook on your bet, if he left without holding up his end of the deal he would be in constant pain until he made things right. Believe me, he will hold up his end of the bargain."

The Cat Sí accepted Ailsa's answer and the two began searching for Lugh in the rubble. They dug through piles of wooden splinters, gold coins, and emerald shards until they noticed rubble covered in the sickly green of fae blood. They finally found Lugh half crushed underneath a portion of a palace spire. The king was in terrible shape, and his wounds weren't healing like the Cat Sí's. His arms and legs were twisted at odd angles and dark bruises were already forming where he smashed against tree branches. Green blood with flecks of gold splashed against the grass, giving it a bright shimmer.

The Cat Sí watched Lugh's labored breathing and couldn't help but see traces of the god she once called brother. His name may be different, but Lugh still had Hermes's red curls and perfectly straight nose. While the curse of the fae may have shrunk him in size, he still had the lean muscle and lanky frame of the god who ran across Greece in the blink of an eye to deliver messages.

While he was never the kindest of the Cat Sí's false, second family, he was far from the worst. The Cat Sí wiped a fresh drop of moisture from her cheek.

"Is he going to die?" Ailsa asked as the Cat Sí joined her by Lugh's side.

"Possibly," she answered. "But he's always been a stubborn one."

A pained smile appeared on the Leprechaun's face, but his eyes remained closed. "As are all our kind... come here, sister."

The Cat Sí knelt close to Lugh.

"Place my crown on the Lia Fáil to open the door," Lugh winced, taking his crown off his head. "You do not have to return it. I won't be needing it anymore."

"Thank you," the Cat Sí said softly as she took the crown which grew and expanded in her grasp until it would comfortably fit her. She lowered her hood, revealing her catlike ears, and placed the silver crown on her head. Ailsa thought it fit her better than the hood ever had, and was disappointed when the Cat Sí immediately raised her hood to hide the royal circlet.

Lugh let out a pained chuckle. "This is the first time I've seen your whole head."

"No point in hiding from you now," The Cat Sí said. "Besides, you already knew."

The Leprechaun King smiled and closed his eyes. "It's a shame you kept them hidden; they suit you." Lugh paused and took a few pained breaths. "In Tír na nÓg, unchain the fae... restore them..."

"I will."

"Please... take my sandals. They should let you enter secret places. Then take them with you, and someday give them to Hades, so I may see them again in his hall."

"Consider it done."

"Thank you."

A peace fell over Lugh the Leprechaun King as he took his final breath. The Cat Sí wiped away tears and pulled out a single coin larger than the Leprechaun's head and placed it on his chest. She carefully wrapped his arms around it to keep it in place.

"For Charon," she said to Lugh as if he was still there. "May he ferry you to Elysium."

The Cat Sí carefully unwound Lugh's golden sandals from around his limp legs and slipped them off his feet. Much like the crown, the sandals grew in size while in the Cat Sí's possession, but unlike the crown, she did not wear them. Instead, she reverently folded the straps and placed them within her satchel.

Without a word, the Cat Sí picked up Lugh's lifeless body and gazed around the wreckage. She found a smooth stone, extended the claw of her index finger, and carved a single line with two snakes entwined around it. She added the simple lines of two wings protruding from the top of the line where the heads of the snakes met.

The Cat Sí gently placed Lugh's body on the ground and began to dig a small hole. She was so entranced by the scene she did not hear Tragos, Fotini, and Jaimie arrive, but she noticed when Tragos hobbled over and gently picked up Ailsa.

"Thank goodness you are alive," Tragos said to the pixie. "When the tree fell, we feared the worst. Are you okay?"

"I don't know how to feel," Ailsa admitted. "I'm alive though."

Tragos wrapped his fingers around Ailsa as a sort of hug and placed her back on the ground to process her emotions. The group continued to watch as the Cat Sí finished digging her small hole and placed Lugh inside.

"Until we meet again brother," the Cat Sí said just before she stood and turned to the rest of the group. "Well, there's nothing else we can do here. The humans will surely return soon, we should go."

The Cat Sí got up and disappeared into the trees while the rest followed.

30

Gorm

"What the hell happened?" John asked Gorm as he appeared in the basecamp a few miles from the fae kingdom.

Gorm walked past the angry old man and made his way to his tent. He collapsed onto his bedroll and buried his face into his hands but couldn't erase the pair of glowing golden eyes from his vision. His ears still rang with the sound of its roar and his shoulders stung where long claws scraped against his skin. Worst of all, he could still feel the creature's hot breath against his throat from when it prepared to sink its massive fangs into his flesh.

"Don't ignore me!" John yelled as he stomped into the tent behind Gorm. "Why is the camp filled with injured men? I thought these belts of yours would make us impervious to the fairy's attacks, but all the men are coming back battered, bruised, and bleeding."

"The belts worked perfectly," Gorm said. "The fairies couldn't touch us, but there were more than just fairies out there. Jaimie had some sort of monster with him."

John bristled at the mention of his son. "You mean the changeling was there? So, this is where it escaped to."

It took Gorm a moment to remember John would rather believe his son was a fairy trickster than accept his sexuality. "Yes, sorry, it is hard to keep straight since it wears your son's face, but its new ally is something far worse than a fairy, and the belts have no effect on it."

"What did you see?"

"I am not sure. It was part woman, part beast. Unlike the pannites, her animal features were not taken from some passive animal we keep in a barn. It was a wild predator with claws, teeth, and glowing eyes to stalk prey in the night. It was like a cat, but bigger and meaner. I have only heard of one such creature before, but I swore it was a legend because it is only mentioned in the oldest of stories."

It couldn't be the same beast, could it? The beast Thor fought thousands of years ago was supposed to be cloaked in flames and had an insatiable blood lust. It wiped out armies and none of the gods could stand against it. The creature at the fairy tree was powerful but didn't seem powerful enough to compete with a god like Thor. It must be something else.

"So, what is this creature then?" John's question snapped Gorm out of his thoughts.

"You would probably call it a demon in your tongue. It is a monster who devours any who refuse to bow to it in worship."

Gorm expected this revelation to cause John to call off the quest and cut his losses, but the older man smiled and wrapped Gorm in a tight fatherly hug.

"If a demon is truly aligned with the fairies, then there is no greater enemy worth fighting. Our mission is surely ordained by God. We will triumph with the Lord on our side."

Gorm sunk into John's embrace and felt the man's confident words wash over him. Maybe John was right, maybe God would protect them and fight on their side. His heart began to feel lighter, but then the memory of the glowing golden eyes brought it back down to the pit of his stomach.

John released Gorm from the hug and led him out of the tent into the starlit camp. Gorm was so caught up in his own thoughts he didn't realize what John was doing until the pair of them were standing in front of the entire camp.

"Fear not!" John said using his best preacher impersonation. "While the enemy is powerful, we will prevail for we have God on our side!" The men from Whitfield cheered at John's words, but the Vikings stayed silent or groaned in response. "The fairy folk have made a pact with a demon to increase their strength, but with all the enemies of God aligned, He is surely on our side!"

This was too much for Sigurd who stood up in protest. "Easy for you to say! You didn't see that beast herd an army of deer to defend the fairies! I saw several men gored to death and we have nothing to show for their sacrifice!"

The dim glow of the campfires cast shadows on John's face exaggerating the smile that grew across his lips. "The Lord works in His own time. You will feel His presence before the night is over and know that we will be victorious!"

Sigurd opened his mouth to protest but was interrupted by a loud crack, like wood splintering apart. All eyes looked past John and above the treetops to the fairy tree that pierced the sky. The branches of the tree swayed, and a second louder crack rang through the forest. The tree tilted away from the camp and slowly fell out of sight with the sharp sound of splitting wood followed by a deafening crash that shook the forest.

"Behold the power of God!" John exclaimed. "When we cannot defeat our enemies ourselves, He will smite them for us! You can have all the treasure you can hold but the crown of the Leprechaun is mine!"

Gorm was in awe as all the Vikings, mercenaries, and men of Whitfield charged between the trees back to the fairy kingdom without fear. The whole group felt invigorated by John's speech and the benefits of divine intervention, but Gorm gripped his sword tightly as he ran. The demon surprised him earlier and he would not let his guard down again.

When Gorm reached the wreckage of the former treetop he was surprised, but relieved, to find it deserted by all the fairies, the two pannites, and even the demon. The only people around him were human men and women furiously filling sacks with shards of emerald and fistfuls of gold coins from the smashed vault. He did not join his companions in filling his pockets, he had a specific piece of treasure to find.

Gorm scanned the ground for any sign of the Leprechaun king or his crown. He spotted a few dead elves, but none with crowns on their heads. He was about to attempt to wade through the largest pile of emerald shards when he saw the first sign that his search may be in vain. In the soft earth was a trail of distinctive footprints. At first, they appeared to belong to a barefoot human, but sharp impressions disturbed the earth at the end of each toe. Gorm abandoned the pile of emeralds and followed the trail left by the demon instead.

The tracks led to a small patch of recently disturbed earth. The loose dirt was easy to dig through, so Gorm quickly dug down more than a foot where his fingers brushed against a tiny body. Gorm easily exhumed the largest fairy he had ever seen. The figure wore an intricate green tunic and had bright red hair and a matching beard. It was clearly the Leprechaun King, but it was missing a key feature for a king; he was not wearing a crown.

31

Tragos

F otini's heavy breathing drowned out all the sounds of the forest, including the pounding of her hooves. The trees thinned out considerably hours ago, but the group kept on running through the forest to put as much distance between them and the humans as possible. Tragos tried to run but his injured leg slowed him down considerably, making him Fotini's burden for the rest of the night.

Tragos felt an uncomfortable knot in his stomach as he dwelled on his pathetic state, but at least he normally wasn't as pathetic as the human. Humans were embarrassingly slow, and Jaimie was no exception. It barely caught up to Fotini whenever she stopped to rest, though it was slightly unsettling how it didn't seem to need to stop for rest as often as everyone else. So, while slow, it managed to keep pace through the night.

"Come on!" the Cat Sí yelled from up ahead. She seemed to have the stamina of a human combined with the speed of a centaur. "We need to reach the Lia Fáil before sunrise!"

"They're trying!" Tragos yelled back for Fotini and Jaimie, who were both unable to speak while running and gasping for enough air to push forward. "We cannae go any faster! Be patient!"

The Cat Sí stopped and let everyone catch up to her. She waited motionlessly and breathed slowly but deliberately, as if to force down an unproportional amount of rage. "I have been patient for a thousand years; I am not waiting another day."

"Stop exaggerating already! I get it, you have been trying to get to Tír na nÓg for a long time, but you can wait a bit longer!"

The Cat Sí shook her head and resumed running.

"I swear to Artemis... I am... going to kill that... malaka... when we stop," Fotini said between gasping breaths while Ailsa suppressed a quiet laugh.

Even with Fotini and Jaimie pushing themselves to their limit, the first rays of a new day filtered between gaps in the tree branches before they reached the edge of the forest. They caught up to the Cat Sí standing in the darkness beneath the last tree at the edge of a wide field of green grass surrounding a hill with a tall spire at the peak. They finally reached the Lia Fáil, the ceremonial coronation stone of the old Irish kings atop the Hill of Tara.

"Well, we made it," Tragos said proudly as he slipped off Fotini's back. "Happy now?"

"No," the Cat Sí seethed. "We are too late. The sun is up and shining on the stone. I can't go further until nightfall."

"What?" Tragos asked. "What do you mean? The entrance is right there!"

The Cat Sí ignored Tragos and gazed across the field at the Lia Fáil, lost in thought. "Thanks to your slow pace, we are stuck here until dark. Might as well set up camp."

Tragos boiled with rage. "The Lia Fáil is right across that field! We are too close to stop now!"

"We cannot go further until the sun sets," the Cat Sí said with a biting tone.

This was the last straw. What started as a simple con to steal a tournament prize had spiraled so far out-of-control Tragos found himself in a foreign country arguing with a creature he swore was made up to scare away gullible intruders. Now she wanted them to rest out in the open while a literal army marched towards them!

Tragos lowered his head, bent his knees, and pushed off the ground with all his strength. He shot forward and smashed his horns into the Cat Sí's chest with enough strength to knock an oak door off its hinges.

The Cat Sí was unfazed. Smashing into her was like headbutting a stone wall. The force of the headbutt failed to knock her over or even make her stumble.

"Are you done with your tantrum?" the Cat Sí said to Tragos as he sat on the ground rubbing his sore horns. "I cannot be seen by the sun so we will camp here in the shade until it is safe to cross the field."

"You cannae be 'seen' by the sun? What are you? Some sort of vampire? Let's go!" Tragos limped out onto the field and into the sunlight, but the Cat Sí did not follow.

"I will not go where the light touches," the Cat Sí said plainly but with a tone that left no more room for discussion. "I will camp here until nightfall, and you cannot open the door in the Lia Fáil without me or the crown, so you might as well get some rest and tend to your wound."

Tragos was about to give a snide remark when Ailsa buzzed up next to his ear. "Let me talk to her. You should rest and I'll see if I can help with your leg in a bit."

Tragos relented and made his way back to the comfortable shade, but a short distance from the Cat Sí. He gingerly lowered himself onto the grass beneath the tree and stretched out his injured leg. Maybe a rest would be a good idea.

The cool grass felt wonderful against Tragos's sore body as he lay in the shade, but it did little to improve his mood. He grumbled to himself as he pouted and repeatedly failed to stop himself from glancing at the Lia Fáil atop the sun-covered grassy hill. Every time he looked at the stone, his anger bubbled in his stomach like soured milk.

Everyone had a separate method of passing the time as they waited for nightfall. Fotini stalked the forest for a meal to restore everyone's strength. The human cleaned and pointlessly sharpened his sword. Tragos felt there was no point in carrying a weapon if you were not willing to take a life. The Cat Sí lounged in a tree with her limbs dangling from a large branch. Her yellow eyes were slightly open, so Tragos couldn't tell if she was asleep or simply resting.

"How's your head?" Ailsa asked, landing on Tragos's chest. With the pixie so close to his face, Tragos could see her more clearly than normal. Her golden hair hung loose around her chin and was slightly out of place and wavier than normal, adding a hint of wildness to her beauty. Glittering pixie dust coated her hair, luminescent skin, and even her clothing. She reminded Tragos of the golden idol they worked so hard to steal, except shinier, and if she were made of gold the craftmanship would have been without equal.

"Sore," Tragos responded. "Is the witch made of granite?"

"She seemed soft enough when she saved me from the Leprechaun. Maybe she's wearing a magic belt protecting her from satyrs."

Tragos laughed. One of Ailsa's more endearing qualities was her ability to break tension with humor.

"Whatever the case, I do not recommend head-butting her. Tell me, how do I look?" Tragos asked with his ever-present sarcastic tone. If he looked half as bad as he felt he probably resembled mashed porridge.

"Handsome as always," Ailsa answered immediately before glowing pink. "...What I should say is there doesn't appear to be anything broken. Maybe a slight red tinge at the base of your horns, and a few bruises from last night."

Ailsa's first statement shocked Tragos. She always seemed annoyed by him, so he always assumed her feelings were purely antagonistic. If Fotini had called him handsome, he would assume it was a joke, but Ailsa couldn't lie...

"Anyway," Ailsa said awkwardly, "let's have a look at your leg. I suspect you might need to run before this quest is over."

Tragos sat up and unwrapped a strip of cloth he hastily tied around the wound while waiting for the Cat Sí to rescue Ailsa. Congealed blood matted the fur on his leg turning the warm brown coat into slick black clumps. Sticky yellow strands of goo oozed out of the wound and stuck to bandage as it was peeled away.

Ailsa turned slightly green. "Well, you are healing poorly. This is going to be unpleasant, but if I don't act quickly the festering will spread and you will lose your leg. I can help, but I'm going to need you to do what I tell you. Do you trust me?"

Tragos nodded without any snarky comment. He no longer doubted Ailsa's inability to lie.

"Good. Wait here." Ailsa flew off into the forest and quickly returned with a fresh stick with soft green bark. "Put this in your mouth so you don't bite off your tongue."

Tragos quickly put the stick in his mouth as his heart began to race. This was not how he wanted to spend the day. He watched as Ailsa fluttered next to the wound and shook her head releasing a shower of glittery dust on the injury like magical dandruff. The dust coated the wound and mixed with the blood and puss causing the liquids to bubble and froth before rising into the air. Ailsa flapped her wings creating the smallest gusts of wind to push the infection into the sky.

Ailsa danced around sprinkling fresh pixie dust on the cut until all the floating droplets came out a healthy red instead of with a milky yellow tinge. Tragos was relieved the puss had all been leeched out without any additional pain. In fact, the pixie dust felt warm and comforting instead of painful.

"There, the sickness shouldn't spread any longer," Ailsa said. "Now all that's left to do is close the wound, so it doesn't fester again." Ailsa danced and spun her hands in graceful circles until sparks ignited at her fingertips and grew into stable handfuls of flame. She stopped her dance and pressed her burning palms against Tragos's open flesh.

Tragos clamped down on the stick and tried to suppress a muffled scream. He closed his eyes but could not block out the sizzling pop of burning flesh or the smell that was eerily close to cooked mutton.

"There, it's done," Ailsa announced, and the sounds of cooking meat ceased. "You should be able to keep your leg now. Sleep and you will feel a bit better by nightfall."

Tragos tried to clear his mind and ignore the pain as he succumbed to exhaustion and drifted off into an uneasy sleep filled with dreams of demons and fire breathing dragons.

Tragos spent the rest of his day drifting in and out of sleep near the base of the Hill of Tara where the Lia Fáil proudly stood. For a monument sacred to fae, Celts, and Druids, it wasn't very impressive. It was tall, but not massive, and had worn etchings of knotwork patterns barely visible through years of rain and sun. Tragos couldn't fathom why Irish kings insisted on being crowned at this stone instead of in their castle halls surrounded by the symbols of their wealth.

Tragos sat up to get a better look at the Lia Fáil in the grey evening haze and noticed a small but increasingly familiar weight nestled in the curls between his horns. Ailsa's glow illuminated the trees and grew brighter then dimmed in a rhythmic pattern as she steadily breathed. After the events of the previous night Tragos was relieved she was getting some much needed sleep.

"It's nearly time," the Cat Sí called out from her perch in the tree. "As soon as the sun disappears, we can go."

"Why cannae you go into the sun?" Tragos asked without any snark. "Are you cursed like the fae?"

The Cat Sí dropped to the ground and gazed up the hill at the sacred stone silhouetted against the setting sun. "To be honest, I don't remember what will happen if I walk openly in the light, but the thought feels me with such fear and revulsion I would rather not find out."

Tragos bit back his desire to make an inflammatory comment. He didn't like not knowing why they waited around all day, but if the Cat Sí was openly afraid then he wasn't going to argue again.

The last rays of the sun disappeared behind the horizon, and the only light came from the nearly full moon. The Cat Sí started her march up the hill with Tragos, Ailsa still asleep between his horns, Fotini, and the human not far behind.

The group quickly reached the top of the hill where the Lia Fáil stood like a pale obelisk in the moonlight. Ailsa awoke and fluttered around the stone illuminating the faint knots carved into it.

"Since you seem to be in a talkative mood, why exactly do you want to go to Tír na nÓg?" Tragos asked. "Ailsa mentioned the Leprechaun wanted you to go there to help the fae, but you were already going there."

The Cat Sí's normally stern and angry expression softened slightly.

"Before he was the Leprechaun, Lugh was known as Lugh Longarm, king of the Tuatha Dé Danann, and the malaka stole a precious boar skin from me."

Tragos vaguely remembered an old Celtic myth about Lugh Longarm sending thieves around the world to steal weapons for a war against other gods, but the Cat Sí being involved was preposterous. "Even if the myth of Lugh was based in history, that would have been a thousand years ago. I dinnae believe you are that old."

The Cat Sí's anger barely stayed at a simmer. "Believe what you want, it doesn't change anything."

The Cat Sí motioned for everyone to be silent, pulled down her hood, and removed Lugh's crown from atop her head. "Doors to other realms normally only open for individuals from the realm to which they lead. However, they can be tricked with two ingredients. An object from the realm on the other side of the door and..." the Cat Sí paused a moment to extend a single claw and slide it across her palm, "ichor."

Tragos watched in disbelief as she wiped actual golden blood across the stone and then licked her palm clean, revealing a fully healed hand.

The smeared ichor seeped into the Lia Fáil and flowed into the etched swirls, changing the color of the pattern from white to gold as it went. The design grew out of the sacred stone in a wave until it reached the lush grass at the base of the monument, making the grass shine in beautifully complex knotwork.

With the reaction of the ichor running into the earth, the entire hill shook with the roar of rocks scraping together like an underground symphony. A spot of grass near the Lia Fáil rose into the air and peeled away as a large, curved stone pushed through the earth. The monument grew from the innards of the hill until it towered over the Lia Fáil. At first glance, it looked like an archway, except instead of an empty space to walk through, the arch was a solid half circle of marble.

Once the solid arch stopped rising out of the earth, a ray of light shot from the tip of the Lia Fáil against it. Wherever the light touched, the arch changed into the empty air of a deep tunnel, faintly lit by the occasional glowing fae stone.

The Cat Sí calmly strutted into the dark cave, turned around, and addressed her stunned companions.

"Welcome to the door to Tír na nÓg!" she said.

Tragos, Ailsa, and Jaimie walked forward to the entrance of the tunnel, but Fotini stayed behind. Tragos turned to his oldest friend and saw her face had grown deathly pale. She slowly skittered backward away from the tunnel. It was the same reaction she had whenever she faced the tunnel to their home in Coille Sealgair.

"Wait a second," Tragos said to the group as he walked back to Fotini.

"I can't go in there," Fotini said plainly. "I won't."

"That's fine. No one is going to make you go in there."

The Cat Sí returned to the opening of the tunnel and called with an impatient tone. "What's the holdup?"

"Fotini disnae deal with tight spaces where she cannae turn around," Tragos explained. "She won't go through the tunnel."

"Then she can stay behind." The Cat Sí didn't waste any more time but disappeared into the darkness.

"We won't be long. You can be our lookout, blow your horn if you see the humans." Tragos patted the salpinx horn Fotini kept strapped to her side. "And when we get back, we will finally get paid, and we can afford a ship of our own where we can sail above deck. You can finally show me the rolling hills of Thessaly."

Fotini nodded, and Tragos trotted into the tunnel to catch up to the rest of the group.

The tunnel seemed to stretch on forever, with the only source of light being glowing fae stones on the walls in regular intervals. Unlike the entrance to Coille Sealgair in England, someone had purposely arranged the shining crystals instead of using the jagged stone exposed when the tunnel was dug into the deep rock. These magical gems were also delicately carved into unique figures instead of being left in their natural state. Ailsa remarked on each figure she recognized from the stories she heard in her youth.

"This one shows the three forms of the Morrígan, the goddess of war, fate, and death. She sometimes appears as a young maiden, a motherly figure, or as an old hag," Ailsa said as she buzzed around a lime green statuette that cast an eerie light in the tunnel. She zoomed forward to investigate the next statue, this time carved out of a blue stone with white swirls. "And this must be Manannán, god of the sea."

Tragos felt strangely calm as he listened to Ailsa jabber about the gods and stories of her people. It reminded him of Fotini talking about Artemis, but without the implication that her god was better than everyone else's.

The tunnel gradually changed as the group walked deeper and deeper into the darkness. Creeping vines with violet flowers began to slowly cover the smooth walls. Their sweet scent filtered through Tragos's nose and swirled into his mind.

"I don't recognize this one," Ailsa said hovering in front of a bright red figure with a sword in each hand.

"Well, you should," Tragos said with a grin. "That's Tragos! God of swords and wine!" Tragos posed like the statue and waited for Ailsa to laugh, but she merely looked at him with a puzzled expression before fluttering toward the next statue.

The tunnel gradually widened as if the vines were slowly pulling the stones apart. With additional space the flowers grew larger and began to release regular sweet-smelling puffs of pollen into the air. When Tragos saw a large flower in full bloom, something came over him and he skipped over to the plant and took a deep breath to absorb as much of the smell as possible. The fragrance filled his mind with a rush of peace and happiness. All concerns about money, freedom, and a pursuing army of angry Vikings were replaced with the sweet smell of bliss.

"This is amazing!" he yelled in giddy ecstasy. A voice whooped in reply behind him, and he turned to see a young human with red hair pushing its face into a large flower of his own.

A glowing ball of light appeared and zoomed around flashing every color imaginable. He stared into the light and saw it was a tiny, beautiful woman with dragonfly wings and glittery specks in her hair. When the tiny woman flew close, he reached out and snatched her from the air causing her to flash bright red.

"You are the most beautiful woman I have ever seen!" he exclaimed. "Can I kiss you?"

"Cat Sí! Help! Something's wrong with Tragos!" The flying woman yelled from his hand.

He let go of the tiny woman who didn't want to kiss him and looked around the tunnel but didn't see anyone in distress. "Who's Tragos? Maybe I can help him. Where is he?"

Another beautiful woman appeared from the darkness of the tunnel. This woman was not tiny, but she wasn't tall either. Her features were striking and perfect to the point of being otherworldly, as if she were from a dream. She looked right into his eyes and instead of feeling in awe of her beauty he was filled with paralyzing fear.

"Who are you?" he asked. "Stay away, I just want to stay here and smell this flower."

The terrifying woman walked up to him and grabbed his chin with a firm grasp and tilted his eyes upward. He felt sharp pinpricks from claws protruding from the tips of her fingers prompting him not to struggle.

"His pupils are huge, and not because of the dim lights," the normal sized woman said. "It looks like he's been drugged." The woman gazed at the flower and watched as a pink puff of pollen burst into the air. "Definitely drugged."

He did not like this woman. He wanted her to let go so he could smell the flower.

"Why are only Tragos and Jaimie affected?" the sparkly tiny woman asked.

"Who says I'm not affected? Can't you see I am filled with joy?" The woman held out her arms in a gesture that seemed to say, 'look at me.' The small bug lady didn't seem amused. "Regardless of why, we need to get these lugs moving."

The woman walked over and scooped up the red-haired human in her arms.

"Hey! Let me smell the flower!" The human instantly became enraged and started hitting the woman carrying him, but the blows had no effect.

"Come on Tragos, we need to go to," the fluttering beauty said.

"Who's Tragos?"

"You're Tragos"

"I'm Tragos?" he asked. He didn't remember being called 'Tragos' before, but he couldn't remember being called anything else either.

"Yes, and I'm Ailsa," the beautiful tiny woman said. "We need to go now."

Tragos thought Ailsa's name sounded familiar. When he heard her name, he felt even happier and felt he could trust someone with that name. He hated to leave the flower, but the desire to follow Ailsa was stronger. He left the sweet scent of the flower behind.

It wasn't long until the tunnel expanded so wide and tall that it stopped being a tunnel and became a forest with tall imposing trees and a pinkish fog of enchanted pollen. With each breath Tragos felt himself forgetting, but he kept his eyes fixed on his fluttering friend and her name kept rising to the surface of his memory.

The flowers, and the mist they generated, gradually thinned the longer the group marched through the forest. Tragos began to remember things he had forgotten while breathing in the intoxicating pollen. He clearly remembered Ailsa now, though he remembered pleasant memories of her far more easily than the arguments they had in the past. He remembered his name was Tragos, and he remembered his closest friend who was usually by his side. Once Fotini entered his mind he began to worry about her and hoped she was safe outside the tunnel.

Tragos was so consumed with his returning thoughts, he was taken by surprise when the forest abruptly ended, and he could see more than rocks and trees for the first time in hours. Tragos had seen many fantastic places in his life and expected the underground kingdom to be filled with ornate decorations, impressive architecture, and possibly an enchanted cave ceiling to bring light and cheer to an underground world. What he didn't expect was an open sky filled with bright stars that appeared far larger than the twinkling lights in the sky back home. A lush green and blue orb filled much of the sky like a foreign moon. Even the clouds were unusual, as they consisted of swirls of blues, pinks, and purples instead of white and grey mist.

"Why enchant the ceiling this way?" Ailsa asked. "Why mimic a sky that does not exist?"

"It's not enchanted," the Cat Sí said. "It's a different sky for a different realm. At last, we are in Tír na nÓg, the realm of eternal twilight."

32

Ailsa

Tír na nÓg had always been more of a story than a place to Ailsa. When she was young, her parents would tell her stories of the land of her ancestors as she drifted to sleep so the twilight lands would swirl and mix into her dreams. They described a purple sky filled with bright stars numerous enough to illuminate the world without needing the sun. A majestic tree held a shining city surrounded by fields of grain and canals of crystal-clear water. To Ailsa's childhood mind, Tír na nÓg was everything Crann Na Sióga strived to be, but without the ever-present fear of giant human invaders with iron swords. It was a world of life, color, and magic.

Ailsa's imagination of Tír na nÓg was technically accurate. Multicolored fields stretched for miles before running up against a large, fortified wall marking the edge of the city. Beyond the wall rose a tree unlike any other, a tree so great it could only exist by the will of the gods. The tree supporting Crann Na Sióga was a small sapling compared to this wonder of magic and nature. Miles above the ground, branches reached across the sky and glittering spots of reflected light gave evidence of a city larger than London nestled within the canopy.

The world looked perfect, but it lacked any of the sounds expected from a large city. Tír na nÓg was silent and devoid of life as if it was a mere model of a kingdom placed by a giant hand. A gentle breeze made waves through the pink and purple fields creating the only sound. The gentle rustling grain wasn't drowned out by the buzzing of a thousand pixie wings, the garbled cacophony of countless conversations, or even clear notes of flutes or harps. The sounds that always accompanied Ailsa in her childhood among the earthbound fae were completely absent.

"Where is everyone?" Tragos asked aloud as the group began their march toward the distant city. "You said the fae in Ireland could not return home because the door was sealed. What about the fae here?"

"I don't know." Ailsa was asking herself the same question.

The group walked toward the city in relative silence for several hours. When they talked, their voices sounded too loud and inappropriate within the suffocating silence of their surroundings. They all took to whispering when they felt the need to communicate, as if their voices were forbidden in such a somber atmosphere.

As they approached the ancient city, individual buildings grew into focus. From far away, everything looked pristine, but the closer they got, the more imperfections appeared. Cracks and soot peppered the smooth stone of the city wall and eventually grew into gaping holes in the city's defenses. Wild and overgrown fields of grain spread outside the city. No neat rows of carefully planned crops or picturesque farmhouses, just wide expanses of unharvested grain interrupted by the cobblestone road to the city.

"Did the human's already attack?" Tragos asked as they walked past a rusted plow abandoned on the road.

"I think if my ancestors invaded another realm, we would have heard about it," Jaimie said. "We would have legends and statues of the warriors."

"Then what caused all this?" Ailsa asked. She didn't expect an answer but glanced at the Cat Sí hopefully. The goddess took in her surroundings in concerned silence. So even she didn't know what had happened here.

As they closed in on the city walls, the evidence of a war grew more pronounced. A heap of greened bronze armor lay next to the road, the warrior who wore it was long buried or decomposed till all that remained was dust. An unusually thick arrow protruded from the metal husk below a wide oval gap in the back which would have exposed the soldiers' shoulder blades when they were alive.

Ailsa landed on the armor and inspected the design. Between patches of green wear, the armor showed flourishes of an intricate knot design etched in bronze. The large, unprotected section on the soldier's back was clearly intentional.

Ailsa traced the fabric of her dress where a thin strap hung around her neck to hold the front of it in place while leaving her back exposed to give her thin insect-like wings free range of motion.

"This belonged to a pixie," Ailsa said. "So, the stories are true. We weren't always so small."

Empty armor shells, chipped swords, and cracked shields littered the path as they approached the city. Some of the cuirasses had the same gap in the back for wings, while other designs lacked such openings. These breastplates were larger but sported the same style of design in their etchings and flourishes. These probably belonged to ancient elves.

What was not present in the ever-growing heaps of discarded armor was anything fitted for anything besides fae. None of the armor would have fit the body of a satyr or centaur, and not a single weapon was made of the iron preferred by humans. Everything looked as if it belonged to the fae. Ailsa shuddered at the thought of a civil war so brutal every citizen was slain.

Ailsa and the others reached the edge of the city wall just as the moon started to set and only stars illuminated the violet sky. The twilight fell to near total darkness outside the walls, but large glowing stones hovering in a crisscross pattern lit the empty city. A large section of the outer wall lay in ruin surrounded by thousands of the same empty pieces of armor littering the fields. The light of the glowing fae stones bounced off the ancient bronze giving the area an eerie glow.

"Where are all the bodies?" Tragos asked in a whisper loud enough for the whole group to hear. Everyone paused and looked around at the heaps of discarded armor and weapons, but not a single body, or even a bone, was in sight.

The blood drained from Jaimie's face as he surveyed the ancient battlefield. "I think I've heard about this before. The night before I was locked up by my father, Gorm told me a story of a monstrous beast that feasted on anyone who did not forsake their gods and worship it instead. He said it would decimate whole armies, peel away their armor, and gorge on the dead, drinking their blood and consuming their flesh and bones. The only thing left to show a battle took place would be things it could not digest."

Ailsa imagined an army of pixies being eaten by a large fur-covered creature and felt her last meal begin to bubble up her throat.

"What happened here was monstrous," the Cat Sí said with a completely blank expression, almost as if she were purposely stifling any emotion, "but I don't think this was caused by a creature like that."

"You know of this creature? How do you know it wasn't her?" Ailsa asked. She hoped these fae had a better fate than being eaten.

"The armor doesn't have any claw marks," she said coldly. "I see marks consistent with arrows, spears, and even the deep dents of war hammers. This was a battle, not a hunt."

"Then where are the bodies?" Tragos asked again.

"I don't know," the Cat Sí said, "but we won't get any answers out here."

The Cat Sí marched towards a hole in the city wall. Ailsa hesitated, the thought of moving forward filled her with a frigid chill, but the idea of staying alone in the silent battlefield made her nauseous. A thousand elves and pixies died in this place. No treasure was worth this.

"Let's go back," Ailsa said. "This is too much. It's not worth it."

"Not worth it?" The Cat Sí said as she stopped in her tracks. "I have spent a thousand years trying to get to this place. Crann Na Sióga fell and hundreds of fae died because your enemies want access to this realm, and now it's 'too much?'"

Ailsa flew over to Tragos and took shelter between his horns.

"The last thing Lugh asked us to do when he died was to come here. To fix things. We are continuing on." The Cat Sí turned and hopped over the rubble of the wall. Tragos, Jaimie, and Ailsa hesitantly followed.

The city behind the broken walls was in ruin. Charred rubble replaced the once mighty stone structures and remnants of death littered the ground. Among the discarded weapons were signs of the common folk who once called this city home. A simple shoe without a mate. A broken cup. A stuffed doll with fabric wings. Ailsa's light dimmed as she imagined families running from some creature or invading force in vain.

"Stop looking down and keep your attention on the tree," Tragos said to Ailsa. "Look how beautiful and full of life it is. Do you think it has fruit? I wonder what it tastes like?"

Ailsa looked up at the massive tree growing out of the center of the city. The canopy was miles above the earth and the branches blocked out most of the light of the stars, making the hovering fae stones the only source of light in the city.

"Wouldn't you be afraid to eat the fruit?" Ailsa asked, thankful for the distraction. "They say eating food in the fairy realm will trap you here forever."

"At least it's quiet," Tragos said. "Besides, I like the company here."

Ailsa chuckled and laid on the soft curls between Tragos's horns. As long as she looked up at the branches of the tree filling the sky, she wasn't looking at the evidence of war covering the ground. She focused on conjuring up the Tír na nÓg of her childhood imagination as she stared up at the distant branches. From this far away, she could imagine the canopy palace filled with life and decadent parties. The Morrígan could weave her magic to allow more lost fae to return home while Brigid prepared to heal their afflictions. From her perch on Tragos's head, she could almost forget it was only a fantasy.

As Ailsa pushed her mind skyward, the events of the last day caught up with her. Her heart slowed in the brief respite from running from the Leprechaun or Vikings. Her head grew heavy, and she closed her eyes just as they reached the base of the massive tree.

33

Fotini

Fotini watched her friends disappear into the darkness of the tunnel with a mix of apprehension and relief. Standing alone at the top of a well exposed hill made her feel uneasy, but the alternative was far worse. A chill ran through her whenever she gazed down the narrow passage to Tír na nÓg. She couldn't force herself through the short tunnel to Coille Sealgair, even with a clear view of the sunny village on the other side. This tunnel stretched for eternity with only faint fairy lights marking the path. As she stared into the depths, she could almost feel the walls shrinking around her. She quickly turned away before she collapsed under the weight of the void staring back at her.

Things were better in the open air under the night sky. To the west, the sky was clear, giving Fotini a sense of calm and peace. To the south, clouds rolled in from the sea over the forest, where they mixed with the smoke from the remnants of the fae kingdom. Rain was coming, but getting soaked was preferable to slowly starving while stuck between unyielding stone walls.

Fotini turned her attention closer to the earth. She kept one eye out for any movement from the nearby forest as she waited for the pursuing men. Once the men finished searching every inch of the ruins of Crann Na Sióga, they would surely make their way to the Lia Fáil. This group of humans already proved to be far smarter and more determined than Fotini expected. They wouldn't give up easily.

Jaimie was the first human Fotini had ever spent time with, and he continually surprised her. She always saw humans as the weakest creatures blessed with intelligence. The only reason they fared so well was because more gods favored their kind than favored centaurs, satyrs, or fairies. They had Zeus, Athena, and

Ares as their protectors, while only one of the twelve ruling Olympians and a few lesser gods favored her kind. As mighty as the huntress Artemis was, she could not stand against the combined might of the gods of war, wisdom, and lightning.

As she waited for the impending army to arrive, Fotini prepared an offering to her goddess. She pulled the pieces of the broken idol she needlessly pursued for so long out of her saddlebags and pulled it together again with twine. The beautiful maiden of moonlight once again stood tall with her bow drawn tight. It may be useless to the Cat Sí without the message scrawled inside, but it was still a treasure to Fotini. She imagined the idol once sat in a Roman temple where worshipers prayed to Artemis under her Roman name, Diana. Her meager offerings of jerky and berries would pale in comparison to the feasts presented to this statue a thousand years before, but she knew Artemis would appreciate them just the same. She was the wild goddess after all, patron to poor animals and young women. She did not favor kings and queens with full coffers and an abundance of finery.

With the offering set aside, Fotini attended to her own hunger. Her stomach gurgled in protest from being neglected since the night she met the Cat Sí. She had tried hunting as she waited for the Cat Sí to open the door to the realm of the fae, but she was simply too exhausted to be effective. There would be more time to hunt once everyone had returned from Tír na nÓg safely.

After she met the needs of her body, Fotini stood with her back to the tunnel and a firm grip on her spear as she watched and listened. The storm clouds moved closer and blocked out the stars, casting the world into increasing darkness. Before long the clouds passed in front of the moon and Fotini's range of vision continued to decrease. To better concentrate, she closed her eyes and listened to the sound of the wind over the grass and through the trees. She picked out the sound of leaves rustling in the wind, the hoots of owls waking up for the evening, and one sound not belonging to the usual animals who called the forest home. At the edge of the trees there were heavy footsteps. They moved slowly, but she could sense a small group creeping out of the trees. She was not surprised. The men under Jaimie's father's command had finally arrived.

Fotini took a deep breath and mentally prepared to fight. Once again, she stood between a wall of men, tasked with preventing them from advancing. She failed the fae, and the fresh loss burned in her mind like glowing coals. She would not fail again.

Fotini waited and hoped the company of men was small and manageable. It was possible the men split into groups going different directions as they searched for Fotini and her companions, but she knew it was unlikely. In their rush, the men did little to disguise their tracks and it sounded like a large group was gathered in the shelter of the forest. The footsteps grew louder as the group emerged from between the trees and walked across the grassy field. Even in the near total darkness of a starless night, Fotini could count the advancing men. As they grew closer, Fotini counted higher and higher until the number was too high to matter. She would surely die fighting twenty men simultaneously. What did it matter if there were forty? Eighty?

As the men approached, Fotini ducked as low as possible and hoped she blended into the darkness. The first man to arrive was Jaimie's favorite Viking. He was young, strong, and directed the other men even though he was much younger than most of the group. The young Viking stopped and raised one hand, signaling the rest of the group to fall silent. He raised an enormous bow and pulled back, taking aim in Fotini's direction. Fotini bolted to her left and an arrow struck the earth where she previously stood.

The men yelled and charged toward Fotini now that they had confirmed her presence. She turned and ran away from the tunnel and circled around. Arrows whizzed past her as she ran. The open field did not have the cover provided by the trees in the forest. With one hand, Fotini unbuckled her salpinx and blew into the long brass trumpet. A deep sound spilled from the horn filling the air. She had fulfilled her duty to warn the others, assuming her friends were close enough to hear the trumpet's call.

Fotini would not fail her companions as she had failed the fae. Instead of immediately fleeing, she bolted back to the Lia Fáil, leaped into the air, and snatched the crown off the sacred stone. The ground rumbled, and the gateway began sinking back into the dirt. Without thinking of the consequences, Fotini threw the crown through the archway just before it disappeared below the earth. She then turned and galloped away from the men as fast as she could.

"Níðingr!" the young Viking yelled as he pulled back on his bow in rage.

A single arrow shot through the air and flew through Fotini's heel with a shock of pain. With her muscle cut, Fotini crashed to the ground, unable to run. She propped herself up and twirled her spear around to keep the advancing humans from coming any closer. A second arrow pierced her shoulder, causing her to release her spear to twirl into the darkness harmlessly.

The arrowheads in Fotini's heel and shoulder dug further into her flesh as she forced herself up from the ground. She took on a lopsided trot that leaned to the left as she attempted to flee using only three legs. Even the lightest breeze sent shocks of pain from her injured heel. She could not endure putting her full weight on the injury.

The men continued their advance toward the injured centaur. For the first time since her childhood in Greece, Fotini was slower than her pursuers.

34

Jaimie

Jaimie used to enjoy hiking. He often roamed the hills surrounding Whitfield, regardless of the weather. There was a certain thrill when he reached the peak of a slope. Seeing the world from a more distant perspective gave him a feeling of peace, but those were the hills and mountains of Ireland and not the uncounted steps winding the interior of the noble tree of Tír na nÓg.

The circular path inside the tree was not too different from the tunnel separating the mortal realm from the fairy realm. Both were dark with only the soft glow of fae stones to illuminate the path. The air was cold and stagnant without the slightest breeze, making Jaimie feel that he was deep underground and not thousands of feet in the air. There was one big difference between the tunnel and the tree; the tunnel was a flat, easy walk and the tree was made of a giant spiral staircase where every step felt heavier than the last.

While the exhaustion from climbing step after step after several days of frantic travel was terrible, it paled in comparison to the terror Jaimie felt as he peered over the side of the staircase. Elves and pixies must be extremely sure footed because the architects of the staircase obviously felt no need to add any railing to the inner edge of the spiral. Nothing prevented Jaimie from falling off the stairs into the dark abyss below. He occasionally peered over the side and saw a spiral of fae lights circle downward until they were swallowed by the dark. He couldn't decide if the darkness made the height better or worse.

Jaimie listened to his companions to distract himself from the pain in his blistered feet and fear of falling for eternity into an endless void. None of the other three seemed much bothered by the climb. Ailsa could fly and hitched a ride between Tragos's horns, Tragos must have inherited a goat's propensity for climbing along with his fur-covered legs, and the Cat Sí was the Cat Sí. Jaimie found it difficult to imagine her being afraid of anything. The three of them enjoyed walking past large murals carved from the wooden walls of the tree while Jaimie fought to remain calm.

"This here is the story of the first fae," Ailsa said as they came across a scene depicting the Celtic gods and goddesses sailing to Ireland in a fleet of small boats. "In the story, the Tuatha Dé Danann came from across the sea where they fought against bloodthirsty gods. They built a new kingdom here where they could live in peace and prosperity."

Jaimie noticed Tragos smile while listening to Ailsa explain the history of the fae. He gave her his undivided attention when she spoke about how there were many conflicting stories about the origin of her people and their gods. Many of the humans said they came from heaven and were fallen angels, but Ailsa said she always assumed that was the human way of filling in the missing parts of a long-forgotten story. On these walls, the stories set in wood predated those ideas, carved by the people who lived the tales.

The next mural showed two groups of fae standing on opposite sides of a battlefield surrounded by fallen soldiers. One group, probably the Tuatha Dé Danann, was breaking free from the other group and preparing to cross the sea. The group that stayed behind stood before a magnificent city on the branch of an impossibly large tree not too different from the tree they were currently climbing.

The final mural once again showed the ancient home of the fae on the branch of a tree, but in this mural, the entire tree was visible. Large beings, ten times the size of the fae city, surrounded the base of the giant plant. The figures were massive but still could not reach the cities nestled on the treetop. On other branches were several other cities with drastically different styles of architecture. One showed gigantic mountains speckled by doors with sharp angles. Another branch, near the middle of the tree, showed humble farms and castles very similar to peasant homes in human communities. The largest city, which sat at the top of the tree, overshadowed all the others on the lower branches. Instead of being carved out of wood, this city was carved out of the same strange metal as the Cat Sí's jagged crescent pendant. The white city almost gave off a small glow and seemed to sparkle with every color. The Cat Sí stopped before this carving and ran a finger over one of several small, winged figures depicted flying near the shimmering city. Jaimie watched the normally cold witch gently caress the figure with reverence and slight confusion, as if she was thinking deeply.

"Do you know this place?" Jaimie asked. The Cat Sí did not answer but seemed to be startled out of her thoughts.

"I think I see a bright light above us. We must be near the end," she said as she turned away from the mural.

It was a relief when Jaimie finally emerged from the tree trunk to the ground suspended above the clouds in the tree canopy.

"Thank God," Jaimie said as he collapsed on a small section of grass free of ancient, discarded armor. The long-forgotten battle apparently wasn't limited to the city below. Weapons littered the ground surrounding the palace of the Tuatha Dé Danann. Even the fae gods were not spared from the battle.

"I say we curse whoever made that many stairs," Tragos said as he collapsed next to Jaimie. Ailsa yelped as she tumbled from his hair into the grass.

The only one not ready for a long rest was the Cat Sí. She calmly emerged from the tree trunk as if she had taken a short walk down the street instead of climbing thousands of stairs. As she walked across the grass, she stepped over countless swords, breastplates, and shields but she didn't get very far before she abruptly halted. She pulled off her hood and turned her head towards the glittering palace with her large ears swiveling. After a moment's pause, she sniffed the air, taking long, slow breaths through her nostrils.

"Malakas!" The Cat Sí swore in Greek under her breath and motioned to the group, who she addressed in a whisper. "There is something in the palace. Something that smells of rot and death."

Tragos sat up and groaned in irritation. "Maybe that's where all the bodies this mess belongs to are stored."

"The smell is fresh, not like the dried out remains from an ancient battle."

The Cat Sí readied her bow as she walked forward cautiously. Jaimie drew his sword and followed her in silence. Reluctantly, Tragos trotted forward with his own unsheathed weapon.

Across an extensive field of grass was the glittering palace of the Tuatha Dé Danann. The palace looked like it was made of white marble with gold Celtic styled knot patterns inlaid into the stone. The structure was the largest building Jaimie had ever seen. It made Whitfield Castle look like a meager hut by comparison. The only blemishes on the otherwise perfect building were blackened scorch marks from the ancient war.

The interior of the palace showed the horrors of the war from so long ago, as if the battle had happened the day before. Just like the field outside its doors, evidence of fallen soldiers decorated the tile of the great hall. Unlike the field outside, a strong odor of death and rot filled the room. Something was definitely decaying in the palace.

Jaimie tightened his grip on his sword as he walked deeper into the dark hall. As he walked, he occasionally stubbed his toes on broken fairy stones, their light snuffed out. The only reliable source of light was Ailsa, who currently let off a cool blue glow that did little to illuminate the massive hall.

"Ailsa, can you fly a bit higher so we can see?" Tragos whispered.

Ailsa fluttered toward the ceiling and followed its slope to the center of the room. Her faint light did little to illuminate the darkness.

"Can you shine brighter?" Jaimie asked.

"I'm not a fire. You can't just add another log to increase my brightness. My mood controls the glow and I'm not exactly excited to be here." The faint blue light turned purple as Ailsa's emotions shifted and combined.

"Come on beautiful, you are the first fae in Tír na nÓg in hundreds of years. What's not to be excited about?" Tragos called up.

Ailsa's light flickered.

"I noticed your dress has a fantastic, embroidered pattern. Did you stitch it yourself?" Jaimie asked, catching on.

"I did," Ailsa answered with a yellow burst of pride. "Not much in my size is available in England, so I do all my stitching myself."

"Well, you are very talented. You sew almost as well as you barter, and we all ken you are the best at selling stolen goods back home. Who else could sell silver candlesticks back to the monastery that made them without telling a single lie?" Tragos added.

Ailsa burst into white light that filled the room, but Jaimie almost preferred the dark. In the center of the room was an enormous emerald the size of a man floating in midair, covered in thick chains. On the floor beneath the emerald were several fresh bodies wrapped in smaller chains pinning them to the floor with thick iron nails. The chains were pulled taut, spreading their arms and legs wide apart making it impossible for them to defend from any sort of attack. Deep gashes and missing bites of flesh covered most of the bodies, and golden ichor flowed freely from the wounds of all but one individual. Amidst the gore slept a large gray beast in the basic shape of a human, but twice as large with two overly long arms and hands that could easily grasp Jaimie's whole torso. Where eyes normally would be, a pair of horns curved over the monster's skull. Dripping from its mouth was a golden stream of drool from its last meal.

"What the hell is that?" Tragos whispered to Jaimie.

The creature was unlike any from the folk tales Jaimie heard as a child, but he didn't have long to mull over his memories as the beast stirred. It opened its mouth in a wide yawn, exposing large, pointed teeth, and it stretched out its massive fingers, which cracked and popped with the motion. The creature slowly rose from the ground as if waking from a deep sleep and sniffed the air. It seemed to like what it smelled as it grew noticeably more alert and excited. It walked on all fours, using its knuckles as feet, over to the only body without gaping bite marks, a beautiful woman with pale skin and dark hair.

As the beast approached, the woman jerked away instinctively, though the chains wrapped around her wrists and feet made escape impossible. Jaimie was stunned to see anything else alive in Tír na nÓg.

Jaimie did not think about how the creature was at least three times his size, with jaws that could crush bone. He only cared that it was going to eat a defenseless woman. He rushed at the beast with his sword drawn and swung it hard against the monster's flesh. Sharp pain shot through his hands with the deep vibration of the sword as it bounced off the monster's hard spine without leaving a mark. He yelled and swung again, but only the noise seemed to get the creature's attention.

The creature turned on Jaimie and swung the back of its hand against him with incredible strength, knocking him backwards. It charged at him but stopped suddenly and let out an angry roar. Jaimie looked up at the monster and watched it pull out an arrow embedded in the softer flesh of its black slimy tongue.

"It's a troll!" The Cat Sí yelled to Jaimie. "Run!"

Jaimie scrambled to his feet and ran back toward his companions. He could feel the ground shake each time the troll's massive feet pounded the ground. Arrows whizzed past his head, but the rhythmic gallop barely slowed. Jaimie ran forward without the courage to look behind. His companion's shocked and worried faces made it obvious the troll was nearly upon him.

The Cat Sí stopped firing arrows and ripped the metal crescent from the chain around her neck. She threw the pendant past Jaimie, and it connected with the creature's massive forearm.

The troll let out an earth-shattering scream and stopped just before it reached Jaimie. It dragged its hand across the ground with a loud scraping sound, like two rocks sliding together. The monster's arm turned to motionless gray stone where the crescent stuck into its hard flesh. Using one of the many breastplates scattered across the floor, the troll scraped the crescent out of its arm. The stone instantly stopped spreading, and the troll stopped screaming in pain and began roaring in anger. It swung its frozen hand like a club striking Jaimie and knocking the crescent across the floor in a single motion.

Ailsa flew in an overhead arc across the room after the crescent. She landed and a moment later shouted, "I can't lift it!"

"I'm on my way!" Tragos yelled as he took off toward Ailsa's light. The troll turned to the noise and ran after the satyr with an awkward three limbed gait while dragging its large stone limb behind it.

Jaimie climbed to his feet and realized the troll would reach Tragos before he reached Ailsa and the pendant. The Cat Sí continued to launch arrows at the beast, but they mostly bounced harmlessly off its thick skin. It was a long shot, but Jaimie had to do something. He picked up a metal gauntlet left behind by one of the troll's many victims and began hitting it with the flat side of his sword. "Over here you brute!"

The troll stopped and turned its head toward the louder sound. It let out a deep growl and barreled toward Jaimie instead, leaving Tragos and Ailsa behind. Jaimie raised his sword and prepared to strike the charging beast.

The room spun as a shadow pounced on Jaimie and rolled him out of the troll's path. The creature charged through the spot where he was just standing and smashed into a nearby wall.

"What were you thinking?" The Cat Sí whispered in Jaimie's ear. In the dim light shining from Ailsa in the distance Jaimie could barely see the Cat Sí's face, but he would have sworn she looked terrified. "This beast feeds on gods; you don't stand a chance."

The Cat Sí leaped off Jaimie and ran toward the troll with her claws click clacking against the smooth stone under her feet. She jumped in the air, landed on the creature's head, and raked her claws across its face leaving a trail of sparks and shallow scratches, but not even a single drop of blood. The beast groped in the air until it grasped the Cat Sí's tail and yanked her off its head. Jaimie watched in horror as the troll slammed her against the floor with a sickening smack. It lifted her in the air and flung her to the ground again, and again, sending golden droplets through the air.

"Jaimie!" Tragos's voice echoed across the darkness behind him. Jaimie turned and saw Tragos sprinting across the room by Ailsa's light. He raised his hand with the crescent firmly in his grasp, skidded to a stop, and flung the pendant toward Jaimie.

Jaimie stuck out his hand and caught the pendant. It radiated an unexpected heat as if it sat in the bright sun on a summer's day, making it almost too hot to touch. Jaimie turned and bolted at the beast. It was standing over a whimpering Cat Sí, its jaws open wide about to bite into her dazed form. Jaimie took his chance and leaped toward the creature's face. He stabbed the crescent right between the beast's horns and it let out a painful scream. Its skin hardened around the wound and spread across its head. The scream turned into a gurgle before abruptly ending as the troll's jaws and tongue froze into a grotesque statue.

Jaimie stepped back in relief as he watched the troll convert to stone. He ached, and was undoubtedly bruised, but they were all still alive.

35

Fotini

F otini awoke with a pounding ache pulsing from the back of her skull and throbbing pain throughout her body. She sat propped up in an uncomfortable position with her legs curled beneath her body and her arms bound behind her back. The tight leather cord binding her wrists together made blood pool in her fingertips until they felt hot and swollen. The only positive thing about this predicament was that she was still alive.

When she fully came out of unconsciousness, Fotini looked around to assess her situation. Small iron lanterns lit the interior of a large yet simple tent. While decoration was sparse, the fabric walls and ceiling were clean and free of holes or patches, and the cot in the tent's corner looked warm with soft furs for comfort. Carrying all these supplies would have taken several horses. This was not the tent of the average mercenary, but of someone who prioritized comfort over practicality.

"Awake, are we?" an older man asked as he entered the tent. He was fairly tall with thick arms that may have been well defined in his youth but had since grown a thin layer of softness. His hair was mostly gray but with streaks of red and a matching thick but well-trimmed beard. The color of his hair and the splash of faded freckles on his cheeks made it easy to see this was Jaimie's father, John Whitfield.

"Sorry if Gorm and his men were a bit rough. They aren't always the best with animals," John said in a calm, almost sweet tone. He walked behind Fotini where she couldn't see him, but she heard some rustling of items being moved around.

She braced herself for a blow to the back of the head, but it never came. Instead, she felt soft fingers untie her hands, allowing the tingle of unhindered circulation. Her hands were now free, but her legs were still bound and useless.

John reappeared from behind Fotini holding an apple and the clumsily repaired idol of Artemis. "You must be hungry." He handed her the apple and she hastily bit into its crisp flesh to ease her growing hunger.

"When I first saw this statue, it was being awarded to the knight who just won a jousting tournament in London. It shocked me when the knight turned out to be a centaur trying to steal the prize. That was you, was it not?"

Fotini nodded but kept her gaze fixed on John. Her trust cost much more than an apple, no matter how sweet.

"I next saw it when Gorm and the changeling found it on the side of the road. Inside was some note with directions to the fairy realm. I was interested as an Irishman to hear the answers to questions I had about the stories I was told as a child, but as a father and caretaker of my community, it was far more worrying than exciting. Fairy folk have long been a scourge on my people, and I hesitated to follow any leads to their realm. But when I learned they had taken my only son..."

John barely contained his anger as he put the statue on the ground in front of Fotini.

"I can understand why a fairy changeling would want to alert his people that I had discovered their secrets, but why is a half-beast like you caught up in this? What does this statue mean to you?" John's face twitched as he struggled to maintain a gentle composure.

"I was hired to retrieve the statue, nothing more." It was more or less the truth.

"Then why aren't you safely on a boat back to England? You had the statue in your possession, but Gorm says a centaur was at the cursed fairy tree, and now we found you guarding the door to the cursed realm."

"I saw your army. Your son said-"

John stood up and his mask of kindness dissolved.

"The changeling trapped *my* son in the fairy realm with all the other kidnapped children! Admit you warned the fairies we were coming to take back our sons and daughters!" John practically roared.

"They didn't take your son, you idiot! Stop this madness!" Fotini yelled in response.

"All lies. I can't trust a pagan beast." John slapped Fotini across the face. His unwashed fingernails scraped across her cheek, leaving growing spots of blood. "Tell me where my son is!"

"He's in Tír na nÓg!" Fotini was never one for lying under pressure. "He's with my friends, safe from you."

John balled his fist and gave Fotini a proper punch in her stomach. "I love my son, which is why I must destroy the fairy who stole his face. Only then will he be free to return home to me."

"You have heard too many fairy tales. There's no such thing as changelings." Fotini flinched away from the impending assault, which came as a punch to the same shoulder an arrow had pierced a few hours earlier. She screamed as burning waves of pain tore through her.

"More lies!" John unsheathed a small knife from his belt and came close enough to Fotini for her to feel his breath. "But there are ways I can make you tell the truth."

Fotini fell in and out of consciousness over the next few hours. By the time John finished, small shallow cuts and words like "liar," "beast," and "pagan" were carved into the fur of her hindquarters. She was exhausted and could not escape the pain, but was relieved when John grew tired of torturing her and retired to the cot beside her.

The tent flap was slightly open, allowing a sliver of moonlight to shine into the tent. In the silence and the soft light, Fotini remembered the idol of Artemis. It was still on the ground where John placed it when he was still pretending to treat her nicely. The moonlight reflected off the gold plating, and Fotini felt some small comfort that her goddess was near in some form.

"Please," Fotini whispered in a voice so quiet, she could barely hear herself. "Please mighty Artemis, bless me that I may live to see the morning sun. But if it is your will that I should die, please guide me to Elysium, where I may join your band of maidens in your eternal hunt. Please, please answer my prayer and help me in my time of need."

The tent remained silent. There was no booming voice from the heavens, no shower of arrows from the maiden of night, but Fotini somehow knew someone, somewhere, had heard her prayer.

36

The Cat Sí

The Cat Sí pulled back in horror when she opened her eyes to the large teeth of the troll taking up her entire vision. Thankfully the jaws remained unmoving. The troll was completely frozen in stone, with the broken solar disc protruding from its forehead between the creature's large, curved horns. The Cat Sí climbed to her feet and yanked the precious crescent from the beast's head, cracking the fossilized skull in the process.

"Are you okay?" Jaimie asked, his face contorted with worry and confusion. "If the troll had slammed me to the ground like that, I would be dead."

"I'll be fine," the Cat Sí said. She instinctively licked a deep gash on the back of her hand and felt relief as the wound closed under her saliva. She tried to ignore the hunger growing in her stomach with the sweet, honeyed taste of her own ichor.

Jaimie glanced at the Cat Sí's hand and then met her eye's. "What are you really?"

The Cat Sí opened her mouth as if to speak but paused with her mouth hanging open. Should she tell him? Ailsa already found out who the Cat Sí really was, or at least one of her past identities, but she had watched the pixie from afar for years. She had only known Jaimie for a few days, yet something about Jaimie made her trust him completely. She felt she could be truly honest with him.

"I am..."

"You did it!" Tragos interrupted and slapped Jaimie across the back in a masculine show of uncharacteristic comradery. "I cannae believe you tried to face that thing alone. Great catch by the way, I have to admit, I am impressed. Maybe not all humans are that terrible."

Jaimie stuttered and turned slightly pinkish in the dim light. It seemed the human and satyr were finally beginning to bond.

"You really were fantastic," the Cat Sí agreed. "I haven't seen bravery like that in a very long time, but I believe there is still more to be done." She motioned to the stone troll.

"Is it dead?" Ailsa asked as she hovered over the group to illuminate the dark hall.

"I think so, but let's make sure it can't come back," The Cat Sí said as she started pushing against the side of the stone beast until it tilted. Jaimie and Tragos joined her and together they tipped the monster over until it fell and shattered against the ground, scattering hundreds of small chunks of stone across the floor. "There, now it should stay dead."

The Cat Sí stared at the rubble and wondered how a troll could have ended up in Tír na nÓg. The beast belonged to Jötunheimr; a frozen realm associated with a completely different pantheon than the gods of the fae.

A soft whimper behind the Cat Sí broke the silence and reminded her of the woman the monster was about to feast on. The Cat Sí, Jaimie, Ailsa, and Tragos all hurried over to the circle of beings chained to the floor around a large, green, floating crystal bound in iron.

The young woman was still alive, but that was little comfort to the Cat Sí. Sores circled her wrists and ankles where iron manacles restrained her. Golden ichor flowed from her wounds revealing her divinity. She was a goddess of the fae, one of the Tuatha Dé Danann. The Cat Sí looked at all the bodies chained to the floor and noticed dried puddles of honey colored liquid coating their remains. Who, or what, could have done this to an entire pantheon?

A loud clang rang through the dark hall as Jaimie struck the lock on the chain pinning the woman to the floor with a large rock that was once a piece of troll. "Help me with these," Jaimie asked his companions as he hit it again.

"Use this," Tragos said as he jammed a small dagger into the manacle lock. Jaimie hammered the end of the dagger with the stone until the lock burst apart releasing the goddess's wrist.

The Cat Sí approached the whimpering goddess and licked her wounds while Jaimie and Tragos worked on the rest of her bindings. Sad faint lines from the old, repeated injuries remained on the goddess's otherwise perfect pearly skin as she began to heal. The Cat Sí ripped long pieces of clean cloth from her cloak, wrapped them around the wounds, and gently sealed the wrappings with a kiss. "Heal well my friend"

The goddess stirred awake and rubbed her wrists and twitched her feet. "Thank you." Her voice was still weak, barely a whisper.

"Anything we can get you?" Ailsa asked as she fluttered down and landed on the Cat Sí's shoulder. "Food? Water?"

"Water."

Tragos pulled out a canteen from his satchel and tilted it against the goddess's lips. At first, she sipped slowly, but she quickly gathered enough strength to guzzle the water in earnest. Tragos didn't wait for her to ask for food, but handed her a piece of bread, which she ate slowly.

Color returned to the goddess's cheeks as she ate, and her skin took on a faint glow similar to Ailsa's.

"Thank you," she said with slightly more strength than before. "I cannot thank you enough."

"Why were you chained to the floor?" Tragos asked abruptly without any trace of tactfulness. "What were you doing in this graveyard?"

The goddess let out a painful and mirthless laugh barely louder than a whisper. "They chained me to this floor because I had the gall to resist the Æsir. I was in a graveyard because that's where you put the dead."

Tragos laughed nervously. "Well, whoever put you here acted too quickly."

"What makes you say that?" the woman asked.

"You dinnae look dead, and you seem too solid to be a ghost." Tragos gently grabbed the woman's hand.

"I'm not dead now, but I was dead yesterday, and I would have died again today if you hadn't come along and slain that cursed troll." She spat on the ground toward the chunks of rubble. "That Jötunn has gnawed on my bones and gotten drunk off my ichor for so long I can scarcely remember what it feels like to be free."

"You were dead before?" Jaimie asked, joining the conversation.

The goddess stood with no lingering signs of pain from the wounds on her ankles. "I was, but now I can finally live again for more than a fleeting moment of pain. Can I ask but one more favor? Can you help me free my family? Iron saps our strength and I cannot free them myself."

Jaimie seemed confused, but nodded and got to work hammering the manacles binding the dead bodies still pinned to the floor, but Tragos looked hesitant to join him.

"I'm sorry, but your family is..." Tragos began to say before glancing at the Cat Sí who glared at him to shut up. He really was a tactless fool.

Tragos silently joined Jaimie in unchaining the bodies.

Ailsa hovered over the group, still providing light that shifted with her thoughts. The room flickered brighter just before she spoke. "You're one of the Tuatha Dé Danann, aren't you?"

"I am." The young woman confirmed she was a goddess as casually as someone would say what region they were born in. "I am called the Morrígan, the mightiest of all queens and master of magic."

A tinge of fear ran through the Cat Sí. The Morrígan was also a goddess of war with a fearsome temper.

"All of my family here are Tuatha Dé Danann," the Morrígan said as she gestured to the bodies on the floor. "The old cyclops couldn't kill us in a way that stuck, so he devised a fate far worse than death."

With a loud crack Jaimie brought the stone down on Tragos's dagger and the last chain broke. Tragos looked down at the half-consumed body he just unchained with a disgusted expression on his face. "This is a terrible fate, but it is also death. The sooner you face this, the sooner you can heal. We can help you bury your family outside if you wish."

A sad smile graced the Morrígan's lips. "There is no need to bury those who do not stay dead, but I thank you for the sentiment. What can I do to repay you for freeing me and my family?" As the Morrígan spoke, she seemed to age. Her hair lost some luster and faint creases appeared at the edge of her eyes and smile.

The Cat Sí stepped forward; she might as well get to the point. "I am here to retrieve what was stolen from me. Lugh sent thieves to lands ruled by my family and stole the hide of the Calydonian Boar."

"The Leprechaun King also asked us to 'unchain' the Aos Sí," Ailsa added hastily.

"I would love nothing more than to let you take everything from Lugh's vault for all the trouble it caused." Streaks of grey slithered through the Morrígan's hair and the imperfections in her skin grew more pronounced as she spoke. "The one-eyed king of the Æsir invaded this realm to access those stolen weapons. None of us could open the vault, the door will open for Lugh, and Lugh alone. As you can see by the state of this realm, the Æsir were not pleased when they learned this."

The Morrígan gestured around the dark hall.

"As for 'unchaining' the Aos Sí? That I can do."

The Morrígan closed her eyes and was once again a young maiden, beautiful and filled with the strength that comes from youth. Despite the tattered and ichor-stained state of her dress, she appeared regal and summoned visions in the Cat Sí's mind of beings glad in white chitons with gold trim dancing around a marble hall above the clouds.

With the grace of a goddess, the Morrígan walked to the center of the circle of bodies and stood beneath the dull emerald hovering in the center of the carnage. Dust covered chains etched with sharp angular runes wrapped around the crystal with the ends hanging motionless in the stagnant air. The Morrígan raised her arms, swayed, and twirled as if dancing to music only she could hear. In response to her movements, the crystal emitted a green light that slowly grew in intensity until it filled the palace hall.

The chains did not respond well to Morrígan's spell. The runes grew red hot, and flames engulfed the cursed bindings.

A song spilled from the Morrígan's lips, and the air crackled with energy and the runes etched into the chains turned blue. The words were unfamiliar yet evoked images of deep seas and unscalable mountains. Like those images, the words seemed filled with beauty, power, and terror.

The chains went from blue to white before succumbing to the Morrígan's magic and melting away to nothingness. With the barrier removed, the magic flowed from the Morrígan's song into the floating gem until it shone like a green star, bathing the palace interior with warm light.

Ailsa let out a small, surprised yelp. Under the glow of the new star in the palace hall, her own glow intensified. "What's going on? This feels strange, but... amazing!"

The Morrígan finished singing and approached the hovering pixie. "Small one, are you one of the Aos Sí? Your magic has been restored and with it, the curses placed on you by the king of the Æsir should also be removed. Come, show us your strength!"

Ailsa flew over the largest piece of the vanquished troll and shook out a shower of pixie dust. The magical powder melted into the stone and disappeared. Ailsa moved aside and slowly raised her hands above her head. The rock followed her movements and rose into the air. She waved her hands to her left, and it moved as directed. She moved her hands to her right, and it changed direction. In a swift motion, Ailsa pulled her hands in opposite directions, stretching her arms wide and the stone cracked and then ripped itself in half sending pieces sailing across the room until they smashed into the walls with a bang.

"Hahaha! Good show!" the Morrígan laughed and praised Ailsa as a mother praising her child, which in a way, she was.

Ailsa fluttered over to Tragos and hovered in front him, radiating joyful yellow hues on his battle worn face. "I hate this magic so much I'm turning red!"

Tragos looked confused half a second before he excitedly responded, "You liar!"

Ailsa shot around the great hall in glee. The Cat Sí had never seen any pixie so happy or free, but she knew the joy could not last. This kind of happiness never did.

As if a sudden realization washed over Ailsa's mind, she abruptly stopped and landed on the ground. She closed her eyes and focused, but nothing happened.

"Grow!" she yelled. "Fás! Vokse!"

Nothing happened. Ailsa remained a tiny pixie.

"I don't get it?" Ailsa shouted, her mood suddenly sour. "Why am I still small? The ancient fae were just as tall as everyone else."

The Morrígan kneeled beside Ailsa. "You have had your magic restored for only a moment. Give it time, you'll figure it out."

Ailsa hung her head but she retained a hopeful yellow hue.

"Thank you for restoring the fae's magic," the Cat Sí interrupted the magic lesson impatiently. "But we still need to enter Lugh's vault."

The Morrígan's hair grew silver as she turned to the Cat Sí. "As I said before, we were unable to open the vault even when faced with an eternity of torment. Only Lugh can open it, but the coward fled at the first sign of trouble. Get him to open it for you."

"He's dead," the Cat Sí said plainly. "I saw him die last night. There must be another way."

The Morrígan closed her eyes and sighed. "That complicates things. Since he is not here, he must still hold some allegiance to his first family in Olympus."

The Cat Sí sighed in frustration. "Are you sure there isn't another way into the vault? I don't think you understand how important it is for me to get what Lugh stole."

"I understand more than you possibly could!" the Morrígan walked up to the Cat Sí to use her height to look down on the shorter goddess. "*I* am the goddess of fate, and when I looked into Odin's eye, I saw the torment I would receive if I didn't let him into the vault. I knew I would wake every morning for centuries in this hall. I knew I would feel the beast's jaws rip my flesh and drink my ichor until the pain grew so great, I would pass into dark oblivion only to reawake again and again. This is the realm designated to the souls of the Aos Sí, so I cannot escape this place even in death. If I could open the vault, I would have opened it a thousand years ago."

The Cat Sí looked at the floor in shame. She had never experienced such physical torment. "I cannot pretend to understand your pain. My trials have been numerous, but they do not compare with a millennium of death, but I still must ask you to at least take us to the vault. Like Hermes, Lugh, I was not born to the realm I have long called home. I need a relic from that realm to open the door. Whether he meant to or not, Lugh stole my only way home and locked it in the vault in this palace. At least take me to the door."

The Morrígan gazed into the Cat Sí's eyes and a flicker of recognition flashed across her face. She slowly grew younger in appearance as her heart softened, and she approached the Cat Sí tenderly. "Very well, follow me."

37

Tragos

Tragos felt the hair on his arms rise in anticipation; they were finally at a vault containing treasure for the taking! The group stood in front of the round door made of a smooth marble slab reflecting the colored lights coming from Ailsa and the Morrígan. Like every piece of architecture in Tír na nÓg, a geometric pattern covered the door frame, but unlike every other door, the pattern was not made of swirling knots with soft curved edges. Instead, angular swirls, like squares growing ever smaller, surrounded the vault opening.

"This is the door to Lugh's vault," the Morrígan announced. "I tried every spell I knew to open this door to save my people, but it remained locked. The door will open for Lugh, and Lugh alone. It is unfortunate he is not here, he could open the door, and I could kill him again for abandoning us. Though if the rumors are true about his uncle, then he is likely having a miserable time in the underworld."

"His uncle?" Jaimie asked.

"Before Lugh came here and joined the Tuatha Dé Danann, the Romans called him Mercury, and the Greeks knew him as Hermes. You no doubt heard of him?" the Morrígan caught Tragos's eye.

"The god of messengers, thieves, and gambling. If I believed in gods, I would make offerings exclusively to him," Tragos said. As much as he disliked listening to Fotini drone on about the gods, he had to admit the stories of Hermes were almost tolerable.

"Not surprising." The Morrígan let the insult linger a moment before she continued. "Anyway, I have had enough talk about Lugh and his antics. When your pointless pursuit is over, you can find me again in the throne room attending to my family as they awaken." With that, the Morrígan marched back down the corridor.

The four companions stared at the door in the darkness, puzzling over how to open it. Tragos rammed it with his horns, but all it did was let out his frustration. Ailsa lied and declared herself Lugh Longarm, King of the Tuatha Dé Danann, but the door wasn't so easily convinced.

"Did Lugh, Hermes, ever tell you how to open the door?" Tragos asked the Cat Sí. After seeing her bleed golden ichor he was starting to suspect she might have some experience with gods, or the beings who called themselves gods.

"No," she said. "I haven't heard a blasted thing about this door."

"Didn't he say something to you before about bringing his sandals here?" Ailsa asked as she fluttered around the room casting long colorful shadows.

"He did!" The Cat Sí said with a look of recollection. She quickly reached into her satchel, removed a small pair of winged sandals, and tossed them to Jaimie. "Put these on."

"Why don't you?" Jaimie attempted to hand the sandals back to the Cat Sí, but she shook her head in protest.

"I think they would suit you better," she said. "Besides, I would like to keep my claws free."

Jaimie removed his boots and replaced them with the golden sandals which grew in size as he brought them near his feet. The golden straps wrapped around his legs to give them a secure fit, and the wings magically fluttered once the sandals touched his skin.

"Here goes nothing," Jaimie said as he approached the door wearing the winged sandals. "Open!"

Nothing happened. Jaimie yelled his command again, but the door stayed shut.

Tragos thought about the last magical door they opened. The entrance to Tír na nÓg opened with Lugh's crown combined with the Cat Sí's golden blood. Tragos turned to the Cat Sí. "I think it needs some of your ichor."

The Cat Sí approached the door and ran a claw across her palm. She smeared golden ichor across the entrance to the vault, once again demonstrating she was more than just a witch.

Jaimie stepped forward once again. "Open!"

With the scraping of stone, the marble slab rolled into the wall and the vault opened. Torches around the room burst into flames, illuminating the large vault filled with gold, silver, and precious gems. Swords and shields from ancient legends, armor and the fine clothing of gods and kings, and artwork from faraway times and places hung from the walls. In the center of the room was a deep pool of still water with a metallic glint from something deep within its depths. It was more treasure than Tragos had ever seen in one place.

"Maybe this is some kind of heaven," Tragos said as he ran his fingers across a small pile of coins. Ailsa could easily sell any of these items for enough money to purchase an entire ship, let alone enough money to smuggle Fotini and himself to Greece. With this, they would have the freedom to stop stealing and finally start living.

Tragos began stuffing his pockets with anything that would fit and made his way to the pool in the center of the room. The metallic glint he saw earlier was the white pearlescent tip of a spear submerged at the bottom of the basin. Tragos reached into the pool, and when his fingers clasped the handle of the weapon, he felt a surge of hot power run through his veins.

Visions of himself at the head of an army flooded Tragos's mind. He saw himself leading a legion of Children of Pan against armies of humans. He knew he could conquer any obstacle, defeat any enemy with this weapon. He looked at the shining white blade at the end of the spear and felt a burning desire to kill any who wronged him flow through him. With this spear, he and Fotini would never need to fear for their safety again.

"Look what I found!" Jaimie said breaking Tragos from his trance. He turned towards Jaimie and saw him holding a sword made of the same strange metal as the spear tip, like light forged into iron. The blade of the sword glowed bright with every color Tragos had ever seen. It was glorious, but another voice inside his head assured him the sword was no match for the spear.

"I found the boar skin!" Ailsa called from the far side of the room. The Cat Sí, Tragos, and Jaimie rushed over with their new weapons in hand to find the treasure that provoked this entire quest.

Compared to the rest of the treasure, the skin was a hunk of trash. It was clearly ancient, and rough bristles matted in dried blood covered nearly every inch of the hide. As a cloak, it would be itchy and as a blanket it would be stiff and uncomfortable. Tragos couldn't understand why the Cat Sí wanted it so much.

"This is what all the fuss is about?" Tragos said. "A disgusting old piece of fur?"

"This old piece of fur was once the mightiest of all boars," the Cat Sí said with reverence. "The Calydonian Boar eluded or vanquished thousands of arrogant hunters until my chosen champion, Atalanta, finally hit it with an arrow. Meleager gave it to her for being the first to wound the beast and I blessed it to cure any injury caused by mortal weapons. It was a relic to rival all other gifts... until Hermes' thieves stole it."

"You blessed this for Atalanta?" Tragos knew Fotini's favorite legend by heart. She recited it repeatedly by the campfire. The story of Artemis's champion, who started the tradition of praying to the goddess of the hunt. His suspicions were all but confirmed, but Tragos wanted to hear the Cat Sí say the name. "Are you saying you are..."

The Cat Sí held up her hand to silence Tragos. "Quiet."

The long ears on the witch's, or goddess's, head swiveled as if searching for a sound. The Cat Sí stood motionless, and the entire company remained silent as she listened for something even Tragos couldn't hear.

"We need to go now!" The Cat Sí shouted as she unceremoniously stuffed her prized hide into her satchel and ran out the door. "Fotini's in trouble!"

38

Jaimie

The Cat Sí moved as if spurred by the wind and fueled by the fires of a thousand forges. Jaimie struggled to keep up as he chased her through the dark corridors of the ancient palace. Tragos ran alongside him with his new spear gripped firmly in one hand and Ailsa on her usual perch between his horns. The Cat Sí didn't pause when she ran through the hall where the Morrígan was embracing a handsome man with a silver arm. She also did not slow in the slightest when she reached the edge of the field outside. When she met the ledge, she leaped into the cloud filled sky without hesitation.

"Cat Sí!" Jaimie yelled in surprised as the Cat Sí disappeared below the clouds.

Jaimie continued to run toward the edge of giant canopy and felt an intense urge to follow the Cat Sí's lead. He couldn't quite explain it, but there wasn't the slightest bit of fear at the thought of leaping off the cliff into the open sky. When he reached the edge of the field, Jaimie pushed off from the ground and leaped towards the clouds, but instead of falling, he soared by the wings on the sandals he wore.

"Keep running," Ailsa yelled to Tragos, who had slowed considerably and fallen behind the others. She shook her hair and wings violently, releasing a cloud of golden powder that cascaded around the satyr.

Tragos pushed forward, gaining speed in his last few steps. "I hope you ken what you're doing!" Tragos yelled as he leaped into the sky. As he reached the height of his jump Jaimie almost expected the satyr to plummet to the earth, but instead he coasted on the air like a child sliding across a frozen pond. He yelled out again, but this time in relieved glee as he floated next to Jaimie.

"Quit dawdling," Jaimie said. "We need to catch up to the Cat Sí." Tragos's demeanor grew serious as he seemed to recall why they were chasing after the Cat Sí in the first place.

Jaimie and Tragos soared through the sky with the aid of winged sandals and pixie dust like a pair of arrows launched from a giant's bow. Dipping below the clouds, Jaimie could see the entire city of Tír na nÓg, most of the destruction from the ancient war faded away from so high in the clouds, and the world seemed calmer as the landscape changed from the city to rolling fields of grain. At this height everything looked simultaneously smaller and larger than ever before. Jaimie felt a sense of peace as he took in all the beauty before him without the harsh details he normally couldn't see past.

On the ground, a small shape ran through the fields at an impossible speed. As Jaimie coasted lower, the shape grew clearer, and he saw it was the Cat Sí running on all fours like a graceful lioness. Clumps of dirt trailed behind her as she ran, dug up by her claws piercing the earth. Her tail was free of the confines of her tunic and whipped back and forth, stabilizing the queen of cats as she ran. The hood, which normally hid her face in shadow, flopped behind her uselessly in the wind. Without her disguise hiding all the parts of her that made her unique, Jaimie thought she looked truly free for the first time since they met.

The closer he flew to the ground the easier it was for Jaimie to see how incredibly fast he was moving. Fields of unfamiliar crops blurred together in pink and purple swirls. His throat seemed to drop into his stomach as an old barn appeared in the distance and within moments was behind him. Jaimie's heart pounded with such intensity he felt each beat but did not know if it was spurred by excitement or terror. The dark forest filled with mist of forgetfulness loomed on the horizon and Jaimie swung his legs forward in a desperate attempt to slow himself.

Landing was unpleasant, but thankfully he had slowed enough to prevent a complete disaster. Jaimie crashed into the soft earth and rolled across the ground for a few feet before he came to a complete stop just outside the edge of the enchanted forest. Tragos crashed just behind him in a heap. They were just standing up when the Cat Sí leaped past them barreling into the forest with enough speed to blow a path through the swirling mist. Jaimie, Tragos, and Ailsa groaned and followed, trying desperately to keep up before the mist returned to the path and invaded their minds.

The forest and tunnel seemed much shorter when the group traveled at a sprint instead of calmly walking and taking in the ancient artwork. It didn't take long before the group found the Cat Sí stopped by a solid wall of earth where the tunnel should open up to the Lia Fáil. The Cat Sí bent and picked up the crown of Lugh from the tunnel floor with her claws. "She sealed the door to stop the humans from following us."

Jaimie's heart sank. How would they get out from this side? Jaimie looked over at Tragos and saw his hands clench around the handle of his newly acquired spear. His face contorted in a potent mixture of fear and rage.

The Cat Sí placed the crown atop her head and spoke in a loud and clear voice.

"I command the earth to let us go forth!" She bit her finger and ran the golden ichor from its tip across the wall of dirt and marble, but nothing happened.

The Cat Sí let out a flow of curses in languages Jaimie had never heard and began swiping at the wall. Her claws left deep grooves in the stone, so she swiped again, and again, until her claws hit soft dirt.

"Help me dig," the Cat Sí commanded through tired breaths. Jaimie and Tragos started pulling out clumps of dirt and scraped the earth until their fingers grew numb from working with the cold soil. After nearly an hour of frantic digging, the Cat Sí's claws raked away the final bit of dirt and moonlight spilled into the tunnel.

"Wait here a moment before you follow," the Cat Sí said before turning to Tragos. "Fotini is still alive, but she might not be for long if we burst out of the ground all at once."

The Cat Sí squeezed through the fresh hole in the ground and slipped silently into the tall grass around the monument. She crouched down and stalked out into the night like a large predator cloaked in shadow. Her perfectly woven braid had come apart as she ran through Tír na nÓg and her thick black hair curled around her back and shoulders, making her look like a feral lion approaching its prey.

The rest of the group waited a moment before leaving the tunnel one-by-one. They crouched by the Lia Fáil to watch as the Cat Sí slowly crept over the grass toward a newly erected camp at the base of the hill. Jaimie wondered if anyone could see her in the moonlight with her black fur and clothing against the dark green grass of the Irish field. He got his answer when a horn blew, and men burst from their tents with weapons drawn. Several arrows shot towards the Cat Sí, but the lioness easily swatted them from the air before letting out a roar that dwarfed the sound of the Viking horn.

"Wait!" Jaimie heard his father yell from the center of the camp. "Hold! We have something of hers and she has something of ours." John turned and faced the Cat Sí who was now standing upright with her long black claws and reflective pupils shining in the moonlight. "I propose a trade, demon! Give me the crown and I will give you your half-breed companion."

"Or I can kill you all and take back my friend!" the Cat Sí yelled. Her entire countenance had changed, and Jaimie thought he could see the rage radiating off her as if her body were a living furnace.

"Move any closer and it dies!" Jaimie's father yelled. He waved his hand and four large men led Fotini out from within a tent and into the field. Jaimie's skin turned cold as he took in the hopeless situation. Two men held the ends of a long rope wrapped around her arms and humanlike torso, preventing her from fleeing or fighting. A third man walked beside her with the tip of a spear pressed against the spot where her large second heart beat in the horselike portion of her body. The fourth and final man rode on her back as if she were a common horse and held the edge of a dagger against the vulnerable skin of her neck. Even if Fotini escaped the ropes and avoided the spear, her dominating rider would slit her throat.

The Cat Sí immediately stopped moving.

"Good kitty," Jaimie's father said. "Now place the crown on the ground and walk back to your companions.

The Cat Sí relented and left the crown in the grass and walked backwards toward the hill, never turning away from Jaimie's father.

Jamie noticed Gorm for the first time as he confidently marched forward and retrieved the crown. The Viking picked up the headpiece and raised it in the air triumphantly, causing cheers from the surrounding men. Gorm gazed past the Cat Sí toward the top of the hill where Jaimie, Tragos, and Ailsa watched. Jaimie swore he locked eyes with his dearest friend for a brief moment, but there was no love in his old friend's expression.

Gorm's eyes lingered on Jaimie and his companions until a surprised look twisted his angry features. He hurried back to Jaimie's father and said something to him that Jaimie could not hear from atop the hill. Jaimie's father nodded as Gorm spoke, growing more and more excited as the young man relayed his message.

"Gorm here says you have brought us one of the fae's stolen weapons as a tribute!" Jaimie's father yelled. "Bring me Areadbhair, the legendary spear of Lugh Longarm!"

Jaimie turned to Tragos and studied the spear he was holding; he hadn't noticed that the white metal of the end of the spear gave off its own light and seemed to glow every color all at once. There was no doubt in his mind the spear must be the murderous spear of legend.

Tragos gripped the spear tightly and silently took a step forward.

Jaimie put his hand on Tragos's back and whispered, "let me take it. If I go with the spear, he may let the rest of you go without harm." Jaimie attempted to take the spear from Tragos, but the satyr would not release it.

"If you take the spear, your father will kill you with it thinking you are a changeling. I'll take it to him." Tragos emerged into the moonlight and made his way down the path with the spear in hand.

All eyes fixated on Tragos as he walked across the field towards Jaimie's father. When he passed the Cat Sí, Tragos caught her gaze. She closed her eyes and nodded with approval.

Jaimie watched Tragos approach his father with growing dread. When he looked at his father waiting with outstretched hands, Jaimie saw him in a new and unflattering light. He wasn't the wise, just, and moral pillar that Jaimie saw throughout his childhood. No, John was ignorant, greedy, and selfish. Jaimie no longer respected him, and with this realization, he no longer hungered for his approval.

"Look, a demon comes bearing gifts. Too much of a coward to bring it yourself changeling!" Jaimie's father spat toward the entrance of Tír na nÓg.

Jaimie's father greedily grabbed the spear out of Tragos's trembling hands. He gripped the handle firmly, raised it above his head, and turned to his men and exclaimed, "Areadbhair, the spear of the fairy king, the spear that never misses and hunts your enemies in a thirst for blood!" The men cheered and the tip of the spear glowed brighter, as if fueled by Jaimie's father's hate. "Shall we test if the legends are true?" The camp cheered again. John pointed the spear toward Fotini and released his grip. "Kill the centaur!"

The weapon shot forward without being thrown. It simply needed to know the target, and its own desire to destroy propelled it forward. In a blink of flame, the spear went clean through the center of Fotini's chest and embedded itself in the man who rode her. The man screamed as the spear tip burned his flesh and ignited his clothes in flame, but Fotini did not make a sound. Her eyes, wide with fear, darted from John to the Cat Sí, and stopped when they landed on Tragos, who was already rushing to her side. The flaming rider tipped over and fell, pulling Fotini to the ground with him.

Jaimie's father raised his hand again, and the spear pulled itself from its victims and returned to his hand. "It works!" he yelled as the crowd cheered.

Jaimie watched his father in horror and disgust. John killed Fotini with glee, as if her life was worse than meaningless. Who was this horrible man? Surely the man who cared for Jaimie his whole life would never find such enjoyment in death and deceit. Jaimie no longer recognized the man who raised him. He no longer saw his father, instead he saw the monstrous John Whitfield.

Without further hesitation, Jaimie rushed down the hill with Ailsa buzzing at his side. When he reached Fotini, the Cat Sí held her head in her lap, gently stroking her hair, softly giving words of comfort. Jaimie reached into the Cat Sí's satchel and yanked out the old boar hide and threw the skin onto Fotini's wound. The leather turned red as it soaked up her blood, but Fotini remained motionless.

"Don't be afraid, Fotini," the Cat Sí said with a cracking voice. "I heard your prayer. You will join all the mightiest huntresses in Elysium. I am so sorry I was not here sooner."

Silent tears ran down the Cat Sí's cheeks, and Fotini's expression relaxed as she seemed to find peace in the Cat Sí's words. Jaimie lifted the skin and saw that the minor bruises and cuts Fotini had collected through their adventures together had disappeared. The hide of the Calydonian Boar healed all her wounds, except for where the spear had pierced through her chest.

"Why isn't it working?" Jaimie sobbed as he stared at the burned and gaping wound. "You said the boar skin could heal people."

"No magic can heal a cut from an adamantine spear," the Cat Sí said softly. She held Fotini and gently kissed her forehead as her eyes closed for the final time. "Celestial metal cuts far deeper than iron."

As Jaimie watched his friend pass on from this world, the surrounding field of men continued to celebrate, and why shouldn't they? They got a mythical weapon that would assure victory in all future battles. A weapon that could turn a minor lord like John into a unifying king. Watching their enemies suffer was an added benefit to their success, which only intensified the cheering. With Fotini gone, the growing glee and celebration reached Jaimie's ears and sliced through his grief, giving room for rage.

Jaimie drew his new fae sword from its scabbard and ran toward John paying little heed of the men celebrating around them. The sword had the same glowing white gleam as the spear, and he felt a surge of power flow from the weapon through his arms as he ran.

Jaimie lunged directly at John while the old man was still busy celebrating, but the spear must have sensed the attack was coming with its own magic and positioned itself to protect its current, although distracted, master. A flash of light illuminated the night as the sword met the tip of the spear, alerting the crowd to the attempted strike.

"So, the changeling does have some courage!" John said in a loud voice so his army could hear his taunts. "You dare attack me now that I have the weapon of your god king? It is time for you all to perish! Attack!"

John's army of men snapped into action and turned toward Jaimie, but were quickly stopped by the Cat Sí darting between them and their intended target. She drew her bow and loosed arrow after arrow into the fray preventing them from coming closer. Ailsa joined the battle by streaking through the sky with a stream of pixie dust wafting over large stones below her as she flew. As she twisted and turned in an airborne mystical dance, boulders were yanked from the earth and hurled at anyone daring to approach her companions. Unlike the others, Tragos stayed motionless by Fotini's side, holding her blood-soaked hands while gazing deep into her unmoving gaze.

John regained his composure to defend himself in earnest with a flurry of attacks using the mythical spear. The anger at Fotini's death opened the floodgates of emotion within Jaimie, forcing him to feel the anger and sadness he long kept buried deep inside his heart. He swung the shining sword with strength fueled by feelings of rejection, unworthiness, and loneliness in his own home. He attacked with all his strength and deftly deflected John's attacks. In many years of practice, Jaimie had never achieved this level of swordplay. It was as if the sword guided his movements while his feet danced at inhuman speeds with Hermes' sandals.

"Why did you take my son!?!" John yelled as he blocked Jaimie's sword and pushed against the blade, sliding it off the spear. "He was all I had, and you took him from me, changeling!"

"There are no such things as changelings!" Jaimie yelled as he brought the blade down again and hooked the hilt of the sword on the spear shaft, pulling the weapons together. Jaimie pushed against John, sending him tumbling to the ground. "I am Jaimie!"

John scrambled to his feet and threw the spear. Even with enhanced speed and skill, Jaimie barely stepped to the side and deflected Areadbhair with his sword sending it sailing into the sky behind him.

"Enough of this! I am Jaimie! I am the same man who has been by your side learning from you day after day! I am the same man who mourned with you when *my* mother died giving birth to *my* brother! Just because you do not approve of my feelings toward Gorm, does not change who *I* am!"

Jaimie walked forward with his sword ready, but desperately hoped he wouldn't need to use it.

John held his hand out to the sky. "Give me my son. Areadbhair!"

The whistling of the rushing spear filled Jaimie's ears from high in the sky behind him.

"No!" The Cat Sí dived from the fighting masses to stand between Jaimie and the spear. She raised her bow and shot an arrow at Areadbhair, but the small wooden projectile splintered and burned on contact with the spear without changing its trajectory. The legendary weapon continued on its path until it pierced through the only obstacle on the way to Jaimie, the Cat Sí's shoulder.

"Areadbhair!" John yelled again and the spear yanked itself through the Cat Sí's shoulder, emerging on the other side coated in sizzling golden blood. Free of the Cat Sí's flesh, the spear returned to John's open hands.

The Cat Sí knelt in the grass, pressing her palm into the gaping wound, but kept her eyes on John as she struggled to stay conscious. "Jaimie! Look out!"

Jaimie turned his attention back to John, who held the spear high above his head.

"Areadbhair! Hunt down and destroy those who imprisoned my son!" John threw the spear forward toward Jaimie, but the weapon sailed harmlessly through the air above his head, arced through the sky, and plummeted back towards the man who threw it.

John held out his hand to call the spear to his grasp, but the spear already had a target. It ignored its master's new command and impaled itself through his chest.

"No!" Jaimie rushed to his father's side. The sparkling tip of Areadbhair stuck through the older man's back, igniting his clothing, and cooking his flesh with the blade's burning thirst for violence.

"Why?" Jaimie asked with tears streaming down his cheeks. "Why didn't you listen to me?"

John stared up at his son in shock and horror. Jaimie searched his eyes, desperate for a glimmer of regret. He placed his hand against his father's cheek and bent close for a final embrace, only to for John to use the last of his strength to spit a mouthful of blood in his face.

39

Gorm

G orm dived out of the way of a large stone as it sailed past his head. A scream followed by a dull thud reverberated through the air as the Viking behind him took the hit. He ran through the frantic crowd away from the fairy attacking from the sky above, wondering how this particular fairy had enough magic to lift something larger than a pebble.

"The belts aren't working!" Sigurd yelled as he caught up to Gorm. "You said their magic couldn't harm us!"

"It can't!" Gorm yelled back above the sound of screams. "We would be fine if it were throwing balls of magic at us, but stones aren't made of pixie dust!"

Gorm crouched down just in time to avoid being hit by another large chunk of earth, but Sigurd was too slow. The rock hit the side of his head with a sickening squelch sending him flying backward.

Rage and fear fueled Gorm as he ran away from the fighting to search for another way past Jaimie's bodyguards. He broke away from the group of Vikings, ran up the hill, and hid behind the Lia Fáil to get a better vantage point.

He couldn't help but be impressed with Jaimie and his demonic companions. A single fairy and the cat beast were successfully keeping the army of Vikings and mercenaries from rushing to John's aid in his fight with his son. Gorm had never seen such a fight. The fairy used magic unheard of in Ireland for over a millennium. It ripped stones out of the hill and threw them at the army with ease. On its own it would have been a formidable foe, but it paled in comparison to the horrors unleashed by the cat demon.

The cat who nearly bit Gorm's head off at the fairy tree, started the fight by unleashing arrow after arrow in a blur. Every shot hit a man or woman square in the eye, killing them instantly. Unfortunately, the demon only had about a dozen arrows before it had to change to more brutal tactics.

Gorm watched as the beast tossed aside its bow and roared with enough ferocity to split the sky. It pounced on a fleeing mercenary and sunk its teeth into its victim's neck and pulled out his throat. Another woman charged at the creature but was taken out by a single swipe of the monsters' claws. The cat moved with godlike speed and the fury of the fires of Muspelheimr. Gorm squeezed the grip of his sword to quell the shaking fear spreading through him. He must be living through a nightmare.

Gorm hid behind the Lia Fáil and watched the beast release its latest victim when it noticed John's newly acquired spear sail through the air towards Jaimie. The creature dove at the spear, stopping it momentarily with its shoulder before it returned to John's outstretched hand leaving a gaping hole. Blood gushed from the wound, but even from where Gorm stood he could see it lacked the crimson hue of mortal blood.

The creature bled golden ichor, the blood of a god.

Old bedtime stories flooded Gorm's mind. He could almost hear his mother's voice as she told the legend of the only creature to ever best the Æsir gods in battle.

A giant cat cloaked in flame came from a land of scorching heat to devour any Viking loyal to Odin. It consumed whole villages, whole armies, until blood flowed like a river into its thirsty jaws.

Could this demon be the creature who once bested Thor? The creature the hammer Mjölnir was forged to finally defeat?

Gorm left the safety of the hill to get a closer look at the beast, when he heard John direct the spear to hunt down the person who imprisoned his son. Gorm stopped. He knew the truth. He understood what John had really commanded the spear to do.

He turned just in time to see the spear arc through the air and slide through John as if he were made of nothing but air, and not flesh and bone.

"No!" Gorm yelled but was drowned out by the sounds of war. The young Viking forgot about the cat demon and ran toward John. He shoved Jaimie aside and held his master close. "No! You can't leave now!"

Gorm pulled on the sizzling spear sticking out of John's chest, but it cut clean through and was wedged deep into the stones of the earth beneath John. The wound seared closed around the spear stopping the blood flow, but it made no difference as John's organs burned from the heat of the weapon releasing a smell like cooking pig.

John was dead, and without him Gorm had no future. John hadn't told anyone of his plan to name him as his heir.

Gorm turned his attention to Jaimie, who stood silently staring at his father's body with wide eyes and a blood-spattered face. Not his blood, but John's. "What have you done?"

"I didn't do anything." Jaimie's voice shook as he spoke. "I just wanted to stop him from hurting anyone."

"It doesn't matter what you wanted," Gorm said quivering with rage. "You chose to fight him and now he's dead, and with him my future is gone." Gorm's expression grew dark as he met Jaimie's eyes. "You took everything from me! John was going to name me his successor when we returned! Now I am left with nothing!" Gorm stood and swung his blade at Jaimie with wild fury, but Jaimie raised his own sword to deflect it as if by instinct.

"Please Gorm," Jaimie said as Gorm continued to strike. "We don't have to fight. You can have Whitfield for all I care. Just stop the attack!"

"I will take Whitfield after I take your head!" Gorm lunged at Jaimie, let his sword be deflected, and struck his former friend in the face with a closed fist.

Gorm saw something break deep within Jaimie. "I took everything from you? He was my father! You were my friend! And I see now I have truly lost you both!"

Jaimie attacked. He fought with an intensity Gorm had never seen before. His swings were no longer aiming to disarm or deflect, but to cause pain, to kill. For the first time ever, he feared Jaimie. He glanced around the hill for aid, but knew no one would come for him. The hillside was in chaos. Men were crushed as the fairy blasted them with stones and the cat demon mauled anyone within reach of her one good arm. Roars, screams, and the tinkling of magic filled the air. Even if one of the other men wanted to help, they would be unable.

With his lungs burning with exhaustion, Gorm brought down his sword with all his remaining strength, passion, and rage. His blade sparked against Jaimie's fairy blade and a current of energy traveled from Jaimie's magic weapon into Gorm's hands, forcing him to drop his sword.

Jaimie pointed his blade at Gorm's throat, his face twisted with grief. "Leave here now. I will not show mercy again."

Gorm scowled at Jaimie in his defeat. "I cannot defeat you, or the monsters you travel with, but I know someone who would love to finish this fight. When I was younger, I was told stories of the first Vikings," Gorm said, turning his gaze away from Jaimie toward the cat demon. "I was told of a feline fire demon from a kingdom of heat and sand who burned villages and drank the blood of my ancestors. The monster almost wiped out my people, and hid in fear when the gods forged a weapon powerful enough to vanquish her."

The cat demon stopped fighting and released a terrified mercenary, but she didn't seem to care. She was too absorbed in Gorm's words.

Gorm raised his fist into the air, dangling his precious pendant in the shape of the hammer, Mjölnir.

"Almighty Thor! I give you my life to open a door between realms so you may have your revenge!"

Thunder shook the world as lightning split the sky and struck the pendant. Heat and pain filled every inch of Gorm's body. His veins boiled as lightning coursed through them, but he held firmly to the pendant. He would face death unafraid and take his well-earned seat at Odin's table in Valhalla.

Gorm collapsed and the lightning ceased. Calm filled the air for a moment before a low rumble of thunder filled the sky and an enormous hammer crashed into the side of the Hill of Tara. The last thing Gorm saw before he closed his eyes forever was a large hand picking up the real Mjölnir from the earth.

40

The Cat Sí

A ncient memories from when the gods were young filled the Cat Sí's mind for the first time in centuries as she looked upon the god standing before her. She could almost feel flames enveloping her flesh and her muscles clenched in response to the mere memory of her unending rage from their last encounter. Her ears swiveled in vain, searching for the echoes of ancient screams from armies watching their god swing a crude bronze ax against her impenetrable skin. The tips of her claws remembered peeling back the young god's flesh in thick savory ribbons and she salivated with thirst for the sweet intoxicating flow of his golden ichor on her tongue. After devouring the god, she remembered turning on his worshipers with her unending thirst.

Was that who she really was? The flaming embodiment of bloodlust and destruction? The Cat Sí shuddered and wretched her mind through millennia to the present. Instead of wondering about the person she used to be, she wondered how a god she killed thousands of years ago now stood before her in perfect health.

Morrígan's voice filled her mind, *"I'm not dead now - but I was dead yesterday."*

The not so young, and not so dead, god from her visions now stood before her as a much more intimidating presence. Thor, prince of the Æsir pantheon, was no longer the scrawny fledgling god of a few nomadic tribes, but a massive god fueled by the prayers of a nation. He was nearly twice the size of a mortal man with long, copper hair and a matching beard braided below his chin. His bright red tunic swirled with the golden accents of Nordic knots depicting the monsters he reveled in fighting, so naturally there was little empty space for additional stitches on the garment. Most importantly, His crude human forged axe was replaced by Mjölnir, an overly large hammer forged out of celestial light with a handle too short to wield with both hands, so only the strongest gods could wield it.

The god of Thunder looked across the field and locked eyes with the Cat Sí for the first time in three thousand years and smiled.

"Finally!" Thor yelled and charged forward with lightning crackling off his impressive frame. A few stray bolts struck nearby Vikings knocking them to the earth. The remaining men fled to the cover of the forest to watch from a safer distance.

The Cat Sí turned and ran away as fast as she could across the field of dead and dying men. She scanned the area as she moved, searching for anything able to match Mjölnir. There, near the bottom of the Hill of Tara was John's crumpled corpse, the flaming spear Areadbhair still embedded in his chest.

"Coward!" Thor yelled as he continued his pursuit.

The Cat Sí was so focused on reaching the spear she almost didn't notice when Thor's heavy footsteps abruptly stopped, and their furious pounding was replaced by a steady whistle rapidly growing louder. She turned just in time to see the hammer, but not in time to avoid being struck in her already injured shoulder. A crack like thunder split the air and lightning surged through the Cat Sí's veins as the hammer spun her off her feet to tumble down the hill past the spear.

The world twisted and turned until the Cat Sí skidded to a stop far from her intended destination. She tried to push herself off the ground, but immense pain shot through her body from where she was struck. She carefully stood up using only her uninjured arm for support. The slightest movement of her left side made her want to scream in pain, but she wouldn't give Thor the satisfaction.

A glance at her shoulder confirmed it was dislocated. The Cat Sí clenched her teeth and quickly pulled her shoulder joint back into place with a small pop. Relief flooded her and the bumps and bruises from tumbling down the hill finished healing, only leaving the seared flesh from the spear and thin spidery lightning burns.

There was no more time to waste. The Cat Sí started running up the hill toward the spear half expecting Thor to have already reached it, but Areadbhair's only company was the dead. She skidded to a stop at John's crumpled body and unceremoniously yanked the mythical spear from his corpse. The white glistening metal at the point of the spear ignited under her touch. It felt good to grasp an adamantine weapon again, she couldn't remember the last time she felt so powerful.

The Cat Sí turned her attention to her attacker and a wave of panic coursed through her as she began her sprint across the hillside. Thor was locked in combat with Jaimie and Ailsa. Jaimie swung his glowing sword wildly as Thor gracefully avoided each thrust, laughing as he easily moved from side to side. Even though the celestial blade could injure the god, he was completely unconcerned with his opponent. He reminded the Cat Sí of a cat toying with a mouse before devouring it.

Thor let out an obnoxiously jolly laugh as he stepped to the side of Jaimie's latest lunge, but failed to notice a pixie dust-coated boulder sailing through the air. The rock smashed against the back of his skull making him stumble forward slightly. The laughing stopped as Thor whirled around in rage and flung an open palm through the air. Ailsa narrowly avoided Thor's assault, another inch and she would have been slapped out of the air.

"Leave them alone!" The Cat Sí roared as she leaped into the air with the spear in hand. She took aim and Thor took notice. The thunder god raised an open hand toward the Cat Sí as if to grasp her from thirty feet away. The Cat Sí pulled back the spear and was about to release it when the whistling sound of the hammer once again filled her ears. Mjölnir pounded against the center of her back between her shoulder blades, sending enough lightning through her veins to kill the toughest men and disorient any god. The Cat Sí, Areadbhair, and Mjölnir crashed into the ground with a sickening crunch.

An angry yell pierced through the Cat Sí's daze as Jaimie finally landed a blow against the distracted Thor. His sword sliced through the god's tunic exposing an adamantine chainmail shirt. As sharp as his new mythic blade was, Jaimie was not strong enough to drive it through celestial metal links.

"Enough!" Thor yelled and picked Jaimie up by the front of his shirt while the Cat Sí was still gathering her wits. "Prepare to meet whatever pathetic god you follow!" Thor yelled as he punched Jaimie in the face, instantly knocking him unconscious. The god then threw the mortal through the air with his limbs flailing in the wind like a young girl's doll. He landed near where Tragos still held the hide of the Calydonian boar against Fotini's unmoving body.

The Cat Sí's mind snapped out of the fog and struggled to push herself from the ground through all the pain. A small bright dot of light fluttered to her side.

"What should we do?" Ailsa asked with a note of panic in her voice. "We cannot take on a god!"

The Cat Sí spat out a glob of golden ichor. "Use the boar skin to revive Jaimie and then leave here while I distract Thor."

"On it," Ailsa said. "Then meet us at the camp near Whitfield when this is over."

"I doubt I will be joining you," the Cat Sí said with a wince as she pushed herself off the ground. "He has the strength of all the Viking's prayers, and only you and Jaimie still believe in me. There is little chance I see the next moonrise."

"Then come with us," Ailsa said as her glow turned a sickly green. "Lets all flee this place."

The Cat Sí wished it were so simple.

"No. Thor won't stop now that he's found me. I couldn't save Fotini, let me save you, Jaimie, and Tragos."

Ailsa looked like she was about to argue but stopped when she looked at the Cat Sí's expression. She solemnly nodded and took flight.

"Do not stop till you are safe!" The Cat Sí called after the dim light as Ailsa flew away.

The Cat Sí pushed herself from the ground and forced herself to run at Thor even though her fresh injuries had barely begun to heal. She roared and thrust the burning spear at the center of Thor's chest. Alerted by the roar, Thor had just enough time to turn and smack the flat side of the spearhead downward with his hammer to avoid injury.

"I will enjoy this," Thor taunted as he raised his hammer and swiped at the Cat Sí, coming so close to his target she could feel the crackle of lightning from his weapon. The Cat Sí retaliated by swinging her spear at Thor's legs, but she also missed.

The world seemed to blur as the Cat Sí engaged Thor in battle. Every time one of them attacked, the other would dodge or parry, only to follow up with an attack of their own. The spear and hammer were evenly matched as the embodiments of fire and lightning encased in celestial adamantine, and neither god was able to firmly gain the upper hand. Thor had the advantage of size and strength, while the Cat Sí had the advantage of speed. They clashed, and clashed again for hours until the horizon changed from black to deep blue with the approaching morning.

Satisfied that she had provided enough time for her companions to escape, the Cat Sí grew ready for the fighting to end one way or the other. She hurled Areadbhair at Thor knowing that if she missed she would be defenseless. Thor swiped at the spear knocking it away from his heart, but the blade turned, found a new target, and pierced his thigh.

Thor yelled as the sizzling smell of burned flesh and boiling ichor filled the air. The Cat Sí lunged at Thor with her claws outstretched. This was her chance to end things. "Nk.Tw aA!" The Cat Sí cursed in a half remembered language and raked her claws across Thor's face, leaving deep gashes leaking golden ichor into his scarlet beard. Thor howled with pain, but instead of submitting to the furious onslaught, he grabbed the Cat Sí by her braid, pulled her off him, and swung her against the ground, knocking the air from her lungs. He slammed her again, and again, and then threw her with all his incredible strength into the Lia Fáil atop the hill. She smashed into the monument, the impact ringing through her ears and the taste of ichor on her tongue.

The world moved slowly as the Cat Sí forced herself into a sitting position. From atop the hill she could see the aftermath of the night's battles. The hill was littered with bodies, weapons, and pixie dust coated stones. Among the dead was Jaimie's father and the man he once loved. Faithful Fotini, the first victim to fall, lay dead and exposed to the air with Tragos still stubbornly by her side. There was no sign of Ailsa or Jaimie, at least they should live another day. Thor limped slowly up the hill with Mjölnir in one hand and Areadbhair in the other, no doubt he would be the last thing The Cat Sí saw before being sent to whichever afterlife she belonged to.

As the first rays of dawn broke over the horizon and the Cat Sí felt sunlight for the first time since she joined the Olympian pantheon. Its rays fell upon her broken form and illuminated her mind along with her body. A river of thought and memory flowed through her like the winding banks of the Nile cutting across a landscape of sand. Limestone monuments in honor of her, and her true family, came to her clearly as if she saw them only yesterday. She could almost feel the hot wind as it blew through great halls where she conversed with Maat, Hathor, and Anubis. She felt at home.

With comforting memories of family came something she wished could stay forgotten. She remembered how the sun was the first eye of her true father, plucked from his head and placed in the sky to light the world. She also remembered why she feared to be seen by its rays, how her father relentlessly pursued her because she dared defy him, leading her to leave her family and live her lies. He could see her now, but it no longer mattered. After three thousand years, he would finally witness her defeat and she was satisfied it would not be by his hand.

"I'm going to kill you!" Thor yelled as he slowly limped up the hill, practically dragging his injured leg. "But before you die, I want you to know one thing."

Thor smiled as he slowly crested the top of the hill. It was clear he had waited a long time to torture the Cat Sí in both body and mind. He spoke as he took the final few painful steps toward his victim, savoring her final moments as she once savored his ichor. He raised Mjölnir high above his head and said, "Your death means nothing. I will not rest until everyone you care for is destroyed."

Thor swung the hammer down at the Cat Sí's head, but she rolled to the side just before impact. Mjölnir struck the earth so close she could feel the blow reverberate through the earth. He lifted the massive hammer for another swing, but the Cat Sí latched onto the hammer's anvil and let him swing her in the air with it. With the little strength she had left, the Cat Sí leaped from the hammer and landed a good distance away from Thor down the other side of the hill.

A strange feeling came over the Cat Sí as she rose to attempt to fight once more. She felt warm, like she was being held in the arms of a comforting friend and an unfamiliar whisper flowed into her ears and reverberated in her mind.

Cat Sí, Artemis, I believe in you.

The pain in her skull subsided slightly as other voices joined the first.

Thank you for freeing us from the curse of the Æsir. Please take our strength so that you may continue to defend us from their wrath.

All the voices of the fae streamed into her consciousness in prayer. Many gave thanks for unlocking the door to Tír na nÓg, freeing the Tuatha Dé Danann, or returning magic to the fae. Other voices pleaded for safety from Thor and the rest of the Æsir who cursed the fae so long ago. All of them gave their strength to the Cat Sí in hope they would be enough to stave off the God of Thunder.

Please come back to us, Jaimie's voice rose above the others and it was as if a dam broke deep inside the Cat Sí's soul releasing all her pain and replacing it with love. Gone was her peaceful acceptance of death, replaced by the determination to defend those she cared about. She embraced the support of the fae, and the love of her friends. She remembered who she was and how to grab hold of her true power.

In a swift motion she broke the chain holding the crescent shard of the second eye her father sacrificed to create her. If Amun hadn't noticed her before he certainly would now as she claimed his power as her own.

She placed the crescent remains of the Eye of Amun in the air above her head and released it. Instead of falling the eye hung suspended in air and began to shine in the dim morning light. The Cat Sí flicked the eye with her claw, and it started spinning, faster and faster, until it spun fast enough to appear as a flickering orb burning above her head.

The Cat Sí drank in the once familiar power. She was no longer the shape shifting witch prowling the British Isles, or the huntress goddess stalking prey by moonlight in Greece. Her long-forgotten name flowed through her mind until it took root, and she recalled all the parts of herself. She was once again her true self, the goddess of the sun and Eye of Amun, Bastet of Egypt.

Thor ran down the hill as fast as his injured leg would allow and threw Areadbhair. The burning spear sailed toward Bastet's chest. She rolled to the side and snatched the spear out of the air, twisted around, and flung it back at Thor. The thunder god swung his hammer, and the two weapons collided in a flash of lightning and flame. Areadbhair ricocheted through the air and disappeared into the distance.

Bastet rushed up the hill, her body bursting into flame as she ran. She pounced toward Thor who slammed Mjölnir down toward her head. The hammer met the Eye of Amun and glanced off the equally powerful orb of light. The impact of the two celestial weapons reverberated through Thor's arm causing the god to release the hammer to bounce down the hill carving deep trenches as it went.

Thor punched and kicked as Bastet pinned him to the ground. She roared, baring her long teeth causing Thor to pull back in fear. Three thousand years earlier she pinned this same god down and drank every last drop of his golden ichor. She yearned to consume him once again, but she fought against her darker impulse.

"Yield," Bastet commanded as she held Thor against the ground. "Yield and promise never to return and I will let you leave here unscathed."

Thor pushed against Bastet, but she did not let go. "I will never yield! I will hunt you across every realm until I have your head mounted on my wall!"

Bastet dug her claws into Thor's wrists releasing a trickle of ichor. He yelled and stretched out his palms in agony.

"Yield!"

"No!" Thor yelled with a voice like thunder, but a faint whistling could be heard above his cacophony. He used his incredible strength to force one hand off the ground. "I will not be defeated again!" Thor struggled to reach out as Mjölnir twisted through the air.

Bastet released Thor's arm, flung out her hand, and plucked Mjölnir out of the air with a fiery fist. She roared as she brought the hammer down against Thor's skull.

The world was calm as the sun rose higher into the sky while Bastet lay on the grass, sticky with ichor and sweat. The remaining Vikings had long since fled after the defeat of their god, letting silence fill the air around the Lia Fáil. Never had a silence felt so uneasy. The battle was over, and while Bastet had defeated Thor, she felt far from victorious. She should have felt relieved, but Fotini was dead, and the rest of her companions would bear the scars of the night for the rest of their lives.

Bastet turned and looked at Thor's motionless form and the Morrígan's words filled her mind, *"I'm not dead now - but I was dead yesterday."*

41

Tragos

Fotini was dead. Tragos couldn't let go of her, even when chaos erupted around him. He held her as Jaimie fought and defeated his father. He held her when a literal god appeared and faced off against the Cat Sí as if they were equals. He even held her when Ailsa and Jaimie begged him to flee with them into the forest to contact the fae. When the dust settled, and the world grew quiet, he still held her. He would continue to hold her as long as he could.

Tragos was young when he met Fotini, old enough to not be considered a child, but lacking enough experience to be cautious of the world. He jumped into fights with humans whenever he could, so he didn't hesitate when he saw a group of men pulling centaurs along by ropes tied around their wrists and necks. Tragos gained two things in the fight with the humans: a scar on his arm and a lifelong companion.

For years the pair traveled around England stealing from the humans who looked down on them, but they otherwise avoided human interaction. They occasionally stayed in Coille Sealgair, but the cramped village never suited either of their wandering hearts. Regardless of the location, it had always been the two of them. Tragos didn't need anyone else, but Fotini always yearned for more. She dreamed of returning to the sunny fields of her home in Greece. Because it was Fotini's dream it became Tragos's dream as well.

Fotini's sun-kissed cheeks grew colder as Tragos ran his thumb across them. As he stroked the warm chestnut braids and wisps of hair on her head, an emptiness grew within his heart. Fotini was the guiding force of Tragos's life, his only genuine friend and the closest person he had to family. Without her, who was he?

When the sun rose above the treetops, Jaimie and Ailsa returned and sat with Tragos where he had stayed through all the fighting. Ailsa hovered around for a while. She opened her mouth a few times as if to speak, but she always thought better of it. Tragos hoped she would land on his shoulder and share her comforting glow, but after an awkward few seconds of hovering, she flew off leaving him to his sorrow. Jaimie gave Tragos a hug but said nothing. The attempt at comfort didn't last long before Jaimie also left to avoid the awkward silence. Fotini's wound was still a gaping hole where the spear had impaled her. Tragos would carry the guilt of bringing that spear from Tír na nÓg for the rest of his days.

Jaimie walked around the trampled grass and laid the hide of the Calydonian Boar on humans who were still breathing, but too injured to flee into the forest. Some of them had broken bones from stones smashing into their arms or legs, others had arrows piercing their armor, and a few had deep bites and claw marks. The magical skin healed all these mortal wounds, and the humans were directed to leave the hill at the point of Jaimie's shining sword.

Tragos watched the men walk away with anger slowly filling the emptiness inside his soul. The skin could heal their wounds, but the ancient relic of the gods had no effect on Fotini. What use was the skin if it couldn't save his dearest friend? Why did violent, hateful men live while Fotini had to die?

The Cat Sí eventually came down from the hill and stopped by a trampled tent. She pulled the golden idol of Artemis out of the mess of cloth and gently placed it next to Fotini. She then approached Tragos and placed her clawed hand on his shoulder, but he swatted it away in disgust.

Throughout the night, Tragos secretly hoped the Cat Sí would die in the battle. She tricked them into sailing across the sea to this godforsaken land with the promise of enough wealth for a brighter future, a future Fotini would never see.

Jaimie came and rubbed the skin over every inch of the Cat Sí. All the cuts and bruises from her battle faded and disappeared. The only wounds remaining were the hole where the spear Areadbhair had pierced her shoulder and a large, burned circle of Nordic knots between her shoulder blades where Thor's hammer, Mjölnir, had struck her. Angry burned veins branched off the circle where lightning surged through her, boiling the sludge she called ichor, and scarring her flesh. The adamantine weapons left wounds the boar hide could not heal. Unfortunately, none of her wounds were fatal, so she would eventually heal.

"So, I think it's about time you gave us some damn answers," Tragos said to the Cat Sí, speaking for the first time since Fotini died.

The Cat Sí opened her mouth to speak, but Tragos wasn't going to settle for half-truths. "None of your damned excuses this time. You will tell us what Fotini died for."

The Cat Sí caught Tragos's gaze and looked away in shame. "I owe you that much. What do you want to know?"

"What are you?" Tragos asked. "Are you Artemis or something else? That didnae look like the power of the moon earlier."

The Cat Sí was silent for a moment, but just when Tragos was about to hit her, she started to speak. "For the past thousand years, the people in these lands called me the Cat Sí, so that was my name. I am indeed also known as Artemis by the Greeks. I spent two thousand years in Greece as a pale reflection of my former self as the light of the moon is but a reflection of the sun. I lived as the goddess of the hunt and protected young maidens who reminded me of the woman I loved but lost."

Tragos stared at the goddess in silence, waiting for her to continue.

"Before I was the Olympian Artemis, I had another family, another name. I was worshipped by the people of Egypt out of fear as the goddess Sekhmet. I was the burning goddess of the desert sun who devoured any who stood against my father and creator, Amun." She ran her fingers over her broken crescent hanging from her neck as she continued. "I killed thousands in his name, including gods from other lands, until the day my father's hold over me broke. From that day forward I was called Bastet.

"My father eventually grew frustrated with his inability to control me, and I had to flee for my life. I searched the world for a place to hide and eventually met Leto on the island of Delos and helped her give birth to Apollo, who I grew close to as if he were my own brother. He told everyone I was his twin sister once we left the island to meet his family on Olympus." Bastet's eyes began to fill with the glisten of tears. She pointed to the idol at Fotini's side. "Apollo used to send me secret messages hidden in idols when I traveled outside of Greece."

Tragos had argued endlessly with Fotini about the existence of celestial beings. He always maintained the gods and goddesses were merely stories to explain the natural world, but Fotini worshiped the Greek Olympians with constant prayers and offerings. She was especially devoted to Artemis. She sacrificed the best part of everything she had to the cursed goddess, never enjoying the best slice of meat, the freshest berries, or even the sweetest wine. If the Cat Sí, Bastet, was indeed Artemis, she owed Fotini for a lifetime of devotion.

"Bring her back," Tragos said. "If you are a goddess, you must bring her back."

"I wish I could," Bastet said. "But I am not that kind of goddess."

"She devoted her life to you!" Tragos shook in anger. "She prayed to you every night! She set aside a portion of every hunt for you! There must be something you can do! What is the point of gods if you cannae save her?"

Bastet stayed quiet as Tragos cried, and her own tears formed in the corner of her eyes. "There is no point. Prayers give us power, burnt offerings give us strength, but gods are seldom willing or able to truly help mortals. I tried to save her. I came running when she prayed for aid, but I wasn't fast enough. I am the goddess of many things, but not death. All I can do is tell Charon what path to take her across the river Styx to honor her final prayer."

Bastet reached into the small satchel she always carried and pulled out a shining gold coin. She dragged the tip of a claw across the metal, scratching in the curve of a crescent moon crossed by an arrow. She carefully opened Fotini's mouth and placed the coin under her tongue. "She will join my past maidens on their eternal hunt in Elysium, the most beautiful realm of the underworld. It was her dying wish and the least that I owe her."

For the rest of the day, Tragos watched as Bastet carefully prepared Fotini for burial. She cleaned the body and anointed it with perfumes smelling of things Fotini loved: forest pines, summer winds, and fields of flowers. By evening, she made Fotini look as beautiful as she was in life. Her warm brown hair was clean and framed her face as if styled by the wind. Tragos braided the long hairs of her tail with yellow flowers woven between the strands. Her blood-soaked shirt was replaced by a clean white cloth with golden trim that did not have a pierced hole in the center. She looked perfect.

Jaimie dug a large hole that the centaur would fit in if placed on her side. Ailsa filled the hole with a layer of flowers and made a wreath of leaves to act as a pillow. Bastet carried Fotini to her final resting place as Tragos held her hand one last time before carefully lowering her beneath the earth.

"I will miss you," Tragos said. "You were always there for me. I'm sorry I was not there when you needed me the most."

Tragos didn't have the presence of mind to say all the things he would later wish he had expressed. He hoped Fotini knew how much he loved and admired her. How she was the one constant in his life, the one thing he could always count on. He felt lost without her leading him from adventure to adventure. Who would he joke with, who would he rush to talk to? Now she was gone.

After taking one last look at his friend, Tragos covered her in a large blanket as a makeshift shroud and sprinkled the first handful of dirt. It would be the last time he saw her in this mortal world.

42

Jaimie

J aimie awoke the next morning to a throbbing back and stiff neck which refused to fully turn to the right. His body yearned for his soft bed in Whitfield. He wondered if he would ever acclimate to the hard damp earth. The sun peaked over the trees letting its rays fall on him and his companions with a gentle warmth. Tragos slept silently on his back, tears mixed with dirt leaving streaks of mud across his cheeks, while Ailsa slept in the folds of the plaid tartan slung over his shoulder. The pixie slept soundly with a soft warm yellow glow to match her dreams.

The rays of the sun touched Bastet's clawed foot, and she shot awake with a look of panic across her face. She looked around the Hill of Tara in sharp sudden movements before yanking the broken eye of Amun from beneath her tunic. She clutched the jagged half-moon pendant, and her breathing slowed to a normal rhythm.

"Are you okay?" Jaimie whispered.

"I'm fine," Bastet said, though Jaimie had his doubts. "It's been thousands of years since I have felt the sun on my skin, it will take some getting used to."

"You said you avoided the sun to hide from your father. Why show yourself now?"

Bastet sat in silence for a moment before responding. "I had to choose between staying hidden in shadow or stepping into the sun to save you all from Thor. Worse, I had to embrace my father's power to defeat him."

She looked down at the jagged piece of metal in her hands.

"I'm sorry we put you in that position." Jaimie began his apology, but Bastet put a finger to his lips to shush him.

"I never want you, of all people, to apologize to me. I put us all in this position and cost you all dearly, for what? An old trinket from a false life?" Bastet waved at the hide of the Calydonian Boar laying in the grass, covered in fresh flecks of blood and sweat. "I did what gods always do. I was selfish, and mortals paid the price. Tragos is right to blame me."

Jaimie looked down the hill at all the bodies lying in the thick grass. He easily spotted his father's crumpled form and the charred remains of what was once Gorm. His chest felt heavy, and moisture pricked at the edges of his vision. He lost everything over the past few days, his home, friend, and even the man who raised him. Grief and anger washed over him, and the tears finally burst forth with a quiet sob.

Bastet put her hand on Jaimie's back as he cried. "Let it out. Tears can help heal wounds healing balms and potions cannot touch. I am sorry for what I have cost you, I truly am."

"Stop," Jaimie said. "Tragos is wrong. You may have sought the hide, but you did not kill my father, Gorm, or Fotini. My father is to blame for all that happened here yesterday. If it weren't for you, I would have been the first victim of his delusions back in Whitfield. Do not blame yourself."

Jaimie embraced his new friend and they both cried as the sun rose higher, but their tears were dried by the time Tragos and Ailsa awoke.

"Good morning," Ailsa said as she stretched.

Tragos grunted and pushed himself to his feet. He glanced at Bastet with a scowl and turned to Jaimie who suddenly seemed to be in his good graces. "Where do we go now?"

"How should I know?" Jaimie said. He hadn't had time to think about the future since leaving Whitfield. "I've been following you all the whole time. Anyone have any ideas?"

Jaimie thought about all the past visions he had for his future, and they were all out of reach. He was surprised to find the idea of not knowing to be more liberating than terrifying. Before he stumbled on the idol his father had his entire life laid out for him like a rigid map with no stops or detours. For the first time he would decide the next turn his life would take.

Ailsa suddenly fluttered high into the air for a brief second before returning with a sly smile. "You should all be quiet for a moment, listen, and look to the forest."

Everyone fell silent and turned to the forest at the bottom of the hill. Jaimie strained to hear anything except the wind, and after a few silent moments he heard a low rumble from behind the trees.

"What is that?" Tragos asked.

"An army of trolls," Ailsa said to Tragos. "They are here to avenge the troll you killed in Tír na nÓg.

Tragos unsheathed his sword and stood ready to fight.

"I'm lying you goof," Ailsa said. "Who do you think would be coming to Tír na nÓg after all these years? It's the fae."

Jaimie looked back to the forest and noticed a cloud of blinking lights forming above the treetops. The ground vibrated with the buzzing of thousands of pixie wings and the tiny pitter patter of legions of displaced elves.

The fae streamed out of the forest and stopped at the base of the Hill of Tara. A pixie and an elf trekked up the hill and stopped before Jaimie, Tragos, Bastet, and Ailsa.

"The night before last we all felt a sudden change in ourselves," said the pixie to the group. "Our magic has grown a hundred-fold, and we no longer feel bound by every word we utter. We were shocked and confused until this young pixie," the pixie turned to Ailsa and nodded, "appeared and told us how you three broke the curse on our people and opened the door to Tír na nÓg. We thank you and are anxious to reunite with the rest of the Aos Sí in our true home."

Jaime stood awkwardly attempting to think of how he was going to politely let the pixie know the ancient fae weren't in the realm of twilight.

"Thank you for listening to my story and coming to our aid," Ailsa said. "Bastet, the Cat Sí, would not have been able to defeat Thor without your outpouring of prayers. For that, I am eternally grateful."

"As am I," Bastet said, kneeling before the fae. "Not only did your faith give me strength to continue on, but it also reminded me who I am and who I want to be. I have spent many lifetimes hiding in fear and your prayers gave me the strength to finally move forward."

Bastet bowed her head in thanks and the fae bowed to her in return.

"Now there is something you should know," Ailsa interrupted. "Tír na nÓg is not what you will expect."

Ailsa's glow dimmed as she explained how they opened the gate to the lost realm of the fae, and the signs of an ancient war we found inside.

"We freed the Tuatha Dé Danann from their shackles and a troll who tormented them for nearly a thousand years," Ailsa said. "All that remains of Tír na nÓg are empty homes and fields. There are no other fae waiting for us through the tunnel."

The pixie and elf both turned a deep shade of blue.

"I am sorry to hear this," the elf said. "We were hoping to be accepted back to Tír na nÓg now that Crann Na Sióga has fallen. Where should we go now? There is nowhere safe for us in the human realm."

"Then you should still return to Tír na nÓg," Ailsa suggested. "I met the Morrígan, and I am sure she, and the rest of the Tuatha Dé Danann, would welcome you back home. There is nothing but space and safety through the tunnel into the hill."

The elf and pixie exchanged looks and nodded simultaneously. "That sounds like the best solution, though I noticed you don't seem to be including yourself when you speak of returning to the realm of our ancestors."

Jaimie had noticed the same thing.

"I was banished by Lugh for attempting to steal from his vault many years ago," Ailsa said without a hint of shame. "I am forbidden to live among the fae."

The elf and pixie glanced at each other, and both nodded. "Lugh's dead," the pixie said. "Who cares what he decreed. What do you think, Aodhán?"

The elf turned to Ailsa. "You went through unspeakable pain to warn us, you have proven more than worthy of a place among our people."

Ailsa turned slightly pink. "I am worthy," she said confidently. "Not only was the pain unbearable, but most of the fae cowering at the bottom of the hill spat on me as the curse of our people inched me towards death. I am worthy of Tír na nÓg, but are any of you worthy of me?"

The elf turned red and took a step toward Ailsa before the pixie grabbed him by the back of his shirt. She turned a shameful red and meekly spoke, "you are right. You deserve a place of honor among our people. With Lugh gone it is only fitting for the pixie who returned our magic to wear his crown. What do you say?"

Jaimie looked at Ailsa and was surprised to see she seemed to be struggling with the decision. Her colors pulsed from yellow to blue to correspond to her mixed emotions.

"I have dreamed of returning to life with my people for many years," Ailsa said slowly as if she were choosing her words very carefully. "I haven't been able to live with another elf or pixie for a mortal lifetime, and I have missed being with other fae. However, I have grown attached to the people who did accept me. I will go where they go."

"And where exactly would that be?" Aodhán the elf asked.

Ailsa looked up at Tragos, Bastet, and Jaimie. Her expression asked them all where they should go now.

"I cannot return to Whitfield Castle," Jaimie said. "Not after what has transpired here."

"I haven't had a home for thousands of years. I will go where you all go," Bastet answered.

"My home is buried here, at the base of this hill," Tragos said with a sour expression. "I have no desire to return to England. I will go where Ailsa goes, the rest of you be damned."

Ailsa turned a warm yellow before addressing the elf and pixie. "Instead of a crown I will have my friends by my side. We will all settle in Tír na nÓg and help rebuild the realm of the fae."

The last elf disappeared into the tunnel to Tír na nÓg as the sun dipped below the horizon. Jaimie, Tragos, Ailsa, and Bastet watched as their light faded into the darkness as they made their way to their new home.

"That's the last of them," Bastet said. "Go ahead inside and I will reseal the entrance behind you."

Without a word Tragos entered the tunnel with Ailsa sitting comfortably between his horns. Her warm yellow-orange glow lighting the path to their new life without Fotini by their side.

Jaimie took a step toward the tunnel entrance and stopped. While he was excited to begin his new life with the fae, there was one thing he felt he must do first. He hung back with Bastet as Tragos and Ailsa silently disappeared after the fae.

"Now that everyone is gone, can I have a moment to bury Gorm and my father?" Jaimie asked. "They may have caused so much pain here, but they were still my family."

"You don't need my permission; everyone deserves a proper burial," Bastet said. "Do you mind if I help?"

The numbness Jaimie felt ever since the battle broke, and tears burst from his eyes as he sobbed. Bastet wrapped her arms around him, comforting him with her warmth.

Silently Jaimie and his new friend and ally spent the night digging and grieving, so when dawn came, they were both ready to embrace their new lives without the weight of their past.

www.ingramcontent.com/pod-product-compliance
Lightning Source LLC
Chambersburg PA
CBHW020420110726
47899CB00006B/2059